SEX,

—not—

love

VI KEELAND

SEX, NOT LOVE
Edited by: Jessica Royer Ocken
Cover model: Fabian Castro
Photographer: Rafael Catala
Cover designer: Sommer Stein,
Perfect Pear Creative, www.ppccovers.com
Proofreading and Formatting by Elaine York,
Allusion Graphics, LLC www.allusiongraphics.com

*Life isn't about the big win.
It's about the person you call first
to tell that you've won.*

Chapter 1

— Natalia —

"Do you think there's any correlation between intelligence and being good in bed?" I inhaled from the tiny remnant of rolled-up paper and held it in my lungs as I passed the joint to my best friend. At least this round I didn't choke and cough for five minutes. Neither of us had smoked pot in ten years, not since high school. It seemed fitting to mark the official end of our childhood by lighting up what Anna had confiscated from her sixteen-year-old brother yesterday.

"I'm about to marry a man who creates robots that can learn how to think. Of course I'm going to say smart guys are better in bed. I mean, Derek can solve a Rubik's Cube in less than thirty seconds. A vagina is a lot less complicated."

"His friend Adam's sweet. But he spent the last hour talking to me about some algorithm he's building for an artificial intelligence robot named Lindsey. My only contribution to the conversation was alternating between *wow* and *that's fascinating*. Can you tell Derek he needs to find stupider friends?"

Anna inhaled and spoke while trying not to exhale, causing her voice to rise two octaves. "He went to MIT and works at a tech firm—not much of a pool of stupid people to pick from." She bumped her shoulder with mine. "That's why I need you to move out here. I can't handle being surrounded by smart people all the time."

"Very nice." I sighed. "At least Adam is sort of cute."

"So, I take it you'll be breaking your dry spell tonight?"

"Maybe tomorrow night after the wedding." I smirked. "If he's lucky. I'm still on New York time. Tonight I'll be ready to go to bed alone by the time they serve dessert."

The bride-to-be and I were hiding from the rest of the rehearsal dinner guests behind an ivy-covered lattice arch in the courtyard of the restaurant. A deep, throaty voice scared the heck out of me, and I almost knocked the damn thing over.

"He'd be the lucky one, huh? Do you look as good from the front as you do the back, or are you just full of yourself?"

"Who the hell...?" I turned to find a man walking toward us in the dark. "Why don't you mind your own damn business?"

The guy took a few more strides and stepped into the overhead spotlight Anna and I had attempted to avoid. My eyes nearly bulged from my head. He was gorgeous. Tall, damn tall—I was five foot four and had on five-inch heels and still had to crane my neck to look up at him. He had dark, sexy hair that looked like it could use a haircut but totally worked for him. Tanned skin, carved square jaw, a five o'clock shadow that probably grew back in two hours from all the testosterone this guy exuded. His eyes were a light blue that popped out from his dark complexion, and tiny crow's feet flawed the skin around his eyes in a way that made me think he smiled often. And *that smile*. It wasn't really a full smile—more of a crooked, cat-that-swallowed-the-canary smirk.

The entire package of man was a lot to take in at once. But while I stood there speechless, Anna threw her arms around his neck.

I hoped she knew him and wasn't just more wasted than I thought.

"Hunter! You made it."

Whew.

"Of course I did. I wouldn't miss my best buddy tying the knot with his girl. Sorry I'm so late. I was up in Sacramento on business and had to rent a car and drive back when they canceled my flight this afternoon."

The gorgeous eavesdropper turned his attention to me. Starting at my feet, he did a slow, incredibly rude, yet seductive sweep over my body. My nipples hardened while I watched his afternoon-blue-sky eyes darken to hazy sunset as they traveled all over me.

When he was done, our gazes met. "Yep, you do."

Huh?

Reading the confused look on my face, Hunter clued me in. "You look as good from the front as you do from the back. You're right. Whoever you're planning on sleeping with is damn lucky."

My mouth hung open. I couldn't believe the nerve of this guy...yet my skin was beginning to tingle.

"*Adam*," Anna offered. "He's her partner in the wedding. She's going to sleep with *Adam* tomorrow night."

Hunter extended his hand to me with a nod. "Hunter Delucia. Got a name, beautiful? Or should I just call you the Adam-fucker?"

For some inexplicable reason, I knew in the pit of my stomach that putting my hand in his was a bad idea. My body and his should never touch, not even once. Yet I did it anyway.

"Nat Rossi," I said, giving him my hand.

"Nat? Is that short for something?"

"Natalia. But no one calls me that."

He smiled again. "Very nice to meet you, *Natalia*."

Hunter kept my hand cupped in his as he turned his attention back to Anna. "And why is Adam paired up with the beautiful Natalia and not me?"

My friend snorted. She was definitely stoned. "Because you two would kill each other."

He seemed to like that answer. His eyes crinkled, and he returned his gaze to me. "Is that so?"

I felt electricity zapping between us, although something told me this was electricity harnessed from lightning in a storm. The last time I'd felt a physical reaction so strong to anyone was when I met Garrett. My delicate heart still had a hole in it from that lightning bolt.

"Do you remember when Derek's brother Andrew lost his job and was having a hard time in social situations?" Anna asked him. "He started to stay in too often, and I was nervous he was turning into an agoraphobe?"

"Yeah," Hunter said. "I remember. It was a few years back."

"I suggested he find a therapist to work with, help him get over a difficult time and his fears. And what did you say?"

"I said you were nuts, and he needed a swift kick in his lazy ass and a job."

Anna smiled. "Nat here is a behavioral therapist. She visits people with anxiety disorders and works on breaking the habits that cause them stress."

His brows rose. "That's an actual thing?"

I slipped my hand from his. "It is. I work mostly with people who have obsessive-compulsive disorders."

"Well, whatta you know? I thought you were making that shit up."

"Hunter is a builder," Anna continued. "He builds large projects like shopping malls. You know, the kind where they need to clear the land of all the trees to build a mile of Gap, Baby Gap, and Abercrombies. He built the one that took over part of the park we used to go to uptown as kids—Medley Park. He and Derek grew up together. They don't get to see each other often because Hunter travels around the country for months at a time on projects."

Mr. Tall, Dark and Handsome seemed proud of that résumé.

I offered him a sugary smile. "I loved that park. Good job blowing up the carbon footprint of the Upper East Side and desecrating our environment."

"Tree hugger, huh? Sounds like Anna's right. We might kill each other if we were partners."

"Mmm...I want cheesecake. Are you thirsty? I'm so thirsty."

Yep. Anna was definitely stoned. "We haven't even had dinner yet," I pointed out.

"Who cares? Let's go get some dessert. Come on!" Licking her lips, she started back into the restaurant without us.

Hunter chuckled. "It was nice to meet you, Natalia. And if things don't work out with that boring shit, Adam, I'm in room 315 at the hotel." He winked and leaned down to whisper in my ear. "We might kill each other, but fucking to death is the way I want to go."

"Are these seats taken?"

Adam and I were just finishing dessert when Hunter walked over and pointed to two empty chairs across from us. The couple inhabiting them had skipped out a few minutes ago.

"Yes," I lied.

Adam was kind enough to correct me. "Actually, Eric and Kim were sitting there. They just said goodbye two minutes ago, remember, Nat?"

A wide, gloating smile spread across Hunter's face. He pulled out a chair for his wedding partner and seated himself directly across from me. "This is Cassie. She's a tech goddess—graduated from Caltech. Have you met Adam, Cassie?"

Adam's interest piqued. "We met briefly this afternoon. But I hadn't realized you were in tech. I'm MIT. I work with Derek over at Clique in robotics programming."

Conversation between Adam and Cassie took off like a runaway train. Neither of them even noticed the scowl I shot at the architect of this match made in geek heaven.

I leaned forward and smiled, speaking through my teeth. "I know what you're doing."

Hunter sat back in his seat with an ear-to-ear pompous grin. "I have no idea what you're referring to."

"It's not going to work."

"Whatever you say. But I'm here if you need an alternate later."

I finished off the coffee in my cup and adjusted the front of my dress to reveal a healthy amount of cleavage. Then I took my napkin from the table and discreetly dropped it on the floor. Picking up my fork, I scooped up a small piece of cheesecake and *accidentally* dropped it onto my cleavage.

Hunter watched the entire show with interest.

Leaning in, I wrapped my hand around Adam's bicep. "Do you have a napkin? They must've taken mine when they cleared dinner, and I seem to have made a mess."

Being a gentleman, Adam excused himself from his conversation and turned to give me his attention. His eyes dropped to the cheesecake, and I knew instantly that I'd won. Triumph roared from my smile as I allowed the techie to help me clean off. Hunter's scowl felt like a victory.

To be honest, during dinner I'd decided I wasn't sleeping with Adam anyway—I needed some sort of physical chemistry with a man, even for a one-night stand. But I enjoyed screwing with Hunter anyway.

"I'm a butterfingers when I'm tired," I said to Adam. "I'm still on New York time. I think I'm going to head back to the hotel."

"I'll join you," he promptly replied. *Cassie who?*

Hunter didn't give up easily—I'd give him that much.

He stood. "I have a car here. I can give you two a ride. Are you ready to go, Cass? The four of us are all at the Carlisle, I'm assuming?"

I flashed Mr. Persistent my pearly whites and hooked my arm through Adam's. "I have my rental car here, so Adam and I are good. Thank you so much for the offer, though, *Tanner*."

"Hunter."

"Right." I smiled.

The hotel was only a mile up the road. As we entered, I spotted a few familiar faces—friends of the groom—in the lobby bar. The party seemed to have moved from the rehearsal dinner to the hotel. As we passed, one of the guys I recognized yelled for Adam to join them for a drink.

He looked to me before answering. "What do you say? You up for a nightcap?"

"I'm actually wiped out—time difference and all. But you go. Have fun."

"You sure?"

"Positive. I'll be sleeping before my head hits the pillow."

Adam gave me a quick hug goodnight, and I headed to the elevator alone.

I really was exhausted. Anna and Derek had reserved the top floor of suites for guests traveling in from out of town, and I'd forgotten that I needed to insert my room key into the little slot on the elevator panel to gain access to the floor. After pushing the button a few times, I finally realized and dug into my purse to find the swipe card. I was preoccupied with the search until I heard that voice.

"Natalia."

My head flew up to find Hunter standing in front of me with a shit-eating grin.

"You..."

"Me," he said.

I looked around his wide, imposing frame. "Where's your partner?"

He winked. "Left her at the bar with yours, so the two of them can get to know each other."

"Won't you be lonely, then?" I said with sarcasm.

"I might. But I can think of a way to fix that."

"Going to take matters into your own hands, huh?"

I finally located my room key in my messy purse. Hunter chuckled and took it from my hand to slip into the slot. *Of course* we were on the same floor since we were part of the same wedding. When the doors slid closed, the elevator suddenly seemed very small. It didn't help that Hunter hadn't bothered to turn around when we started to move. He faced me, standing very close. My body definitely took note of the proximity.

"Don't you have any elevator etiquette?" I asked. "Turn around and stare at the numbers like a normal person."

"Why would I waste my time looking at that when the view is so much nicer facing this direction?"

"I'm not sleeping with you, you know."

"Why not? You were gonna sleep with Adam."

"That's different."

"How so?"

"I've met Adam before. He's a nice guy."

"I'm a nice guy."

"I don't know you."

Hunter slipped his hands into his pockets. "Hunter Delucia, age twenty-nine, single, never been married, no kids. Went to Berkeley for undergraduate and grad school. Degree in architectural engineering. Grew up next door to Derek, been friends since we were in the carriage. He'll vouch for me as a decent guy. Own a home in Idyllwild, about an hour from the happy couple, with no mortgage. I also built it myself and have lots of trees on my property—that should get me extra points, by the way. Last doctor's appointment was a month ago—clean as a whistle. And, most importantly..." He took a step closer to me; our bodies were practically touching. "I think you're extremely sexy. There's some insane chemistry here, and I think we should explore it."

I swallowed. Luckily, the elevator dinged, and the doors slid open on the top floor. Needing some air that didn't smell like Hunter Delucia, I sidestepped around the tree of a man and exited. He followed right behind me. When I abruptly stopped, realizing I was going the wrong way, he walked right into me. His hands caught me, fingers pressing into my hips to stop me from falling forward.

"Wooo. You okay?"

"What the hell? You almost knocked me over."

"You stopped short."

"If you weren't up my ass, you wouldn't have walked into me."

We were still standing in the middle of the hall, and he still had a firm grip on my hips...and it felt *really good*. God, it had been a long time for me. More than *two years*.

Those fingers squeezed a little harder, and his head dipped to whisper next to my ear. "You smell incredible."

A fire burned under his touch. I shut my eyes. *Hmmm.... He and Derek have been friends since they were little. He can't be that bad of a guy. Maybe—*

Thankfully, the other elevator saved me from doing something stupid. A few of Derek's friends stepped off and didn't seem to notice what was going on between Hunter and me.

"Hey, Delucia!" An arm wrapped around his shoulder. "Shots in our room."

I shook some sense back into my head and used the opportunity to escape, practically running down the hall toward my room. Of course, my room had to be the last one at the end. Hunter yelled my name as I fumbled to get the key in the door. I ignored him and rushed inside. Leaning against the closed door, I let out a breath of relief.

What the hell am I doing? Get a grip, Nat. Literally running away from a man instead of just declining his offer or telling him to screw off? But something about this man made me feel restless and nervous—like I *needed* to run the other direction.

A soft knock at the door I was still leaning against made me jump.

"Natalia."

Why the hell did he have to call me that? "I'm sleeping."

I heard him chuckle. "Just wanted to tell you, my room is right next door. Even the hotel thinks we should sleep together."

I shook my head, but smiled. "Goodnight, Hunter."

"'Night, Natalia. Can't wait to see you tomorrow."

Chapter 2

— Natalia —

A team of people worked on the bride-to-be. Jack Johnson crooned about making waves, and the enormous bridal suite smelled of lilac—Anna's favorite scent in the world. Every time I walked through the flower district in New York in the spring, I expected to see her around the corner.

Seeing me come in, she held a champagne flute up in her reflection in the mirror. "I'm getting fucking married."

Normally, anything to do with marriage brought out my bitter and pessimistic side, but I tamped down my feelings on the subject for Anna's sake. I took the flute from her hand and smiled back. "You're getting fucking married."

The stylist busy with her hair grinned and shook his head.

"We're classy, what can I say?" I offered.

In two hours, my best friend would be walking down the aisle to marry a rich, nice looking, young techie, who worshipped the ground she walked on. It was a far cry from what my sham of a marriage had been.

"I saw Hunter follow you out the door last night," Anna said. "Poor Cassie could barely keep up with how close he was to your tail."

I needed my own mimosa for a discussion about that man. I finished Anna's drink and went to the pitcher on the bar to refill hers and grab my own glass. "Do you remember when we were seventeen and I had that crush on Mr. Westbrook, the English substitute?"

"How could I forget? He was twenty-three and gorgeous."

"Hunter's...well, I'm not sure what to make of him, to be honest. He's lewd, forward, persistent...sexy as hell."

"Gorgeous, financially sound, confident, sexy as hell," Anna added.

I sighed. "Yeah. All those. But there's something about him...something I can't put my finger on, that makes him feel as forbidden as Mr. Westbrook did in high school."

Anna's eyes flared at my reflection in the mirror. "Really?"

"What the hell are you smiling at, weirdo?"

"He feels forbidden because he gave you butterflies."

"He did not," I lied.

I wasn't even sure why I was lying about it. Besides, the butterflies he gave me weren't the usual kind that fluttered in your stomach—these flew a little farther south.

"Did too."

"No, he didn't."

"Then why not give in to it? You just said yourself that you thought he was sexy. You were thinking about sleeping with Adam, and he's not half as sexy as Hunter."

I thought back to the way Hunter's hand had felt on my hip last night, and my belly fluttered once again. The damn things were teaming up with Anna to prove a point I wasn't willing to accept.

"He's too cocky for me."

"You like cocky. In fact, every guy you've ever gone out with has been cocky."

"Exactly." I nodded. "I'm over cocky."

Anna smirked and turned to her hairdresser. "She's totally going to sleep with him."

He looked up at me, then back to Anna. "I know."

Derek and Anna married on a bluff overlooking the ocean. Even with my disdain for the institute of marriage, I cried tears of happiness. I'd noticed more than one of the groomsmen's eyes filled, too. One, in particular, seemed to hold my attention. After the second time Hunter caught me checking out how handsome he looked with his tux and slicked-back hair, I'd managed to avoid making eye contact for the rest of the ceremony and the first hour of the reception. It wasn't easy, considering we were in such close proximity for wedding-party duties, but somehow I succeeded.

Until I was dancing a slow song with Anna's dad.

"Can I cut in?" Hunter tapped Mark on the shoulder. "You're hogging the most beautiful guest all to yourself."

Anna's dad smiled and wagged a finger at Hunter. "You're lucky you said *guest*, considering my bride looks so beautiful tonight."

The two men did a bit of backslapping, and then I was in Hunter's arms. Unlike Mark, who'd kept his body a polite distance from mine as we danced, Hunter took one of my hands in his, slid the other down my back and used it to pull my body flush. *Damn, that feels good.*

"You're holding me a little tight."

"Just making sure you can't run away again."

I pulled my head back. "Again? I've never run away from you."

"Call it whatever you want, but you've been avoiding me like I have something contagious."

I mumbled. "You probably do have something contagious."

He ignored me. "You look beautiful tonight. I like your hair up."

"Thank you."

He pulled me still closer, forcing my head to turn into his shoulder, then dipped down to whisper in my ear. "I can't wait to yank it down later."

What balls on this guy.

And, God, why the hell did I want him to yank my hair down?

"You're out of your mind. In fact, just about everything you've said to me since we met has been inappropriate."

"So only *you* can talk about your plans to fuck someone? I can't?"

"I haven't talked about my plans to sleep with anyone."

"You were talking to Anna about sleeping with Adam when we met."

"That was a *private conversation.*"

He shrugged. "So's this."

"But..." I was at a loss—partly because he was sort of right. In my mind, it was okay to talk about sleeping with someone to a third person, yet it was wrong for him to be so blunt when speaking directly to the party potentially involved. It didn't really make sense, but I grasped at a reason that sounded logical. "You're crass about it. I wasn't explicit. It's how you say it that's offensive, not what you say."

"So you don't like dirty talk? Maybe you haven't had it done the right way before."

"I've had it done just fine."

"You *do* like dirty talk, then?"

This man was impossible. Luckily for my sanity—and possibly my willpower—the song we were dancing to ended, and the DJ announced that it was time for dinner. Although Hunter still didn't loosen his grip.

"The dance is over. You can let go now."

"Save me another one later?"

I smiled broadly. "Not a chance."

Of course, Hunter liked that answer. He chuckled and kissed my forehead. "Bet you're a firecracker in bed. I can't wait."

"Enjoy your evening, Mr. Delucia."

I felt his eyes on my ass every step I took to exit the dance floor.

I'd only been legally single for not quite eighteen months. I had no intention of remarrying, so when it was time for the obligatory tossing of the bridal bouquet, I stayed in my seat. Of course, Anna wasn't going to allow that. She grabbed the microphone out of the DJ's hand and insisted that I, along with a few others who were shying away from this particular festivity, get our *asses* out on the dance floor. Rather than make a scene, I complied, though I intentionally stayed all the way off to the side by myself. I wanted nothing to do with that bouquet.

The DJ prompted the audience to count down the toss as Anna stood in the middle of the floor with her back to all the anxious, single ladies.

"3, 2, 1!"

The big toss over the bride's head never came. Instead, she turned and threw the damn thing directly to where

I was standing off to the side. On instinct, I caught the hurtling bundle of flowers.

Grrr. I wanted to kill her.

Especially when I looked across the room and saw Hunter exaggerating the cracking of his knuckles with a big ol' smile on his face as he stared back at me.

Ten minutes later, I stood by Anna's side watching the dance floor fill up with single men eager to catch the garter her husband had just removed. My hand clutched a strong vodka cranberry, should I need some liquid courage.

"If Hunter catches that thing, I'm going to kill you."

"Those who protest the loudest generally have the most to hide."

"Those who cause trouble get their skinny little asses kicked," I tossed back.

"He's a really great guy. I could think of worse people to stick their hands up your dress."

"If he's so great, tell me again why he wasn't my partner?"

Anna sighed. "He's smart, confident, and a total charmer."

"And..."

"And I've also known him for four years now, and every time I see him, he's with a different beautiful woman. I thought after Garrett, you might want a different type."

I downed half my drink at the mention of my ex-husband. "Why am I attracted to assholes?"

"Because they're attractive. That's part of what makes them turn into assholes. And Hunter's not a bad guy. He's really not. I bet he's great in bed, too. If I were in your shoes, I'd pick Hunter over Adam for a one-night stand." She turned to face me. "Hunter's sex, not love. As long as you go in with that frame of mind, I bet he blows your mind."

A sudden loud roar called our attention back to the action. We'd missed Derek's toss of the garter, but there was no missing the cocky smile on the man twirling the garter on his finger and looking in my direction.

"Any chance you aren't sticking with the East Coast tradition where the guy who catches the garter puts it on the leg of the woman who catches the bouquet?"

Anna smirked. "Not a chance in hell."

The drinks went straight to my head. After I downed the vodka cranberry I had while standing with Anna, I proceeded to order another and finish it off in record time. Which meant I had a nice buzz flowing by the time the DJ set up a lone chair in the middle of the dance floor and called my name. Derek and Anna also joined us as the entire wedding guest population looked on.

"Why don't you have a seat, Nat?" the DJ said, tapping the chair. "Our beautiful bride left it up to the gentleman who caught the garter to select the song. I figured we'd give you a sample and see if it works for you since it's your dress he's gonna be under."

The DJ pressed a button on his iPad, and music began to blare—AC/DC's "You Shook Me All Night Long," to be specific. After ten seconds, he hit another button, and the music silenced.

He spoke into the microphone again. "So what do you think? Has Hunter here picked the right song for the evening?"

I shook my head as the crowd laughed, and Hunter's eyes gleamed.

"Alright then. Maybe we're better off letting you pick the song. You have something in mind that seems more fitting, perhaps?"

I thought for a moment and then waved the DJ down so I could whisper in his ear.

He smiled and pushed more buttons on his iPad before speaking to Hunter. "I'm starting to pick up on a little disparity here—maybe some messages you two are hiding in your song choices."

Hunter looked at me, and I shrugged just as the DJ started my song choice. Jason Derulo's "Ridin' Solo" blared overhead, and Hunter bent his head back in laughter. After everyone got a good laugh, the DJ told the crowd he thought things would run smoother if he picked the song.

So Hunter kneeled down on one knee to Beyoncé's "Single Ladies." Of course, he was quite the showman. He twirled the garter around on his pointer finger while gracing the onlookers with a megawatt smile. Then, he slowly lifted my foot, dropped a soft kiss on the top of it, and slipped the garter up my calf.

"Do we have a gentleman today?" the DJ asked over the microphone. "Will he go any higher?"

The wicked gleam in Hunter's eyes told me he was *not* planning on being a gentleman. For the next few minutes, through chants of *higher* from the male portion of the wedding party, Hunter inched the garter up my leg. And he wasn't just moving it along. His thumb lazily stroked the inside of my leg as he went. When he reached mid-thigh, he squeezed my leg to get my attention, and our eyes locked.

Then his hand kept going.

I hated that I didn't stop him. I hated that my hands just sat dutifully by my sides, and my normally boisterous voice seemed to have been muzzled. But the reaction of my body made it impossible to object. The effect of his one hand was profound. My nipples pebbled, my breaths grew shallow, and goose bumps covered my skin. I was way more turned on than I should've been. And it wasn't just his hand—it was the way he watched me. I knew without a shadow of a doubt that he was just as aroused as I was—and that really worked for me.

Hunter's fingers grazed along at a slow and sensual pace, reaching the tippy top of the inside of my thigh. I could feel the heat of his hand radiating between my legs.

Even though we had a crowd watching, thanks to my bridesmaid's dress, no one could see how far he'd gone. And while the entire crazy scene played out in erotic slow motion for me, Beyoncé wasn't even done singing to the single ladies yet.

Hunter let his hand slip down to my knee and squeezed as he leaned in. "Don't try to tell me I was the only one to feel that."

The DJ asked everyone to give a round of applause, and Hunter kissed my cheek, stood, and held out his hand to help me up. I was still in a complete daze.

Anna's brows drew down. "You okay?"

I cleared my throat. "I need a drink."

"How about the four of us head to the bar for a drink?" Anna's new husband said.

One drink led to two, two led to three, and three led to...

Chapter 3

— Natalia —

God, I feel awful.

My head was pounding, and my muscles ached. There was a damp spot on my pillow from where I must've drooled half the night. Without lifting my head, I glanced around the room and saw my suitcase on the stand in the corner—*Jesus, I don't even remember coming back to my hotel room.* But I was damn glad I was here, rather than next door. I tried to think back to the last thing I remembered. Catching the bouquet, Hunter catching the garter, *his hand under my dress.*

Oh God. I felt like royal shit, yet that memory still stirred something inside me.

I remembered the four of us going to the bar—me, Anna, Derek, and Hunter. Hunter toasting to the three things you need most in life—a full bottle, a faithful friend, a beautiful woman—*and to the man who has it all.* I remembered Anna and Derek being called away for some pictures, and Hunter ordering us another round and telling me stories about him and Derek when they were little. He was definitely a natural charmer, but there was also something very endearing about the way he talked about his friend.

After that, things got fuzzy. I couldn't for the life of me remember leaving the wedding or coming back to the hotel. Reaching over to the nightstand, I grabbed my phone to check the time. *Shit.* It was almost ten, and my flight was at one. I was just about to drag my lagging ass out of bed when a noise stopped me in my tracks.

It almost sounded like a snore.

A snore with deep vibrato.

I'd been lying on my side, and my head whipped around to look for the sound.

I froze, finding the source.

Froze.

I was pretty sure my heart skipped a beat or two.

A man lay in the bed next to me, facing the other direction. And from the width of his shoulders, I knew it wasn't just any man. Yet I needed confirmation. Holding my breath, I leaned over the massive body and glimpsed at the face. Just as I caught sight of Hunter, he let out another loud snore, and I leapt from the bed. I stilled on my feet once I'd gotten control of myself, not wanting to wake him.

Shit. What did I do?

I tiptoed into the bathroom with my heart racing and my brain desperately trying to remember something from last night—anything that involved Hunter Delucia inside my room.

Inside me.

This was worse than my worst night in college. How could I not remember anything? My reflection answered me—I looked like death warmed over. My raven hair was a knotted ball—half up, half down with bobby pins falling out all over. My normally fair skin was paler than usual, and my green eyes were red and puffy.

It was then that I finally looked down. I was dressed in a T-shirt and sweats, but underneath I was still wearing a bra and panties. Forget that I didn't remember *getting* dressed; this made me pause and wonder *why* I was dressed. Once my bra came off, it didn't go back on. Not to mention, I wasn't shy about my body—it wasn't my M.O. to get myself fully re-dressed after a night of passion.

Is it possible we slept together and *didn't* have sex?

I reached my hand down into my sweatpants and pressed against my privates. I wasn't sore at all. Although that wasn't proof positive—maybe the giant of a man currently snoring in my bed wasn't anatomically correct and was a gentle lover. Neither seemed plausible.

I checked the garbage can for signs of a condom and the towel rack to see if any towels had been used to clean up last night. Nothing. But yet, I was a mess—it *looked* like I'd had wild and crazy sex...

Unfortunately—or perhaps it was fortunately—I didn't have time to dwell on what had happened. If I wasn't on my way to the airport in the next fifteen minutes, I was going to miss my flight.

After a quick shower, I dried off and tiptoed back out to my suitcase. I collected my clothes, but the garter that had started this mess was nowhere to be found, and I was disappointed I wouldn't have it as a keepsake.

Hunter still hadn't moved. In fact, he was snoring louder and more consistently now. I rushed to dress, pulled my hair into a ponytail, and rubbed some moisturizer on my face before shoving everything into my suitcase.

I was about to sneak out when I decided I needed to know what had happened. Leaving my suitcase at the door for a quick escape, I quietly walked over to Hunter's side of the bed.

Of course, unlike me, he looked just as good this morning as he had last night. I took a moment to appreciate that. His coppery brown hair was disheveled, but somehow even sexier than it had been slicked back last night. Thick, dark lashes framed closed, almond-shaped eyes—eyes that I recalled were a startling light blue.

His gentle snoring continued at a consistent pace, so I took a deep breath and stepped closer. I needed to see what was under the sheet. His chest was bare, but was he wearing pants under there?

One more step.

I stopped again to stare at his face before making my final move. He was still out cold. *Or, so I thought…*

Reaching out, I picked up the edge of the sheet and lifted ever so gently. Then I leaned forward to peer underneath.

Holy shit.

He was wearing boxer briefs.

But…he had a morning erection. A *huge* bulge protruded from his tight underwear. There's no way that thing had been inside of me. I'd have to be at least a little sore.

Feeling relieved (with an odd sense of regret and longing after seeing that behemoth of an appendage), I set the sheet back down and turned to walk away. A large hand gripped my wrist.

"You'd remember it, sweetheart. Trust me." Hunter's gravelly voice carried a hint of amusement.

"I…I was looking for something."

One eyebrow perked. "Oh yeah? What were you looking for?"

"My shoe."

His lip twitched. "What color is it?"

I scrambled to remember what shoes I'd even brought on this trip. "Black with a silver bar across the front."

Hunter's eyes dropped to my feet. *Fuck.*

He looked back up at me. "Found it for you."

I trained my eyes down at my shoes to avoid his intense stare. "Oh. Silly me. I overslept, and I'm out of sorts. I need to run or I'm going to miss my flight." I went to pull away, but his grip on my wrist tightened.

"You're not going anywhere before you do two things."

"Two things?"

"Leave your number and kiss me goodbye."

"I...I...you haven't brushed your teeth."

Hunter chuckled. It felt like he could see through all of my bullshit. Reaching over to the nightstand, he grabbed his phone and held it out to me before getting up. "Toothpaste in the bathroom still?"

"The little one the hotel sets out."

"I'll brush. You type."

While he was in the bathroom, I mulled over not typing anything into his phone. There was no way I was keeping in touch with a man living three-thousand miles away. A guy like him was the last thing I needed. But then I thought better of just *telling* him I'd put my number in. He seemed to have figured me out pretty quick. So instead, I typed my name and number, only I changed the last two digits.

And it was a good thing I did, because when Hunter returned from his bathroom trip, the first thing he did was check that I'd entered something. Luckily, he didn't attempt to call me. Satisfied, he tossed his phone on the bed and nodded.

"Thank you. Now kiss me."

I could see he wasn't going to let me leave without this. So, sacrificing to make my plane, I pushed up on my toes and delivered a quick peck to his lips.

Mmm.... Nice and soft.

(And minty fresh.)

"Well...it was nice to meet you." I turned to dart out the door, but Hunter grabbed my wrist yet again.

"I said kiss me."

"I did!"

"Kiss me the way you kissed me last night."

Before I could even attempt to let that sink in, Hunter yanked me against him. One of his large hands cupped the back of my neck, and he squeezed firmly to direct my head where he wanted it. Then, his lips crashed down on mine.

The shock of feeling his mouth against mine quickly dissipated as he licked my lips, encouraging me to open for him. His tongue dipped inside, and he groaned as he tilted my head and deepened the kiss. The vibration of the sound traveled between us and sent a hum through my body. Soft and gentle went out the window after that. He grabbed a fistful of my ass, and I lifted my body up onto his, wrapping my legs around his waist. As he backed us to the wall, a sense of familiarity overcame me. I couldn't remember the specifics of our previous kiss, but I now knew deep inside what it had felt like.

My cell dropped from my hand so my fingers could tangle in his hair. Yanking on the soft strands, I couldn't get enough. A moan from deep inside my chest moved through our connected mouths. Hunter pushed harder, his thick erection pressing into the center of my open legs. He rocked as he kissed me, causing a friction through two layers of clothing that was leading me to a place I didn't think it was possible to go fully dressed.

It felt like he wanted to swallow me whole, and in that moment, I would have let him. My breasts were crushed to his chest, and a heartbeat raged out of control—only I wasn't sure if it was my own or his. *Jesus, where does a man learn to kiss like this?*

I was breathless and stunned when our kiss broke. Hunter sucked on my bottom lip, tugging it before releasing my mouth.

His voice was strained. "Change your flight. We're not done here."

I swallowed, trying to gain some composure. "I can't." My voice was barely a whisper. It was all I could muster.

"Can't or don't want to?"

"Can't. Izzy comes home today."

Hunter pulled his head back, giving me some room to breathe, some room to speak. "Izzy?"

"My stepdaughter who hates my guts."

Chapter 4

— Hunter —
12 years ago

Damn. I'm going to the wrong school.

It was the hottest day I could remember. The car radio said it was already a hundred and four out, but it was the unusual humidity in Los Angeles that made it unbearable. Since I was a few hours early to meet my brother and didn't know my way around his campus, I took a seat on a brick staircase across from a fountain in a wide-open field, hoping to catch a breeze. That breeze didn't show, but something a fuck of a lot better did. The most gorgeous girl I'd ever seen walked up to the circular fountain a hundred feet away, slipped off her shoes, stepped up on the ledge, and jumped into the thing. She dove under and came up for air, pushing her soaked blond hair off her face.

People passing by glanced over at her, but she didn't seem to notice or care one bit. She floated on her back in what was probably only two feet of water. The smile on her face was contagious, and I found myself mesmerized watching her. It had been almost a month since my mother died, and feeling that happy and free seemed like a lifetime ago.

After a few minutes, the girl sat up and looked in my direction. "Are you gonna join me, or are you just gonna watch from over there like a creeper?"

I looked around to make sure she was talking to me. No one else was in the vicinity. So I got up and walked over to the fountain.

"Is this some sort of a sorority-initiation thing?"

She smiled. "Will it make you feel better if I say yes? Because you were looking at me like I was a weirdo from back there."

"I wasn't looking at you like you were a weirdo."

"It looked that way to me."

I kicked off my shoes and climbed into the fountain. "I was looking at you wondering if you always smile this way or if cooling off just really made you happy."

She tilted her head to the side, studying me. "What's not to be happy about? We're alive, aren't we?"

The cool water felt damn good. We floated around in silence for a while, smiling each time one of us caught the other looking.

"I'm Summer," she said.

"Hunter."

"Do you like the heat?"

"Not like this."

"What's your favorite season, Hunter?"

I smirked. "Summer."

She paddled over to the edge of the fountain and leaned her elbows on the brick, watching the never-ending spray of water in the center. I followed suit, positioning myself next to her and trying not to stare down at her nipples protruding through her wet T-shirt. It wasn't an easy task.

Summer turned to look at me. "Do you go to school here?"

"No. My brother does. Came for the weekend for a visit. How about you? You go to school here or just come to cool off in the fountain?"

Her smile was as blinding as the sun. "I go here. Art major."

She pushed off the ledge and swam to the other side of the fountain. I watched, intrigued by the randomness of her actions. Once she settled again, she cupped both sides of her mouth to yell to me, even though the fountain wasn't that big. "Truth or dare?"

This girl was bizarre. And gorgeous. Who knew bizarrely gorgeous could be such a damn sexy combination.

"Truth," I yelled back.

Her face scrunched in the cutest fucking way while she tapped her finger to her chin. When she figured out what she was going to ask, her face lit up so bright the only thing missing was a bubble over her head with a light bulb. I chuckled to myself.

"What's the one thing you're most afraid of?" she yelled.

The normal answer would have been death, considering I'd recently lost my mother. Or maybe I should've given a generic answer like spiders, or heights. But instead, I did what always got me into trouble—answering with unfiltered honesty.

"You breaking my heart."

Chapter 5

— Natalia —

My cell phone rang as I was about to descend the stairs to catch a train back downtown. Seeing it was Anna, I backed up to the sidewalk so I wouldn't lose service. I wasn't in a hurry to get back home.

"Hey, Mrs. *Weiner*."

She sighed. "Will you ever be able to say my new last name without cracking up?"

"I wouldn't count on it. I still can't believe you gave up Anna B. Goodwin to become Anna *B*. a Weiner."

"I'm ignoring your curmudgeonly commentary because I'm in wedded bliss."

"Curmudgeonly commentary? Your new husband's vernacular is rubbing off on you."

She laughed. "I'm on the way to the airport for our flight to Aruba, but wanted to run something by you."

"What's up?"

"Hunter is bugging my husband for your phone number. He says you gave it to him, but must have entered it wrong. Did you enter it wrong?"

"Nope. I entered the right number...to reach Eden."

"Eden? Don't tell me you're still giving out phone-sex numbers at twenty-eight years old."

"Of course not."

"Then who is Eden?"

"She's an escort who happens to have a very similar number to mine."

Anna sighed. "So I take it you don't want Hunter to have your phone number?"

"He's a playboy who lives three-thousand miles away. What's the point?"

"I guess. Although he's actually a great guy. I thought you guys had a lot of chemistry."

"Playing with chemistry leads to explosions."

"Fine. Derek won't give him your number—even though he's been bugging him for days." She exhaled. "How's Izzy doing? Did she enjoy her week with her grandmother?"

"She said she's never going back. I hate to admit it, but it made me feel a little better that she despises her, too."

"You two needed this break."

My stepdaughter, Isabella, has been living with me for two years now. Well, technically, I guess you could say she's lived with me for three, since Garrett and I had full custody after his ex-wife died. Izzy lost her mother to cancer in seventh grade. Then, mid-eighth grade—October 31st, to be exact—she lost a second parent. Only this time, it wasn't to illness. In the middle of the Halloween party we were hosting, my husband was arrested for running a Ponzi scheme at his prestigious investment firm. He was wearing a pirate costume at the time—irony at its finest.

"Yeah, we needed the break. She's been somewhat civil to me since I got home. But that'll change. Sunday is visiting day. Her crankiness usually ratchets up for a week after visiting Garrett. And this month, I wrote him a letter asking him to tell her she was getting pulled from private school after this year because I can't afford it anymore. So she should be especially unhappy."

Our monthly pilgrimages upstate were always difficult. Since New York state didn't allow unaccompanied minors to visit inmates, I had to see my ex-husband every month, just so his daughter who hates me could visit with her dear old dad.

"You're going to heaven for taking her to visit him once a month."

"I hope not. It'll be lonely without you there."

She laughed. "I gotta run. We're pulling up to the terminal."

"Have a great trip! Don't get pregnant. I'm not ready to be an aunt yet."

"Says the woman who has custody of a fifteen year old."

"Umm...you just made my point."

"Love you. I'll call you when I'm back."

"Love you, too, Anna B. a Weiner."

⸻

"Mrs. Lockwood?" the prison guard manning the desk called without looking up from his clipboard.

"You ready?" I turned to Izzy.

She pulled her earbuds from her ears and went to throw her stuff in a locker. While I always left any banned items in the car, Izzy couldn't be without her earbuds for the short wait to see her father. God forbid I try to strike up a conversation with her. She kept the things in her ears twenty-four-seven, like most kids her age.

I walked to the sergeant at the desk. It was a guy I'd never seen before. "I'm Natalia Rossi, visiting for Garrett Lockwood. You called for Mrs. Lockwood, but my name is Rossi now."

He flipped through some papers in his clipboard. "List of approved visitors says Natalia Lockwood, wife. Are you not her?"

"Yes. Well, no. I was when I first started visiting. But we're divorced now, and I go by Natalia Rossi—like the license I showed you and the name I signed in with."

"You should tell the inmate to update the list of names."

I did, every time I came. But the asshole refused to write my name without his last name.

"Isn't there a form I can fill out myself?"

"Only the inmate can request visitor approval."

Great. Whatever.

"I would have kept Lockwood anyway," Izzy said from behind me. I hadn't realized she'd finished up with the locker. "It's a better last name than Rossi."

I bit my tongue to keep from responding that even *Weiner* would be a better last name than that of a lying thief. Izzy and I were led to a room where a few other visitors waited, and eventually they brought us all to the family visiting room. Garrett was already seated at a table. He stood when he saw us and flashed the dazzling smile that had swindled hundreds of investors out of millions and me out of my pants and dignity.

His eyes were trained on me as we walked, even though his daughter was practically running to greet him. She wrapped her arms around him for the brief embrace allowed at the beginning and end of a visit. In that moment, the vulnerable girl she really was shined through. Izzy did her best to act tough, with an I-don't-give-a-shit-about-anything attitude, but inside, a big part of her was still a little girl who'd lost her mother *and* her father. She idolized Garrett, even with all that he'd done.

34

After she released him, he attempted to physically greet me. I took a step back out of his reach and nodded. "Hello, Garrett."

He frowned. "Hello, Nat. You look beautiful."

"I'm going to grab a drink. Do you want something, Izzy?"

She didn't even turn around to respond. "No."

The rules required a minor to be accompanied by a guardian. It didn't require me to sit at the same table as my ex-husband. I was here for his daughter, whether she appreciated what it took for me to come each month or not. I walked to the vending machine and bought a bottle of water before taking a seat at a small, vacant table on the other side of the room.

During the hour, I glanced over at Garrett and Izzy a few times to check on her. I hated that once my eyes lingered on his face for a minute. I hadn't even realized I was doing it. Even after two years in prison, sallowed skin, and dark circles under his eyes, he was still an incredibly beautiful man. But I'd learned the hard way that a beautiful face is nothing when you have an ugly heart.

When the guard called the end of visiting hours, I walked back to Izzy. I could have waited at the door, but I never wanted her to have to walk away alone.

Garrett used every hello and goodbye as an opportunity to manipulate me. "Can I have a word alone with Nat, Izzy? We need to talk about some finances."

I waited until his daughter was out of earshot. "Did you tell her?"

"The timing wasn't right."

My eyes widened. "You get one hour a month. You don't have the luxury of *timing*."

His eyes dropped to my collarbone. "Remember when we were on our honeymoon and you—"

I interrupted him. "We're not walking down memory lane. Come back to reality. You're about to walk back to your eight-by-eight. You need to tell your daughter that you drained her tuition fund. I can't afford twenty-five thousand dollars for her private school next year."

"I'm working on something."

I scowled. "*From prison*? Don't make me tell her. She hates me enough as it is. *You* need to own up to this."

He reached out for me. I put my hand up. "Don't. You couldn't do this *one thing* for me."

"I miss you, Nat." *Did he even fucking hear me?*

I threw my hands up in the air. "This is pointless."

Then I turned around and walked my stepdaughter out of the state prison, vowing never to come back...like I did every damn time.

Chapter 6

— Natalia —
9 months later

"What time is my shower tomorrow?"

Anna didn't even say hello before asking when I answered the phone at eight o'clock on a Saturday morning.

I shook my head and rolled over with my cell pressed to my ear. "Take a shower anytime you want. I'm sleeping."

"Is it at Sugar Magnolia?"

"I think this pregnancy has affected your brain. What are you talking about?"

"Don't play dumb. I saw the note in my mother's day planner in her purse. And I know you wouldn't deprive me of your presence at my baby shower. It's been forever since I've seen you, and you love me too much."

I sat up and rubbed sleep out of my eyes. "What were you doing in your mother's purse looking at her day planner?"

"Looking for information about my shower. *Duh!*"

"You're horrible. Can't you let anything be a surprise?"

"Well, I don't know the restaurant it's in. She didn't write that down. That's why I'm calling you."

I climbed out of bed and padded to the coffee pot. I feigned sincerity like the Academy was watching. "Anna...

I'm so sorry. Sunday is Izzy's visiting day, and I just couldn't swing it."

"Oh my God. How could my sister have not coordinated the date around your prison visits?"

She actually did.

"The world can't revolve around Garrett. I'm sorry, sweetie. I hate to miss it, too. But I'm swamped at work, and I really want to take some days to come see you when the little butterball is born."

When I heard her voice, I felt a tad bit bad about lying.

"But I miss you. And I can't have a party without you. Remember when I attempted that in eighth grade, and I wore that awful outfit that had pants with a crotch that hung to my knees and a big bow in my hair? I wound up kissing Roger Banya. Kids started calling me Anna Bow Banya—which wasn't bad...until a week later when I told Roger I didn't want go out with him. He got mad and told everyone I gave him a blowjob at my party. Then I became Anna *Blow* Banya. God, you have to come. I can't have a party without you!"

I had to stifle my laugh because her panic was real, even if her reasoning was ludicrous. She was on edge about anything and everything as her due date neared. Though I'd never been pregnant, I remember my own life-altering change making me the same way.

"Send me a pic of the outfit you choose, and I'll approve it. I'm also pretty sure you won't be kissing anyone except your husband at this party. You'll be fine. We'll have to video chat during so I can be there with you in some way."

I heard the pout in her voice. "Fine. But you better stay at least a week when the baby is born. And you're changing all the poop diapers."

I laughed. "You have a deal. But I need to run. I have to be somewhere in an hour." *The airport.*

"Will you at least tell me where the shower is since you're going to ruin it by not being there?"

"Fine. But only because you sound stressed. It's at your house." I lied some more. Hey, why not? I was on a roll. "Derek is going to take you out to lunch to make you think it's your shower. Everyone will be there when you get back, pissed off that it wasn't actually your shower. So smile nice when you walk in."

"Oh my God. Thanks. You're right, I would have been coming home feeling let down. Alright. I'll let you go. I'll video call you tomorrow from my shower at home!"

After I hung up, I finished packing and attempted to wake Izzy on a positive note.

Flicking on the light in her room, I said, "Rise and shine, beautiful. It's going to be a great day."

She pulled the cover over her head. "What's so great about it?"

"Well, the sun is shining, and you don't have to go to school."

"I hate the sun. It ruins your skin and gives you wrinkles when you get old," she said from under the covers. "And I'd rather go to school than go to Nanna's house. I don't see why you keep having to go away."

Keep having to go away. A little dramatic since it had been nine months since I'd left Izzy to go out to California for Anna's wedding and had been home with her practically every night since.

"Awww...you're upset because you're going to miss me, aren't you?"

"*Grrr...*"

"I'll let you wake up a little while I make *Nutella crepes*." I wasn't above bribery to get her to sit down at the table and talk to me.

"Fine." That was teenage speak for *fuck you*.

Fifteen minutes later, she couldn't resist the smell of chocolaty hazelnut that wafted into her room. I plated a homemade crepe and slid it in front of her. "I bought some decaf Starbucks K-cups for you. Want me to make you a coffee?"

"I'd prefer caffeine."

I opened the Keurig and popped in a decaf. "I'd prefer elves to come and do my laundry, but I settle for carrying it down to the laundry room in the basement."

"We had someone who did the laundry when my father was around."

Izzy preferred to remember only the good things about her father. Rather than remind her that the housekeeper was paid for by the life savings of unsuspecting families who'd trusted her father with their investments, I simply said, "Things change."

After I made her a mug of decaf, I joined her at the table with my second cup of regular. "I should make it back by the time your game starts on Tuesday night. If for some reason I'm late, Marina's mom is going to text me the score updates."

She shrugged. "I'm starting. But it's not a big deal if you can't make it."

"Are you kidding? This is a huge deal. When was the last time a sophomore started on a varsity basketball team at Beacon?"

She tried to play it off like she didn't care, but I saw it in her eyes. "Never."

"Well, I can't wait to watch you not only start as a freshman, but kick butt."

She ate her breakfast in relative quiet after that. When I was unloading the dishwasher, she surprised me by starting a conversation. For two years now, almost every conversation had been started by me.

"Are you going alone to California?"

"Of course. Who else would I go with?"

She looked away. "That guy you went out with last week."

I stopped unloading to give her my full attention. "No. That was just a date. And I don't think I'll be going out with him a second time."

Her voiced pepped up. "Because of Dad?"

"No, honey, not because of your dad. My dating choices have nothing to do with your father. Brad and I just didn't connect."

"He was ugly."

I'd recently forced myself to start dating again. I didn't have time to do it often, but when I did, I made sure not to bring them around for Izzy to meet.

My brows furrowed. "How do you know what he looked like?"

"You left your Mac open to Match.com when I borrowed it."

"Oh. Sorry."

"He didn't look like your type."

Translation. He looked nothing like your father. "I'm trying to date outside my type."

"Why would you do that?"

The truth was, I was attempting to avoid gorgeous men who swept me off my feet and out of my senses. But Izzy was smart enough to understand what I meant if I said that. And I'd vowed not to put her father down when speaking to her, no matter how tempting it often could be. Every little girl should be allowed to idolize her father and make her own decisions as she grew up. Someday Izzy might see Garrett for who he was, but I wouldn't be the one to open her eyes.

"To be honest, I think I was too closed-minded when I was younger," I told her. "If a boy wasn't cool enough or good looking enough, I really didn't give him a chance. I judged a book by its cover, so to speak. Since I've gotten older, I've realized that by doing that, you miss out on some pretty amazing people. So I've been trying not to focus on the silly stuff I used to."

Izzy was quiet for a moment. "My friends make fun of this boy Yakshit...well, because his name is *Yak-shit,* and his nose is sort of big. He moved here from India last year. He's in my science research class, and he plays on the boy's basketball team. But he's nice and makes me laugh."

Wow. I was momentarily taken aback by Izzy's sharing of...well, anything. "Yeah. Kids can be cruel. Let's face it, adults can be cruel, too. I'm glad you're friends with Yakshit."

Her eyes dropped, and I realized she was telling me more.

"Izzy, you like this boy...as a boyfriend?"

The tiny bit she'd opened up to stick her neck out slammed shut as she recoiled into her shell. "I didn't say that."

"It's okay if you do. You're almost sixteen. I liked boys at your age."

She chanced a glance up at me. "Dad says I can't go out with boys until I'm twenty-one."

I reached over and squeezed her hand to catch her attention again. "I'm never going to tell you to ignore something your father says. He's your father, and any advice he gives you is worth consideration. However, what goes on day-to-day here in *our* home, so long as we're open and honest about it with each other, is between you and me. We need to trust each other with these things. Just like I told you about my date with Brad. We're in this together, Izzy."

She looked away, but nodded.

It was more than she normally allowed me to have from her.

"I'm going to go finish packing for Nanna's."

I smiled. "Okay. We'll leave in about a half hour, and I'll drop you on the way to the airport."

My planned thirty-minute departure turned into an hour. Since I was running late, I said goodbye to Izzy at the door of Garrett's mother's house. "Be good. I'll only be gone a few days."

"Whatever."

"Oh. And I joined Snapchat. Accept my friend request or follow request—whatever you do on that thing. I figured we can text and send pictures."

Izzy looked horrified. "Please don't do that. I'm not adding you on Snapchat."

"Why not?"

"Because it's not a place where you connect with your mom."

With your mom. She hadn't even realized what she'd said. And perhaps she was just generalizing, but I chose to take it as something more meaningful. I walked back to her and engulfed her in a big hug.

"I love you, Isabella."

Her face softened for a brief moment before her teenage shield set back into place. "I'm still not adding you."

I walked down the stoop. Garrett's mom smiled and nodded her approval. "I'll text you when I land."

"You're going to be in L.A. Text me some pictures of celebrities, or hot guys at least."

"I only post those on Snapchat. You'll have to follow me to see them," I yelled as I got back into the waiting cab.

Pulling the door closed, I waved one last time and mumbled to myself, "Plus, you're keeping away from the good-looking ones, Nat. Remember?"

Famous last words.

Chapter 7

— Natalia —

Flying into LAX always amused me.

Drivers in suits were two layers deep behind a gated area next to baggage claim. I read their signs as I stepped off the escalator, rolling my carry-on luggage.

Mr. Spellman.

Piedmont.

Laroix family.

Mr. Damon.

Hmmm. I wonder if it's Matt Damon. This is L.A., after all. I kept walking as I browsed. Most were hand-written on white boards with erasable markers, although some were typed and printed out. One particular sign caught my eye—not because it had my first name, but because it was written on what looked like a ripped piece of a brown paper bag. The handwriting was slanted and slashy and almost illegible. But as I got closer, I figured out the last name. The sign read:

Natalia Sbagliato-Numero

I said it aloud in my head once before it all clicked together.

Natalia.

Sbagliato. Italian for *wrong.*

Numero. Meant number in Italian.

Natalia Wrong Number?

I felt it before my eyes raised to the face of the man holding the sign. An inexplicable warmth settled low in my belly, and the tiny hairs on the back of my neck rose to attention. But when my eyes met those of the man with the cocky smile, I did the only thing I was capable of—tripping over my own feet and falling flat on my ass.

"Are you okay?"

It was impossible to play it cool sprawled out on my ass in the airport with a pink face heated from a mixture of embarrassment, excitement, and anger. Plus, Hunter was even more good looking than I remembered—ruggedly handsome, kissed by the California sun, and packaged in a casual and confident wrapper that made my knees glad I was on the floor. But as much as I liked the full package before me, I hated that he made me feel off kilter. I rolled with the hate part.

"What are you doing here?"

Hunter had hopped the barrier gate that separated us and was kneeling at my side almost before I came to a halt from my fall. "I came to pick you up. Didn't you see my sign with your name on it?"

"Natalia Sbagliato-Numero? Cute. Very cute. How did you even know I spoke Italian?"

Hunter offered his hand to help me up. "You were mumbling curses at me under your breath the night of Derek and Anna's wedding."

I didn't remember that. Then again, a lot of the evening was fuzzy. I took his hand and stood. "What happened to Samantha? She was going to pick me up so we can run the errands for the shower tomorrow."

Hunter flashed a boyish smile. "I offered to help with her errands."

I knew Samantha. She might've looked just like her older sister, but she didn't have her sister's energy. In fact, lazy might be the right way to describe Sam.

"I'm sure you didn't have to ask twice."

"Nope. And I would've done them all just to get to pick you up from the airport." Hunter grabbed the handle to my suitcase. "Do you have any other luggage to wait for?"

"No. This is it. I hate to check luggage."

"I'm parked in short-term parking, so it's not too far."

We walked through the busy airport and parking area together. Hunter's strides were longer than mine, so when we stopped at the crosswalk for the light and then started again, I might've had the opportunity to ogle how good his ass looked in his shorts. *I bet he does a shitload of squats.*

When we arrived at his vehicle, I wasn't surprised to find a sparkling clean, late-model, black pickup truck. He pressed the button to start it and walked around to the passenger side with me. An electric step lowered as he opened the door, which I was glad for because the truck was really high off the ground. Hunter put my bag into the backseat of the cab and shut my door before jogging around to the driver's side.

The inside was more spacious than I would've thought.

Hunter caught me inspecting his ride. "What?"

"This thing is so big."

A dirty smirk crossed his face. "I've heard that before. Often."

I rolled my eyes. "I meant the truck. I've never actually been inside a pickup."

"Well, what's the verdict?"

Hunter's car was not a typical work-type pickup truck. It was more like a fancy SUV—lined in top-stitched leather, with an enormous amount of electronics and dark wood grain.

I nodded my approval. "It's nice. Suits you."

He put one hand on the steering wheel. "Oh yeah? Suits me? What do you drive?"

"What do you think I drive?"

He squinted as if he was going to give it some legitimate thought, then quickly put the car into reverse. "Easy. Prius. You drive a Prius."

"How did you know? Anna told you."

"Nope. Your friend Anna wouldn't tell me shit about you. Couldn't even get your last name or phone number out of her."

"So how did you know?"

"Fits. Same as you said about me and my truck."

Hunter pulled up to the parking exit gate, inserted a ticket into the machine and paid forty-dollars to park.

"God. That's worse than parking at JFK."

"Traffic's worse, too. And home prices."

"So why do people love it so much?"

Hunter held his hand up to the window. "Year-round sunshine. Can't beat it."

"I like having four seasons."

He chuckled. It was deep and rumbly. "Anna wasn't kidding."

"What?"

"When we first met—she said we were opposites and might kill each other."

Most days, I could barely remember what I'd eaten for breakfast. Yet I recalled the comment Hunter had made after Anna said that more than nine months ago. "*We might kill each other, but fucking to death is the way I want to go.*"

After maneuvering through the maze of LAX, Hunter pulled onto the highway. "So, Natalia Sbagliato-Numero, why did you give me the wrong number and refuse to let Anna give me the right one?"

I looked out the window. "Figured it was best that way."

"Best for whom?"

"Both of us."

"Both of us? So you know what's best for me, do you?"

"Just trying to save you the trouble of a broken heart."

Hunter glanced over at me. The side of his mouth twitched. "A broken heart, huh? You think I'd spend one night in your bed and pine over you for years?"

I turned to face him. "It's been nine months, and here you are still chasing me after one night in my bed. And I didn't even put out. Imagine the condition you'd be in if I did."

Hunter shook his head. "Anna was wrong about one thing. She said we were complete opposites, but you're as full of yourself and as big of a wiseass as I am."

We merged onto the 405, only we were heading north instead of south where Anna's sister Samantha lived. I was crashing at her place tonight so Anna wouldn't see me before the shower tomorrow.

"You're going the wrong way."

"No, I'm not. Sam said you were running errands with her today."

"I am. Sam lives south, not north."

"Ah. I see your confusion. You think you're spending the day running errands with Samantha."

"That was the plan..."

"I agreed to do *most* of Sam's errands, not just pick you up. So you're spending the day running her errands with me."

"Why would you agree to that?"

"Because you can't run away from me when I have you captive in my truck."

"God, these smell so incredible." We were at our second stop on Sam's errand list—Bold Blossoms, a flower store where we were to pick up eighteen lilac-filled centerpieces. The woman behind the counter went to box them up while I roamed the store, sniffing various arrangements and plants.

"What is it?"

"It's a sweet pea." I cupped my hand around the delicate purple flower. "Here, smell."

Hunter leaned in and took a deep inhale. "That does smell good."

"Doesn't it? They remind me of my grandmother. When I was about ten, my mother took us to Italy to visit her. Nonna had them growing wild all over her property. She had a fence around her little house, and they were wrapped around it so heavily that you could barely see the white pickets. Sauce on Sundays and the smell of sweet peas—that'll always be my Nonna Valentina. She died when I was a teenager. My mom kept up the sauce on Sunday tradition, but it's too cold to grow sweet peas outdoors in Howard Beach where she lives."

"You have a big Italian family?"

"Four girls. We get together every Sunday night for dinner at my mom's. Two of my sisters have kids, two girls each. There's not a lot of testosterone."

The florist came out from the back. "We're just finishing packing them all. I'll ring you up, and you can drive around to the back. We'll load them into your car."

"Sounds good," Hunter said. He motioned to the sweet pea plant. "We'll take that, too."

"I hope that's not for me. I can't bring that on a plane."

"It's not. It's for my place. I don't have any flowers." He winked and leaned in so the florist couldn't hear. "Plus, I figured you might like to smell it if after you wake up."

I had to give him credit; he was at least consistent, even after almost a year.

Hunter loaded the boxed centerpieces and his new plant into the back of his pickup and secured the cap back down.

"What's next on our list?" I asked as I buckled into the passenger seat.

"My place."

"Your place? I don't think so. We have errands to do."

"This is an errand. Sam asked me to build a wishing well for the shower. I painted it this morning. It needed to dry before I loaded it into my truck."

Hunter read my face, which called silent bullshit.

"No, really," he said.

"So this isn't an attempt to get me in your bed."

"It wasn't. But now that I get to impress you with my house, I can't be responsible for your actions if you try to take advantage of me."

"You're nuts."

"Maybe so, sweet pea. But you haven't seen my house yet."

Hunter's house was incredible. It was also nothing like I'd expected. Surrounded by trees in the middle of a large piece of land sat a rustic-style cabin that blended industrial materials and natural wood and rock. The large stone exterior with towering picture windows looked more like an HGTV dream home than what I would have expected from Hunter Delucia.

I exited the truck, still taking in the house. "Is this really yours? It's amazing."

"Designed and built it myself. Took me six years."

"Wow. This is nothing like I expected."

"What did you expect?" He walked to the back of the pickup, lowered the gate, and slipped out his new plant.

"I don't know. Something more in-your-face, I guess— not so natural and beautiful." The sound of water running caught my attention. "You have an actual babbling brook. And trees. Loads of trees."

"Took me twice as long to build because I used small equipment to reduce the number of trees that had to be taken down. I want to look at nature when I have my windows open. Tried to build something that showcased the land, rather than overpowering it."

"Well, you definitely succeeded. I feel like I'm in a cabin in the middle of a forest, not ten minutes off the highway."

"I'm glad you approve. Come on, let me show you inside. This is just the beginning of the tour." He unlocked the door and put his hand on the small of my back to guide me in. "I think you'll like the room the tour ends with the best—my bedroom."

I rolled my eyes, hiding my amusement.

The inside was just as beautiful as the outside. It was simple, understated, and surprisingly eco-friendly. A large stainless kitchen was separated from the living room by a granite-top island. Two sets of French doors led to an enormous deck off the back of the house, where a stone fireplace was being built.

Hunter pointed outside. "The fireplace might take me another six years at the rate I'm going."

"I can't believe you built all of this. It's sort of ironic that you build commercial property and have taken out parks to build malls, yet live in an environmentally friendly home."

"Building is my job. I love it, don't get me wrong. But that doesn't mean I want to live in one of the megamalls I build. Do you live in a big building in New York City?"

"Yes."

"Does it mean you like pollution because you live in a tall building that contributes to a reduction of fresh air and sunlight?"

"No. I guess you're right."

"I'm always right."

"I liked you better when you were giving me a tour and letting your handiwork impress me instead of your mouth."

Hunter chuckled. "Well, then let's continue. I can think of plenty of ways my hands will impress you in the next room. Although I'm pretty sure you'd like my mouth in there even better."

Of course, the next room on the tour was Hunter's bedroom.

"Wow."

My jaw dropped when he turned on the lights. Just like the other rooms in the house, the space was large and open. A king-size platform bed had been elevated to claim the best view of the forest-like yard from two walls. That view included a birdhouse with a blue jay currently perched on top. I stepped to the windows to peer outside. It wasn't until I looked closer that I noticed more than one birdhouse. In fact, there were a lot of them.

"Are you a bird watcher?"

"No. My mother was. I always wanted a big Macaw parrot, though. Every year from the time I was able to swing a hammer, I made her a birdhouse for her birthday. She'd put seed in it and watch the birds outside, and I secretly hoped she'd take the hint and get us a bird for inside." Hunter stood next to me at the window and pointed to a birdhouse hanging from a tree branch off to the right. "That was the first one I made. I was seven. If you look inside, my mother put some plastic birds in there. For the longest time, I thought she did it to attract real birds. But after a few years, she stopped doing it. One year I finally asked her why, and she told me it was because I'd finally learned how to make a good birdhouse. Apparently the plastic birds had nothing to do with attracting other birds. The way I'd built the first couple of houses, I had nails sticking up inside, and she was afraid they were going to impale the birds."

I laughed. "That's funny. It's sweet that she didn't want to tell you. How many are out there?"

"Ten. I made one each year from seven to seventeen. That's the only thing she ever asked for."

"Did you stop making them when you went to college?"

"No. She passed away when I was seventeen."

"Oh. I'm sorry."

"Thank you." He looked around outside. "She would have liked this place. If I put a little birdseed on a few of them, it turns into an aviary out there."

I looked over at Hunter, who was still staring out the window. He looked younger in the natural light. "There's more to you than meets the eye."

He turned his attention back to me. "That's what I tried to tell you the first night we met. There's a lot more for you to see. And we happen to be in the perfect place for me to show you."

His words were teasing, but when he reached out, grabbed my hip, and took a step closer, there was nothing funny about the things my body felt.

Over the last nine months, I'd dated a few different men. None of them had lit my fuse like Hunter could with one simple touch. In fact, the difference was so apparent that I'd talked myself into believing my memory had exaggerated what the man did to me. Apparently, the only thing exaggerated was my denial.

"Kiss me." His voice dipped low, and he reached up to brush his fingers over my lips. "I've had fucking dreams about this mouth."

"That's not a good idea." I didn't sound convincing, even to myself.

"It's a very good idea." He leaned his head down slowly.

"We have errands to do."

"They can wait. One kiss."

I wasn't sure I could control myself after *one kiss* with this man. He moved slowly, as if giving me a chance to stop him, which is what I planned to do. Only my body was at total odds with my brain, and while they were busy fighting it out in a massive tug of war, Hunter's lips sealed over mine.

I'd forgotten how soft his lips were. They directly contradicted the firmness of his touch when he wrapped his arms around me and closed the gap between us. Even though I'd forced myself to forget the way his touch felt, my body had not forgotten how to react. Instinctively, my legs lifted and wrapped around his waist. Hunter walked us back away from the windows, and before I could register where we were going, plush bedding was at my back.

"Hunter," I feebly attempted to protest.

"Just a kiss," he growled. "For now."

It had been years since I'd had a real make-out session. Our bodies were tangled, his hard pressed against my soft. I groped his hair, his back, anything I could get my hands on to bring him closer. Every nerve ending in my body ached for more as I kissed him with more passion than I could remember having with anyone.

I'd been kissed hundreds of times, yet it was as exciting as that first make-out session when I was a teenager— maybe even more so, because no teenage boy's body felt like Hunter Delucia's hard one did pressed against me.

I vaguely felt vibration up against my hip, but my entire body was buzzing, so it didn't register as a cell phone until it stopped and then started again a second time. "Your—"

"Don't care," Hunter hissed.

The desperate edge to his voice made the corner of my lips curl even as they remained glued to his. But ten seconds later, my phone started to ring. I wasn't even sure where I'd dropped the damn thing. Ignoring it worked the first time, though the second time mine sounded, it became impossible.

I extricated myself from beneath Hunter and found my phone on the floor near the window where we'd started kissing. It stopped ringing again before I could swipe to answer. When the missed call registered, Samantha's name popped up.

"It was Sam."

Hunter dug his phone out of his pocket and checked his call history. "Same," he grumbled. "Probably wants to add six more things to my to-do list."

I took a second to smooth what Hunter's hands had done to my hair and then hit *Call Back*.

"Where are you?" Samantha sounded panicked.

"Relax. We already picked up the flowers, and we're at Hunter's place getting the wishing well he made. We'll get everything you need done."

"No! There isn't going to be a shower. Anna's in labor. Forget the errands. We're going to have a baby instead."

"Oh my God! But she's still got six weeks left." I covered the phone and yelled to Hunter. "Anna's in labor!"

"The doctor said the baby is big enough, and since her water broke, they aren't trying to stop it. She's already four centimeters dilated."

"What hospital?"

"Cedars-Sinai."

"We'll be right there."

Chapter 8

— Natalia —

"What? Is the baby here? Did I miss it?"

I woke to a gentle tap after dozing off for a few minutes in the waiting room. Six of us had been here since two this afternoon, and it was now almost two in the morning—and that was California time. For me, it was five a.m.—exactly twenty-four hours after I'd gotten up the day before. The thought that only one day had passed since I'd gotten up for my flight just didn't seem possible.

Hunter spoke low to avoid waking Anna's two sisters sitting across from us. "I'm going to go find a coffee machine for Derek's mom. You were leaning on my shoulder sleeping, and I didn't want your head to fall when I got up."

"Oh. Okay. Thanks." I rubbed at the back of my stiff neck. Looking over at Hunter, I cringed, finding a wet spot where my face had been. I scrunched up my nose. "I think I drooled on you a little. Sorry."

"You were also snoring. Want a cup of coffee or you gonna go back to working on the puddle on my shirt when I get back?"

I stretched my arms over my head. "I'll take the walk with you. I'm stiff from the way I must've been leaning on you."

"Yeah. I'm *stiff* from you leaning on me, too. Had a perfect view right down your shirt. Red bra, by the way, *nice*. Sexy."

"You're even a perv at two in the morning."

"You bring out the best in me, sweet pea."

The two of us wandered the halls of the hospital until we found a coffee machine that actually worked. When we returned with Margaret's coffee, Derek was in the waiting room giving everyone an update. "She's at seven. Been stuck there for a few hours. Doctor's said it's probably still going to be a while before the baby's here."

"You can't rush perfection," I said.

Derek looked as if *he*'d spent the last twelve hours in labor. He raked his hand through his hair. "My feet are killing me. Although if I said that to Anna with what she's going through, she might literally kill me."

Margaret laughed. "I'd keep your foot pain to yourself."

Derek turned his attention to Hunter. "By the way, she's also pissed at you."

"Me?" Hunter said. "What the heck did I do?"

"Remember when we first told you Anna was pregnant?"

"I think so?"

"What did you say?"

Hunter's response was a guess. "Congratulations?"

"Nope. You said maybe we'd have the kid six weeks early to share a birthday with his favorite uncle."

Hunter smiled. "I guess I did say that."

"Yeah, well...my wife thinks the baby would have been born a few hours ago, but it stalled to share a birthday with you."

"So it's my fault she's still in labor?"

Derek smiled. "It's better than it being my fault, which it was until she came up with that crazy theory."

"I'll take one for the team. No problem."

With a promise that the next time he appeared he'd be announcing the birth of his child, Derek headed back through the double doors of the labor and delivery unit.

Since we had some time to kill, Hunter and I decided to go outside and do a lap around the hospital to get some fresh air. It was dark, but Los Angeles still lit the night.

"So, I guess happy birthday is in order?"

"Thank you."

"How old are you, again?"

"Thirty."

I turned to walk backwards. "Wow. That's a big birthday. Do you have any plans?"

"I was supposed to have a drink with Derek while you ladies threw Anna her baby shower. Then we were assigned to load my truck with gifts and deliver them to Derek and Anna's place. My plan was to try to convince their houseguest to pick up the kiss where we left off at the wedding last year."

I laughed. "Looks like you're ahead of yourself. We did that this afternoon."

"Have dinner with me tonight?"

"I'm not sure that's a good idea."

Hunter pouted. "You'd leave me all alone on my thirtieth birthday?"

"Something tells me you don't have to be alone if you don't want to be. I bet you could snap your finger and get a date. In fact, why don't you have a girlfriend, Mr. Delucia? What's wrong with you?"

"Why does something have to be wrong with me because I don't have a girlfriend? I'm guessing you don't have a boyfriend, since you kissed me this afternoon. Does that make something wrong with you?"

"Ummm.... First off, *you* kissed *me*. I didn't kiss you. Second, I don't have a boyfriend, or that kiss wouldn't have happened, no matter who started it. And third, yes, there's something wrong with me."

Hunter stopped in his tracks. It might've been dark, but I could see legitimate concern on his face. "What's wrong with you?"

"I'm divorced at twenty-eight. My ex-husband is in federal prison. I have full custody of a fifteen year old who isn't mine and doesn't particularly care for me. I just borrowed twenty grand I'll never be able to pay back from my mother to cover an overpriced high school so said fifteen year old will hate me less. Should I go on?"

"Do you abuse pets?"

"Pets? Of course not."

"Do you kick people when they're down?"

"No."

"Have you ever committed a robbery, arson, murder, or assault?"

"Never."

"Then there isn't anything wrong with you that can't be fixed."

"What if I don't want to be fixed?"

"Then that's good. Because I don't want to fix you."

"You don't?"

Hunter shook his head. "I just want to fuck you—make you forget what's broken for a while."

"You're really vulgar."

"Maybe. But I'm honest. I don't know what your deal is with your ex, but I'm guessing the reason you're leery of men has to do with him not being so honest."

Of course, he was right—Garrett had cut me deep. Trust was like glass. When it broke, it shattered, and even if you managed to glue it all back together again, there were always fissures. It was never as strong as when it was whole.

"How about if we go out to dinner for your birthday as friends—no expectations of sex. We'll just share a nice meal and call it a night. I'll even pay for dinner."

"Fine. But you're not paying for dinner. That's a deal breaker. I pay for dinner, or you can find someone else to not have sex with after the meal."

I couldn't help but laugh. Extending my hand, I said, "You drive a hard bargain, birthday boy. It's a deal."

Hunter took my hand to shake, but then used it to yank me flush against him. He kissed my forehead. "I drive lots of things hard. And just because I agreed to no sex doesn't mean you're off the hook for another round of kissing and dry humping."

"I can't wait." I laughed as if I was joking, but there was a lot of actual truth in my statement.

―

Caroline Margaret Weiner was born at 3:47 a.m., after eighteen hours of labor. I'd watched plenty of movies where the new dad runs out in his blue scrubs and says the baby is born, but actually being part of that in real life was nothing short of magical. Derek had the blue paper mask and hat on when he walked out with his eyes full of tears.

"It's a girl."

He'd barely gotten the three little words out before the tears started flowing. There wasn't a dry eye in the room after that.

Even though I'd sworn I was never going to have children of my own after my life fell apart over the last few years, a tiny crack ran up the impenetrable wall I'd built around my heart when I saw Anna's baby in the nursery. After another hour of waiting, we took turns going to visit the new mommy.

Apparently Derek hadn't told his wife I'd flown in for the shower. And since I'd told her I wasn't able to make it, she was quite surprised when I walked in.

"You're here! You're really here!"

"Thank God I am. If I hadn't come in for the shower, I would have missed this." The two of us clung to each other, crying tears of joy, until a nurse knocked at the door. She had the baby in a clear carrier on wheels.

"Time for Mommy to show off her beautiful bundle of joy," the nurse said. She locked the wheels on the portable bassinet and gently lifted baby Caroline out. The precious little thing was swaddled so all I could see was her sweetest, little pink face.

While the nurse settled Anna with extra blankets and a pillow to prop the baby up on, I walked to the sink and washed my hands, then pumped some disinfectant on them as an added precaution. The minute the nurse shut the door behind her, I climbed into bed next to my friend.

"Oh my God. She's beautiful. She looks just like you." I unglued my eyes from the beautiful newborn and looked at my lifelong partner in crime. "You have a baby."

"I have a fucking baby," she said.

I laughed. "I don't think you should say that word around my sweet niece."

Her smile wilted. "You were supposed to have one at the same time and live next door so we could wheel them in carriages like we did our dolls when we were little."

I stroked the baby's cheek. Her skin was so soft. "Maybe I can see about getting my ex-husband relocated to a West

Coast penitentiary so I can move out here. Do you think they make extra-large carriages? I'm sure Isabella won't mind if I stuff her in one and wheel her around with you." I leaned in and smelled baby Caroline. "God, she smells so good."

We huddled in the bed in our own little world, so we didn't hear Derek or Hunter enter the room. It was Hunter's voice that announced their presence.

"Did you just *sniff* the baby?"

Derek chuckled. "She sniffs everything."

"I do not." *I totally do.*

Intrigued, Hunter walked to the bed. "What does she smell like?"

"Baby," I said.

Hunter squinted at me, then leaned forward and inhaled a giant whiff of Caroline.

Derek was amused. "God, I hope my kid decided to try out her diaper a minute ago."

The nurse who had wheeled the baby in came back and interrupted our sniff fest. "Are we ready to see how Caroline does latching on?"

Anna nodded. She looked nervous. "Ready as I'll ever be."

"The first few times can be a little frustrating, so why don't I go grab you a support pillow and some breast pads while you say goodbye to your friends. They can go to the waiting room, and I'll come get them when you're done, if you want."

"No. That's okay," Anna said. "They need to go home and get some rest. They've been here all night. Why don't you guys go sleep and come back tonight if you feel up to it."

I really was exhausted. And I was certain Anna needed sleep more than I did. "Okay."

"I'll give you my keys," Derek said.

I'd completely forgotten that my plan had been to stay with Anna and Derek after the shower. It would be weird to stay there without Anna home. Plus, they needed their privacy now that they'd have a newborn at home for the first time.

"That's okay. I'm going to check into a hotel."

"Don't be ridiculous. Stay at our house. Derek will be here most of the time until I come home anyway."

Hunter piped in. "I'll make sure she has a place to stay."

"Are you sure?" Anna questioned.

"Positive. We'll all get some rest and come back later to visit."

Anna yawned. "Okay."

"Bye, beautiful baby girl." I caressed Caroline's cheek one last time and stole one more sniff.

"Do you know of a place nearby where I can stay?"

"Sure do."

I leaned back into the leather seat of Hunter's pickup and closed my eyes. "I haven't stayed up this long since college. My body actually aches from lack of sleep. I feel old."

"We'll get you some sleep, and you'll feel as good as you look in no time."

I mumbled something about him being a charmer and told myself that closing my eyes for three minutes wouldn't hurt. The next thing I knew, I was being lifted out of Hunter's truck. I blinked my eyes into focus. "Where are we?"

"My house."

"You were supposed to take me to a hotel."

"No. You asked if I knew a place nearby, and I said yes. I do. My place." He used a foot to swing the truck's door shut.

"I'm not staying with you."

"It's six o'clock in the morning. Check in at hotels is the middle of the afternoon. Even if I found a place with a vacancy—which in this area is not as easy as it sounds—you'd have to wait to check in or pay for last night when you didn't sleep there."

He had a point. But still... "I can't stay here."

"I have a guest room. You can crash in there for a few hours. I'll take you to a hotel this afternoon, if that's what you want. But I have plenty of room, and you're welcome to stay."

A part of me wanted to argue. But the man had been shuttling me around since he'd picked me up from the airport, and he had to be as exhausted as I was.

"Okay. But no funny business."

Hunter grinned. "Never."

Chapter 9

— Natalia —

A warm stream of light shining directly into my eyes woke me up. Disoriented, I had no idea where I was or what day it was. I sat up in the comfy bed and looked around the familiar room until the morning came back to me. *Hunter's house.* I'd left my phone in my purse, which was still in the kitchen—I think—and there was no sign of a clock in the guestroom. So after a quick trip to the ensuite bathroom, I headed out to quietly retrieve my cell, hoping not to wake Hunter if he was still sleeping.

Only...Hunter was *definitely* not sleeping.

I froze as I turned the corner from the bedroom hallway to the open kitchen and living room. He stood with his back to me at the stove, cooking what smelled like bacon—shirtless, while dancing to Billy Joel.

As far as wake-ups go, this view was up there. Hunter wore gray sweatpants that hung low on his narrow waist, and the muscles in his back rallied together to form a V that led up to broad shoulders. There was no doubt the man worked out—a lot. I stood in silence, taking in the way his hips swayed to the music and remembering how good his rhythm was when we'd danced together at Anna's wedding. *Damn.*

"Hope you're not a vegetarian. I don't make tofu anything, especially not bacon." I jumped at the sound of his husky voice. He'd never turned around to see me, and still hadn't when he spoke.

My heart raced in my chest. "You scared the crap out of me."

He finally turned around. "*Me*? I didn't sneak up on you while you were frying hot bacon to ogle your ass."

I narrowed my eyes. "I wasn't ogling your ass."

"It's okay. I don't mind."

"*I wasn't ogling your ass.*"

Hunter turned back around to the stove, reached up to the cabinet on the right to grab a dish, and then used tongs to pick the bacon from the frying pan.

"The more we deny the truth, the more power it has over us." He set the plate on the table before returning his attention to me with a cheeky grin. "On second thought, keep denying it. It'll just make you focus on it more."

"You're really a big ass, you know that?"

Hunter held a hand to his ear. "What's that? You really dig my ass?"

"Are you always this obnoxious in the morning? No wonder you live alone."

"It hasn't been morning for hours. It's almost three o'clock. Come. Sit and eat. Your eggs will be done in a minute."

"Three o'clock?" I walked to the table forgetting about his ass comment. "I slept the entire day away."

"You needed it."

He poured a mug of coffee and held it up to me. "Cream and sugar?"

"Yes, please. I can't believe how long I slept. What time did you wake up?"

"Around eleven."

Hunter brought me coffee. "Thank you." As he handed it to me, my eyes did an involuntary sweep of his chest. It would have been fast and harmless, had the jackass not watched me do it. God, the man didn't miss a beat. He quirked a brow and smirked.

"Shut up. Go put some clothes on if you don't want me to look."

"I never said I didn't want you to look."

"What are you, a peacock? Walking around fanning your tail feathers, trying to attract a female?"

"That's not a bad idea. Let me show you my tail."

I couldn't help but laugh. "Let's start over. Good morning, Hunter."

His smile was genuine. He nodded. "Good morning, Natalia."

"Did you sleep well?"

"I did. You?"

"I can't remember the last time I was out that cold. That bed is really comfortable."

"I'm glad you enjoyed it. Just an FYI, the one in the master bedroom is the same model if you'd like to try it out next."

I shook my head. "You just can't help yourself, can you? It always comes back to sex."

He chuckled and went to the stove to get the eggs. "I spoke to Derek a little while ago. He said Anna and the baby are doing great, and they'll probably go home tomorrow morning."

"Wow. So fast. I think I'd want a few days at the hospital for people to take care of me before I went home."

"Derek will take good care of her."

"You're right. I forget she has an amazing husband." I scoffed. "I forget they exist sometimes."

"Derek told me you were divorced. That was about all I could get out of him."

"Derek is a gentleman. He goes by the *say nothing if you don't have anything nice to say* rule, so I'm sure he had nothing extra to say about Garrett."

"You mentioned something about prison this morning. What happened, if you don't mind me asking?"

"I'll give you the short version. Married after six months of dating. Lived the American dream in a penthouse with a gorgeous, wealthy man. He was arrested three years later for securities fraud, and I saw none of it coming. I was blindsided in every way. He left me with more than my annual salary in debt that he'd racked up in my name *and* as the sole caregiver of his then-thirteen-year-old daughter who hated me. I'm still working to get both under control two years later."

"Jesus."

"Yeah." I was anxious to change the subject. "Do you know what time visiting hours are?"

"3:30 to 5:30 and 6:30 to 8:30. But Derek said to try to come up for the afternoon hours because he has some big surprise dinner being delivered from Anna's favorite restaurant at 6:30."

"He's so sweet. I guess we should get going soon then. I was hoping to check into a hotel and shower before we went back to visit, but I don't think we'll have time."

"You're welcome to shower here. And stay as long as you want. I have an early flight out tomorrow morning for work up north anyway, so you'd have the place to yourself after tonight."

"That's very nice of you. Maybe I'll take you up on the shower if you really don't mind. And then I can find a hotel after we visit the hospital."

"After dinner, you mean?"

"Dinner?"

"My birthday dinner. You agreed to have dinner with me."

"God. I totally forgot. It seems like that conversation was a week ago instead of this morning. It's *still* your birthday?"

"Yep. But I'm passing the torch to baby Caroline after today. Thirty is the last one I celebrate. After this, it's all hers. So you're going to help me celebrate the very last one I get."

"That's a lot of pressure. Now I feel like I'm going to have put on a dress and be entertaining and witty."

Hunter winked. "Feel free to make that dress cut low in the front and showing off a lot of leg."

⌐━━━

"You look beautiful, Natalia."

After we visited the hospital, Hunter had dropped me off at a hotel so I could check in and get ready for dinner.

"Thank you." It was the second time he'd complimented me since he'd picked me up. Even though he liked to tease me about sex—some of which was not *really* teasing—I was somehow certain his praise was sincere tonight. "You don't look bad yourself *for a man in his thirties*."

"Take it easy. I'm about eight hours *into my thirties*."

The waitress came to our table. "Can I start you off with something to drink? Tonight's special drink is a coconut margarita. It has fresh cream of coconut, lime juice, Cointreau, and Patrón tequila. The glass is lined with salted, toasted coconut."

"Mmmm. That sounds delicious. I'll try one of those," I said.

Hunter ordered a Coke.

"What? It's your birthday. Your *last* birthday. Aren't you going to join me for a drink?"

"I'm driving, and I have a 6 a.m. flight."

I turned to the waitress. "Can you make a virgin coconut margarita?"

"Sure can."

"He'll have one of those. And put an umbrella or something in it. It's his *thirtieth* birthday."

She smiled and looked to Hunter for approval to change his order.

He chuckled. "That's fine. Thanks."

After she walked away, I looked around at the rooftop Mexican restaurant. The view of a twinkling L.A. was breathtaking.

"This place is great. Do you come here often?"

"First time."

"Really? I would think this place would be in your dating arsenal—impressive restaurant with a view and a long drink menu on top of a hotel. It's like a playboy's one-stop-shopping dream. Couple of drinks…grab a room…"

"I prefer to keep a mattress in the bed of my pickup. It's cheaper and easier to dump them off when I'm done."

I laughed. "Smart."

"You know I'm not really a whore."

The waitress delivered our drinks, so I sipped mine. It was the most delicious drink I'd ever tasted—like a melted, toasted coconut ice cream bar.

"Really? So how many women have you dated in, say, the last month?"

He thought about it for a minute. "Three."

"Hmph. That's not so bad, I guess." I sipped my drink again and squinted at him. "Unless you slept with all of them. Sleeping with three different women a month would be thirty-six a year...after ten years of singlehood that would be upwards of three hundred and sixty different women. That's kinda gross."

Hunter frowned.

I smirked. "Slept with 'em all, huh?"

"I travel a lot for work. Sometimes I spend the better part of three months on a job site out of state, so I don't always get to date that often."

"So you don't date when traveling? You've never met a woman at a bar while on the road and brought her back to your room?"

Another frown. "Did we or did we not meet when I overheard *you* deciding to bring some random—boring as shit, I might add—guy back to your room while you were traveling?"

"That's different."

"How?"

"I have a good reason for not wanting anything more than sex from a man these days. Plus, I don't do it very often."

Hunter said nothing. He seemed to like to argue with me, so my guess was his sudden silence was because I'd hit upon something he didn't want to talk about. Perhaps he had his own good reasons for not wanting anything but a sexual relationship with someone.

"So, tell me something about your love life, birthday boy who isn't a whore. I gave you the thirty-second version of my heartache this afternoon. What's your deal?"

"Not much to tell."

"Ever married?"

"Nope."

"Engaged?"

"Nope."

"Serious girlfriend."

"One."

I took another sip. "Now we're getting somewhere. How long was that relationship?"

"A few years."

Although that surprised me, it did make sense. I wanted no part of a relationship because of my sour outlook after my marriage. "Why did you break up?"

He shifted in his seat. "Life."

"*Ah*. That tells me a lot."

"I prefer to live my life looking forward, not backward. You look in the rearview mirror too often, sometimes you miss what's right in front of you."

Huh. Not the answer I expected. But a damn good point.

The waitress came back to our table. Her timing was perfect for a change in the tone of our conversation. After she took our dinner order, and I finished off my large margarita, I shared something I'd been thinking about earlier as I was getting ready.

"My mom's a big gardener. Growing up, she would plant a different flower on my birthday each year—one that would bloom around my spring birthday. Every year, we'd go outside to plant a new one, and all of my birthday plants would be in bloom. When I went away to college, she would snap pictures and send them in my card. It's kind of goofy, but I loved it and looked forward to it each year. Yesterday, when you showed me your mom's birthday birdhouses, it made me think maybe we could start some sort of a tradition for Caroline."

Hunter sat back in his chair. "I'd like that. What did you have in mind?"

"You know the big oak tree that's right outside Caroline's bedroom window in the yard?"

"Yeah."

"I was thinking maybe we could send her plants every year to hang from that tree on her birthday. You could make Anna and Derek a flower box to keep all the flowers in individual containers with hangers. Then on her birthday each year, we could take turns going over the night before and hanging all the plants on the tree—sort of like a Christmas tree, but a birthday tree instead."

Hunter stared at me funny for a minute. I thought it might've been a look of disappointment, which caused me to say, "If you think it's silly, we can just forget it."

"No, not at all. I think it's a great idea."

"Oh, okay. You made a weird face, so I thought maybe you thought it was a dumb idea."

Hunter scratched his chin and did this squinty thing with his eyes that looked like he was trying to figure out a problem.

"What?"

"Nothing."

"Tell me. I saw on your face that you were thinking something."

He stared for another minute before leaning forward and folding his hands on the table. "Alright, when I went to Anna to try to get your telephone number after you blew me off with the wrong one, she refused, and when I asked her why, she said, 'I'm not giving it to you for your own good. She's as beautiful inside as she is out, and she'll break your heart when you realize she's not ready to let anyone in.'" He paused. "Figured she was full of shit and was trying to pass on your rejection so it wouldn't hurt my fragile ego. Now I'm not so sure anymore."

Hunter didn't joke around about us having sex when we left the restaurant. To my surprise, he didn't even attempt to come up to my room after he walked me into the lobby.

"Thank you for dinner, even though *I* should've been the one who paid since it's your birthday. And thank you for picking me up at the airport, letting me crash at your house, and shuttling me all over."

"You're welcome."

I pressed the button to the elevator. "I guess I'll be in touch next year for our first joint Caroline-birthday-tradition present?"

"Going to need to exchange numbers to get in touch next year. Think you can give me the right number now that we've made friends?"

I smiled. "Sure."

Hunter dug into his pocket for his cell and extended it to me, but when I went to take it, he latched onto my hand. "Kiss me once more."

I looked around the hotel. There were people milling around in the lobby, even a family with kids. "I'm not sure our kiss would be G-rated enough for the lobby."

As if it was in cahoots with the man, the elevator dinged, announcing its arrival. Hunter took my hand and pulled me inside. He pressed the button to close the doors and tugged me close. "Now we have privacy. What floor?"

"Fifteen. But I'm not going—"

The rest of my sentence was swallowed into a kiss as Hunter planted his mouth over mine. Perhaps it was *third time's a charm,* or perhaps I was aware that the elevator ride wouldn't last very long and subconsciously didn't want to waste even a second, but I didn't bother to try to fight it. I opened for him, and my body melted into his the minute his eager tongue found mine. The electricity that had been zapping between us since the very first kiss ignited like a two-hundred-and-twenty-volt switch had been flipped on. Hunter gripped my wrists and held them behind my back, which only made my need to touch him even more desperate.

When the kiss broke, I was confused. My heart raced, my breaths were ragged and uneven, and the elevator doors I'd watched close were now open again. Apparently we'd risen fifteen floors, and I hadn't felt a thing. Hunter knelt and picked his cell up from the floor. I'd dropped it without even realizing. That seemed to be a common thing when he kissed me—my ability to focus on anything other than the kiss disappeared.

He held out his phone and cleared his throat, although his voice was still hoarse when he spoke. "If you want me to be a gentleman and stay on this elevator, put your number in. Otherwise, we're going to your room until you give it up."

I collected myself and nodded, still unable to find my voice. Before that kiss, I'd had every intention of giving Hunter my phone number. What was the harm? He lived three-thousand miles away, and I was reasonably assured he wasn't a serial killer. Plus, we now had an annual gift to coordinate for our sweet Caroline. But my still-racing heart reminded me that this was a man I should minimize contact with. There was no specific reason, yet I knew it was the right thing to do. It was like when someone throws a punch and you instinctively raise your hands to protect your face. Hunter's kiss sent my body into self-protective mode. Smiling up at him and taking in his handsome face one last time, I punched seven digits into his phone and offered it back.

"You sure it's the right number this time?"

I lied. "Yes." Then I practically ran out of the elevator. "Goodnight, Hunter. Happy birthday. Take care of yourself."

Chapter 10

— Hunter —
12 years ago

Nine hours on a bus that smells like urine. Happy birthday to me.

The last time I made the trip from Berkeley to UCLA, I'd been fucking miserable. The air conditioning had been crap during one of the worst heat waves to hit southern California in a decade. A month later, summer's heat had cooled into fall, so at least the temperature wasn't making the already bad smell into pungent *hot* piss. Still, next time I needed to get to the terminal earlier so I didn't get stuck sitting next to the nasty bathroom.

The only good thing about this trip was that the seat next to me was empty. And I'd fully taken advantage, spreading my charcoal pencils and sketchpads all over the place. I was shading the angles of a drawing due Monday for my structural design class when my phone buzzed in my pocket. I smiled before even digging it out, knowing it was her.

The season might have cooled, but things were just getting heated with my very own Summer. After spending hours in the fountain together the afternoon we met, she'd had to take off—her parents were picking her up for a weekend back down in San Diego where they lived. We'd exchanged numbers, and I'd wound up texting her at two in the morning that night after having a few too many beers with my brother and his friends. Even my drunken texts that rambled on about how gorgeous she was didn't scare her away. Over the next six weeks, we texted or talked a few times a day, yapping about all sorts of shit that I didn't normally talk about. But recently, as my visit neared, our texts had taken a hot and heavy turn. We'd gone from talking about her stepfather being an asshole, my mom's death, and our plans for the future, to what we wanted to do to each other when we were together again.

I typed in my password, and her new text popped up.

Summer: Truth or dare?

I smiled. Considering I was sitting on a bus, there wasn't much of a choice. Plus, it seemed to be our thing. I always picked truth. Summer always picked dare.

Hunter: Truth.

Summer: Hmm.... Okay. Let me think of something good.

A few minutes later another text arrived.

Summer: What's the grossest thing you've ever done with a girl?

I knew the answer without even needing to ponder, although I wasn't sure she'd like to hear it. I typed back.

Hunter: Are you sure you want the truth on this one? What if it grosses you out?

Summer: Now I'm totally intrigued and need to know...

I chuckled. *Okay, you asked for it.*

Hunter: I sucked a girl's toes once. I should add that she'd just gotten out of the shower, so they were clean.

Summer: Is that something you're into?

Hunter: Not at all.

Summer: You just wanted to try it?

Hunter: No. She asked me to.

Summer: Hmmm...

What did that mean? *Hmmm...*

Hunter: Did I gross you out?

Summer: Not at all. Just the opposite. I think it's sexy that you'll do something you aren't into just to please your partner.

I wanted to demonstrate my dedication to pleasing *her* in the worst way.

Hunter: Your turn. Truth or Dare?

She typed back immediately.

Summer: Dare.

I knew what I wanted. Hell, I had a stiff one growing in my pants from just the thought of what I wanted to dare her to do. But I didn't want to be a dick and type *send me a skin shot.* So I went light, tossing the ball in her corner.

Hunter: Send me a sexy pic.

My phone went quiet after that for a good ten minutes. I'd started to get concerned that I might've upset her when it buzzed again.

Summer: Use your hands to shield your phone so no creepers on the bus see over your shoulder.

Fuck yeah.

A few seconds later, a picture flashed on my screen. Summer was completely naked, even if I didn't get a full look at everything. She was kneeling to the side with her legs closed and had one arm positioned across her chest so it covered almost both her breasts, except she'd left her pointer and middle finger spread wide so her left nipple was on full display. As if that wasn't the sexiest thing I'd ever seen, the face she made was the frosting on the cake.

Her head was tilted down in a shy way, but her lips were parted in a pout as she looked up at the camera from under her thick lashes.

Fuck. She was every guy's wet dream. Open, free spirited, face like an angel, and body like the devil. I stared at the picture so long, I hadn't realized how much time went by until Summer texted again.

> **Summer: Say something. Was that too much? What are you sitting there thinking?**
>
> **Hunter: You want the truth?**
>
> **Summer: Of course.**
>
> **Hunter: You're fucking gorgeous. I'm wondering if I should slip into the piss-smelling bus bathroom to jerk off now or try to hang on until I get to my brother's place.**
>
> **Summer: LOL. Happy birthday, Hunter. Can't wait to say it in person.**

She probably thought I was kidding. I took a deep whiff in. God, this bus reeked. *Jayce's room, it is. Sorry, big bro.* Which reminded me...Summer and I had talked about spending time together this weekend, but we hadn't made any specific plans, and my brother wanted me to go to some party to meet a girl he was head over heels for.

> **Hunter: What are you doing tonight? My brother wants to take me to a party at one of his frat brother's houses. Want to come along?**
>
> **Summer: Hmmm. I promised a friend I'd stop by a party, too. It's off campus. How about we each go make our appearances and meet up afterward back at the dorms?**

Getting two parties over with at the same time so we could be alone sounded like a damn good plan to me.

> **Hunter: I'll text you when I can escape.**

Summer: Can't wait to see you.

I spent the last hour of my bus ride memorizing every detail of Summer's body as I stared at the picture she'd sent. There was something special about this girl—and it wasn't just that she was better than a pinup. I even wanted Jayce to meet her, something I'd never given a shit about before. Neither one of us had ever brought a girl home to meet Mom. That thought made my heart heavy, knowing it would never happen now. But for some reason, Summer was different. We'd only spent four hours together in person, though we'd been talking for over a month. Yet I wanted her to meet the only real family I had left. Jayce would like her—hell, we had similar taste in girls.

Chapter 11

— Natalia —

Since I'd returned from California, I'd missed three Sunday night dinners at my mother's house, and now I was late for a fourth because our train hadn't budged in fifteen minutes.

"Why don't we just take your car, or better yet, an Uber, out to Howard Beach like we always did when Dad came?"

Isabella was a smart girl. She knew the answer.

"Because driving from the City to Howard Beach takes forever in traffic, and an Uber is a hundred and fifty dollars round trip. The A train is faster and three bucks each way."

She raised her perky little nose in the air. "When I grow up, I'm not going to be poor."

"We're not poor."

"So why are we in this stalled sweat box right now instead of an air-conditioned Uber?"

"Because we don't waste money. We make wise decisions on how to use it." I pointed my chin at her feet. "You know, like on those hundred-and-forty-dollar Nikes I just bought you. There's your Uber."

She rolled her eyes, but stopped bitching. A few minutes later, the train finally started to move again. It was just in the nick of time, too. I'm not claustrophobic or anything, but the oppressive heat had me feeling like I was trapped inside a sealed baggie with no air.

Mom's house was a fifteen-minute walk from the train. She lived in the same two-family brick house we'd lived in growing up—only instead of a tenant to help pay the rent upstairs, now my oldest sister and her family occupied the space. They'd moved in two years ago when she had her second baby so Mom could help with the kids.

The smell of sauce wafted through the air as we turned the corner to my mother's block. Of course, this was Howard Beach, so almost every brick house in the neighborhood had an Italian family cooking sauce— or gravy, as most of them called it. But I could actually identify the smell of my mom's sauce. My mouth salivated as we walked closer.

I used my key to let myself in. "We're here! Sorry we're late."

My mother pursed four fingers together while she spoke. "The pasta is going to be overcooked." She power-kissed both of my cheeks and then moved on to Izzy. "You've grown even more in the last few weeks. Now you have more room for meatballs. Come. You can lick the spoons on the cake I just made before you set the table."

I followed the two of them into the eye of the storm, otherwise known as the kitchen. My two nieces were in highchairs, the one year old crying and the two year old banging a spoon against her plastic tray while yelling "Ma Ma Ma Ma" nonstop. My sister Alegra yelled *hello* while dumping sauce from a giant pot into a giant bowl. My sister Nicola screamed *fuck* while pulling bread from the oven—she'd apparently burned herself. And Mom began scolding her in Italian for her language.

Yep. I missed Sunday night dinners.

Jumping in, I grabbed glasses and napkins and started setting the dining room table. When I went back into the kitchen to grab plates, the doorbell rang.

"Will Francesca ever remember her key?"

"Your sister isn't coming. She's in Jersey for the weekend, down at the shore," Mom mumbled. "I hope she brought sunscreen."

"Well, that makes setting the table a lot easier." My sister Francesca had an array of obsessive-compulsive behaviors, one of them being symmetry and orderliness. It took her over an hour to *fix* the table after someone else set it on Sundays. Growing up, I'd shared a room with her, which was how I became interested in cognitive behavioral therapy to begin with—not that she'd let me work with her *or* even go see a different therapist.

The doorbell rang again.

"Natalia, go answer the door."

"Why? It's probably just someone who wants to save our souls." I turned to Alegra. "On second thought, you should probably get it. Your soul needs saving, floozy."

Mom barked, "Go get the door, Natalia. That's our guest. Don't keep him waiting."

"Our guest?"

"Go! And brush your hair before you answer the door."

I shook my head, but headed to the front door anyway. If Bella Rossi said jump...

The peephole was so damn high, I had to stand on my tippy toes and crane my neck to the sky. A man stood on the top step of the stoop, facing the street. From the back, he looked damn good in his jeans. Maybe I should have fixed my hair for the Jehovah's Witness after all. *Wait? Do Jehovah Witnesses have premarital sex?* I smirked to myself. *I really need to get laid. I'm checking out the religious solicitor standing on the stoop next to a statue of the Virgin Mary at my mother's house.*

With a smile still on my face, I opened the door. "Can I help you?"

The man turned, and my breath caught in my throat. I blinked a few times, but it didn't change the face in front of me—the gorgeous face with a smile that slowly curved into something wicked.

"What...what are you doing here?"

"Your mother invited me for dinner."

I'd forgotten whose number I'd punched into his phone when I last saw him in California a month ago. "My mother?"

"Yes. You *accidentally* gave me Bella's number instead of yours, remember?"

Oh. My. God. I'm going to kill my mother. I'd given Hunter the number as a joke, figuring he'd take the not-too-subtle hint. And if not, I'd been sure Mom would send him running the other direction. She couldn't talk to a single man for three minutes without mentioning that her daughter Natalia needed a husband and babies.

I was utterly and completely bewildered to see Hunter standing at my mother's door. "My mother invited you, and you flew across the country for her sauce?"

"I had business in New York this week, and Bella thought it would be nice for us to see each other again. I figured since I was here, it would give you an opportunity to rectify your *mistake* in giving me the wrong number. Again."

"I think you might be a little insane."

My mother startled me when she flung open the door that had swung partially closed behind me.

"Ah, you must be Hunter." She stepped forward and kissed both his cheeks. "So nice to meet you. Why are you still standing outside? Did my rude daughter forget her manners? Come in. Come in."

I hadn't moved since I'd opened the door. Hunter stepped around me into the house, pausing as he passed. He leaned down and kissed my cheek, then whispered in my ear, "I'll take a proper kiss hello later."

—

I still couldn't believe Hunter was in New York, much less sitting at the head of my mother's dining room table. Everyone's hands were joined and our heads bowed to say grace, which gave me the perfect opportunity to stare at him without being caught. God, he was so damn handsome. Dangerously so. As my mother prayed to the Holy Mother Mary, I found myself thinking what it would be like to be underneath this man. Bella would spend a week in church praying for my soul if she knew the thoughts I was thinking during her prayer.

I bet he fucked hard and was attentive in bed. Unconsciously, my tongue ran along my bottom lip as a thousand dirty thoughts flooded my mind. Of course, Hunter picked that moment to open his eyes and glance up at me. A boyish grin crossed his face as our eyes locked. God, my stomach fluttered like a teenage girl's.

I forced my eyes back shut for the rest of grace, which wasn't an easy task. Just like the first time we were together, I found myself amazed that a man had such a visceral effect on me—a lot like things had been at first with Garrett. *That thought* was better than a cold shower. At least my ex-husband was still good for something.

It took less than two minutes after prayer for the Rossi women to start the inquisition. Hunter had no idea what he was in for sitting at a table of *seven* Rossi women and one teenage girl with an attitude.

"So, Hunter, how did you and my sister meet?"

"At Derek and Anna's wedding."

My mother chimed in. "Hunter caught the garter, and Nat caught the bouquet. Isn't that romantic?"

A room full of *awww*s ensued.

Mom added, "Hunter has a degree in architecture. He's in commercial building." It sounded like Mom and Hunter had spent a lot of time on the phone. Of course, my mother probably thought he was ready to give her grandchildren next week. She'd invite Jeffrey Dahmer to dinner if it meant I got married again and popped out a baby. Little did she know, Hunter Delucia only wanted to defile her daughter.

"It sounds very romantic." *Did my sister Alegra just bat her eyelashes and swoon?*

Izzy looked at me. "You're dating that guy?"

"No."

"Because don't you have a date with that dweeb Marcus this week?"

Thanks for keeping my secrets there, kid. "Ummm.... Yes. But like I said, Hunter and I aren't dating. We're just friends."

Hunter smiled at Izzy and winked. "Friends who sometimes kiss."

My eyes went wide. Izzy seemed to find the situation amusing. I put down my napkin and stood. "Hunter, can I speak to you in the kitchen for a moment?"

He looked to my mother before standing. "Please excuse me for a minute, Bella."

I heard Izzy say, "She probably wants to kiss him again," right before the dining room broke out in laughter.

My hands went to my hips as Hunter shut the kitchen door behind him. "What do you think you're doing?"

He feigned innocence. "Having dinner. Getting to know your family."

"You just told them we kiss sometimes!"

He leaned against the kitchen island and folded his arms across his chest. "We do."

"First of all, it's inappropriate. Izzy is not even sixteen yet. And it's none of my family's business. And secondly, it was only twice, and the first time I was drunk, so that doesn't count."

"It was five times, and I'm counting the time you were drunk. By the way, that time, you kissed me."

"Five? It wasn't five times. And I seriously doubt I initiated the kiss. You're just making that up because you know I don't remember it well."

"Five times." He held up a finger. "One—the night of the wedding." A second finger came up. "After the wedding—the next morning against the hotel door." A third finger came up. "At my house—started at the window, ended on the bed." The fourth finger rose. "In the elevator, when I said goodnight to you like the gentleman I'm not."

Okay, so maybe I had forgotten about the house. *Damn. That was a good kiss.* "Fine," I snapped. "But that's four and not five."

The devilish look on Hunter's face made my knees weak. He closed the gap between us faster than I could come to my senses.

"Kiss me," he said gruffly.

He didn't wait for a response before crushing his lips to mine. *God, can this man kiss.* It was slow, confident, and had the perfect amount of aggressiveness that made me want to claw at his skin.

When the kiss broke, Hunter leaned his forehead against mine. "That's five, sweet pea."

He must have sucked the brain out of my head along with my tongue, because I smiled back at him like an idiot instead of telling him to shove it up his ass. *His damn, sexy ass, I might add.*

"I can't believe you're here."

"Me either. But get used to it. I took an assignment out here for a while."

"How long are you in town?"

He looked into my eyes. "Two months. And don't bother to try to hide anymore. Your mother gave me your number a week ago."

***

Seven at one blow.

I remember reading the Brothers' Grimm Fairy Tale where the giant is impressed because he thinks the tailor slayed seven men with one blow. The tailor had nothing on Hunter Delucia, who'd charmed seven Rossi women and one disgruntled teenager over one dinner. Okay, so maybe it was eight Rossis, including me, but who's counting anyway?

After dinner, both of my sisters and my mother peered out the front windows to watch Hunter play basketball with Izzy in the driveway. I sat in a chair across the room, attempting to pretend I had no interest in looking.

"Jesus Christ, every time he does a jump shot, his shirt rides up. I hope he kicks Izzy's ass," Alegra said.

"I haven't seen a V like that in...well, I don't think I've ever seen one like that in person." Nicola swooned.

Mom was Team Hunter all the way. "He's a handsome man. But I invited him to dinner without even seeing him. So that should tell you something. He's just as attractive inside as out."

I rubbed my temples. "How long did you talk to him?"

"Long enough to know he's had one serious girlfriend, his mother died when he was seventeen, he had one brother who died a few years ago, and his hobbies are scuba diving, surfing, and rock climbing."

My jaw hung open. "He had a brother who died? Rock climbing?"

"Yes, his name was Jayce. He's also Catholic. He hasn't been to confession in quite a few years. You should work on rectifying that. It's good for the soul to ask the Lord for forgiveness."

Why in the world did this man show up at my mother's door? Any other man would have run as fast and far as he could without looking back. Instead, not only did he survive the interrogation by my mother—a woman who because of her own experiences is leery of all men—but I got the feeling *my mother* might have had a bit of a crush on the man herself.

I stood and walked to the window where she was still gawking. Standing behind her, I placed a hand on her shoulder. "He sounds great, Mom."

"He does."

"You have my blessing."

"Good. Wait. *What*?"

"You have my blessing to go out with him. I know he's a few years younger than you, but I think you two will make a great couple."

My sisters smirked at me behind my mother's back.

Mom actually blushed. "I'm not interested in him for me. I meant for you!"

"Uh-huh." I hid my smile and made a face that said *sure you are.*

"Natalia Valentina Rossi. You need to get back out into the dating world, and this man has flown all the way across the country to get to know you better."

"He has a job out here, Mom. He travels for work, and his job happens to be in New York this time."

"It didn't happen to be in New York. He requested the project so he could be closer to you."

I was taken aback. "He told you that?"

Izzy blasted through the front door. "He's better than my coach!"

Is that...*a smile* I see on her face? The man wasn't just a charmer, he was a fucking magician.

"But he's not as good as me, is he?"

Hunter walked in behind her and closed the front door. He was sweaty, *so deliciously sweaty.* "You play?"

Izzy scoffed. "When she shoots a free throw, one of her legs goes up like she's Marilyn Monroe. And a few weeks ago, she scored a goal."

Hunter's brows drew down. "She plays soccer, too?"

"No, that's what she said when she miraculously hit a basket. She started jumping up and down yelling that she'd scored a goal."

"I was excited."

Izzy shook her head, but the smile never left her face. "I invited Hunter to come see my game on Tuesday. He's gonna watch and tell me what I'm doing wrong, like Dad used to do."

I looked at Hunter. "Oh, is he?"

"Is that okay with you?" he asked, looking sincere.

Izzy was so excited, I couldn't possibly say no. At least that's the reason I gave myself when I didn't object.

"Sure. That's nice of you. I have plans after the game, but I can make them a little later to stay for the recap."

The Hunter swoon-fest continued during dessert. After we'd finished, when I caught the time on my phone, I was surprised to find it was almost ten o'clock. Normally we were out of here by eight since Izzy had school in the morning and the train ride was over an hour.

"It's getting really late. We better head out, Izzy."

She frowned. But then a thought gave her momentary hope. "What train do you take, Hunter?"

"I drove here. But I'm staying in Manhattan. I can drop you ladies on the way to my sublet."

I said, "No, thank you" at the same moment Izzy said, "That'd be great."

Both looked at me with pouts. I rolled my eyes. "Fine. Traffic should be moving by now anyway."

The car ride was surprisingly quiet. Izzy put her headphones on in the backseat and fell asleep ten minutes into the ride, probably wiped out from playing basketball with Hunter for so long. Hunter looked lost in thought, and I struggled with my own thoughts as I looked out the window. Namely, while the idea of getting involved with this man was very tempting, I was in no way ready for a relationship. I also needed to keep my focus on the important things—my career and stepdaughter.

As we crossed the bridge back into Manhattan, Hunter broke the comfortable silence. "Your family is great."

Knowing his mother and brother were deceased, I felt his words in my chest, and it made me appreciate what normally annoys the crap out of me. "Yeah, they are. But don't tell them I said that."

Hunter smiled and spoke quietly. "I hope you don't mind my coming to the game Tuesday night. I played ball in college. She's really good, and I didn't know how to say no."

"No, not at all. It's really sweet of you."

After a few more minutes, he said, "Those plans you mentioned having after the game, would those be the same plans Izzy mentioned at dinner that involve a guy named Marcus?"

I nodded. "One and the same."

"First date?"

"Second."

Again he went quiet. Eventually, he said, "Poor bastard."

My brows drew down. "What? Who?"

"Marcus. Probably had a nice first date. Won't understand why you're so distant on the second one and never accept a third. Will think he did something wrong."

"What are you talking about?"

Hunter shrugged. "You'll be busy thinking of me on your date Tuesday night. Poor bastard won't even know what hit him."

"You're so full of yourself."

Even though Izzy was sleeping with headphones on, he leaned in close to whisper, "Maybe. But soon you'll be full of me, too."

Chapter 12

— Natalia —

I spent a ridiculous amount of time getting ready so I looked good for my date after the game tonight. It had nothing to do with the man who was going to be *at* the game. I repeat, *nothing to do with Hunter Delucia.*

Marcus was a great guy. Good job—a web developer for a prominent local utility company. Polite—opened my car door and pulled my seat out at dinner on our first date. Nice looking—medium height, medium build, maybe twenty pounds to lose. But who didn't have an extra twenty to lose when they hit their thirties?

I hated that the answer to that question came as a visual *way* too readily available in my mind. Hunter didn't have an extra twenty to lose, *that's who.*

I took one last look in the mirror. My red skirt was the brightest of reds. It wasn't short, yet it managed to pull off sexy because of the way it hugged my curves without being slutty tight. I'd coupled it with a simple, black button-up blouse that had feminine, capped sleeves and a pair of sandals that had heels, but weren't too inappropriate for attending a high school basketball game before my date.

When I arrived at the gym in Izzy's school, the game hadn't started yet, but Hunter was already seated in the stands. He stood when I went to join him and pulled me in for an innocent kiss on the cheek. Although there wasn't anything innocent about what I felt when near this man.

"You look gorgeous."

"Thank you."

Hunter grumbled. "Poor bastard."

I laughed it off, and we sat just as the girls jogged out from the locker room. Izzy was the third one in line.

"She's the only sophomore on the varsity team, and she's one of the tallest already."

"Are both her parents tall?"

"Her father's six foot two, and her mother was probably about five foot ten."

"Was?"

"She died a few years ago."

"Wow. Tough. Dad's in prison and Mom died young. She's lucky she has you."

"Most days she doesn't see it that way."

"She's fifteen. She sees what she wants to see in order to justify brooding. I'm not saying what happened to her is easy, but teenage girls will find a reason to brood even when there isn't one."

"Sounds like you're speaking from experience."

"After my mom died, I moved in with my Uncle Joe and his wife, Elizabeth. He was much younger than my mother, so he felt more like an older cousin than an uncle growing up. We got along great, but him and his daughter—that was a whole different story. When Cara was about Izzy's age, she was one big pain in the ass. Her life was perfect. Parents were happily married. Father's a doctor. Mother stayed home to raise her. She was smart and beautiful— got the best genes from both parents. Yet she found a reason to growl at them daily. Never understood what the hell she was so angry about. I would have given anything to be in her predicament. She's twenty-four now. Grew out of it, and now we laugh about it all the time."

"I'm not sure we'll ever get to the place where we look back and laugh at these years. But I get what you're saying."

"How long is her dad away for?"

"A few more months. He made some ridiculous deal by testifying against a federal regulator he'd bribed and got thirty months instead of the thirty years he deserved."

"What happens when he gets out? Izzy goes to live with him?"

"I don't know. I'm guessing so, but we haven't started talking about it. Taking it one day at a time right now."

The announcer came on to call the starting lineup. Hunter and I stood and cheered when they called Izzy's name. She looked up at the stands and half smiled at us before her eyes shifted a couple of rows up, and suddenly the lame smile she graced us with turned beaming while she waved to someone else. Both Hunter and I followed her line of sight to a tall boy of Indian descent sitting alone on the top row.

"Who's that?" Hunter thumbed toward the top bleacher when we turned back around. He'd only met her once, but there was a protective tone in his voice nonetheless.

I sighed. "It must be Yakshit."

His brows jumped. "Pardon?"

"The boy she has a crush on. His name is Yakshit."

Hunter shook his head and grumbled, "Another poor bastard."

"You hit sixty percent of your free throws." Hunter said to Izzy. "You have a great shot. But you can definitely do better. You're flicking the ball with your thumb on your guide hand as you take your shot, which is making it spray left."

"Coach said the same thing."

"Have you tried squeezing your thumb and index finger on your guide hand together?"

"I've tried, but I forget when I'm in a game."

"You need a shooting strap. Back to basics. A J-strap and at least fifty extra free throws a day after practice until you do it automatically without the strap on in a few weeks. I can grab you one."

"Okay! What else?"

I looked at the time on my phone—it was almost seven-thirty. We'd walked around the corner to a coffee shop after the game so Hunter could give Izzy his thoughts. But the game ran late, going into overtime, and Hunter had to excuse himself for a business call that took close to a half hour as soon as we arrived. Now, I only had a half hour before my date, and it would take me that long to get Izzy home and get back to where I was supposed to meet Marcus.

Hunter caught me watching the clock and smirked. I wouldn't put it past him to have sat outside for a half hour without really having anyone to speak to.

"Excuse me for a minute. I need to make a call of my own," I said.

I stepped outside and pushed Marcus to eight-thirty with an apology. It would cut the date short, because I didn't like to leave Izzy alone at night for long and always liked to be heading home by ten. I could have postponed, but I refused to give Hunter that satisfaction.

When I returned to the table, Hunter stood. "Are we keeping you from your date?"

I flashed him a sugary smile. "No, I pushed it back a half hour."

Hunter and Izzy went back to basketball talk as I sat.

"When you're shooting from long range—three-pointer distance—you should drop your elbow to get more power behind your shot."

"I thought I was."

"Not enough. You're also leaning forward. Here, let me show you." He stood and held out his hand. "Natalia?"

I reluctantly put my hand in his. He helped me slip out of the booth and turned me around so my back was facing him. Gripping my hip in one hand, he used the other to control my arm. I was essentially his puppet.

"You're releasing here." He stopped my hand above my head.

Without realizing it, I had leaned forward, following my extended hand. Hunter ran his fingers down my side outlining the arch my torso had formed. Chills broke out all over.

"See how she's naturally bending here? Now watch her stance when she releases earlier."

He again controlled my arms to mimic throwing a ball, but stopped my hand a little lower for a simulated release. Again, he ran his hand down my side. Only this time, he went slower. Izzy was so enthralled with the knowledge and advice he was sharing, she didn't seem to see anything other than shot counseling going on. But, God, I felt it.

"See? No arch," he said as his hand reached my hip. "When's your next game?" he asked as we sat back down.

"Thursday night."

"Sorry, I won't be able to make that one. How about after that?"

"We have a game Saturday morning. But it's an away game in Westchester."

"Work on what we talked about. I'll be at that one."

Izzy's face lit up. "Okay."

By the time we paid the check, which Coach Delucia refused to let me do, I was already going to be late (again) for my date.

Izzy began texting away on her phone the minute we walked out onto the street.

I turned to Hunter. "I guess I'll see you Saturday then?"

"I'll pick you up. We can drive together."

I said yes only because I didn't like to drive over bridges. *Sure you did.*

"Izzy, say goodnight and thank Hunter."

She looked up from her texting for two seconds and gave him a genuine smile. "Thank you and goodnight, Hunter."

"You're welcome."

Izzy immediately returned her attention to her cell.

"Goodnight, *Natalia*."

I'd given up on correcting him and telling him I preferred to be called Nat. But why did the way he said my name have to sound so damn decadent?

I cleared my throat. "Goodnight, Hunter."

He gripped my hip and leaned in to kiss me on the cheek. His head lingered close to my ear. "Don't sleep with your date to try to get me out of your head. It won't work anyway."

Chapter 13

— Natalia —

"I'm sorry. What did you say?" God, I wanted to punch Hunter. This was completely his fault.

Marcus furrowed his brow. It was just the two of us at a quiet table in the back of a nice restaurant, an expensive restaurant at that. Yet I still wasn't able to maintain my focus.

"I asked if you wanted to go to an art gallery opening on Sunday afternoon."

"Oh. Sorry. It was a long day at work today, and I have a patient on my mind," I lied. "Umm...sure. That sounds nice."

Sadly, I really didn't want to go to an art gallery opening on Sunday. I said yes because I needed to have something blocking the path for Hunter. Marcus was that obstacle.

No matter how nice a guy he was and how much I wanted to be attracted to Marcus, it wasn't there. Being with Hunter an hour ago was a not-so-subtle reminder of what attraction felt like. You can't force chemistry to exist any more than you can deny that it's present. Then again, chemistry wasn't all it was cracked up to be. Chemistry is what brings people together. It isn't what keeps them together. Trust, respect, and compatibility are the glue that keeps a couple together. I had all the chemistry in the world with my ex-husband, but none of the glue that mattered most in the end.

Marcus reached across the table and took my hand. "Don't sound so excited about it," he joked.

"I'm sorry. I'm just having an off day. It's not you. Really. It's not."

He laced our fingers together. "How was your stepdaughter's game?"

"They won in overtime."

"It was nice of the coach to give her feedback after. He must be dedicated." I'd mentioned that I was going to be late because Izzy was getting some coaching tips.

"Oh, it wasn't her coach. It was Hunter—he's a friend of a friend."

"The guy from California?"

My brows drew down. "Yes. He's here for a while on business. How did you know he was from California?"

"You mentioned him on our first date."

"I did?"

He nodded. "A few times. When you were talking about your trip."

"Oh." I felt the need to explain now. "He played college basketball, so he came to the game to observe and give her some tips."

For the rest of the date, I worked at being present. Marcus didn't deserve my half-assed attention.

At the end of the night, outside of my apartment building, he took my hands. He'd insisted on seeing me home. "I know you have to get home to Izzy, but maybe Sunday after the art gallery, I can make you some dinner at my place?"

Third date. Even though I was sexually deprived and had started to date to remedy that situation, I wasn't ready for sex with Marcus.

"I go to my mom's on Sunday evenings for dinner. All my sisters go."

His smile wilted. "Another time, maybe."

"Sure."

He leaned in and kissed me. As it happened, I found myself focusing on the mechanics of the kiss. Almost as if I needed to think about what to do with my tongue, my lips, even my hands. It was the exact opposite of a kiss with Hunter. With him, I was *unable* to think. Raw passion took over, and I had zero control. Marcus's kiss was...*nice.* Pleasant.

I definitely was not panting when it broke.

"I'll see you Sunday?"

"Sunday it is." God, the entire thing felt awkward, and I couldn't wait to hide in my apartment. "Thank you again for dinner."

I knocked on the door to Mrs. Whitman's apartment across the hall to let her know I was home. Izzy was fifteen, past the age that she felt being left with a babysitter was acceptable. But I still asked the neighbor to check in on her when I went out.

Izzy was fast asleep on the couch with the TV blaring when I walked in. Rather than wake her, I covered her with a blanket. Her laptop was open, so I went to shut it, but when I moved it, the screensaver turned off, and the last thing she must've been working on came up. It was the results of a Google search of her father's name.

I'd caught her doing that on a few occasions after he was arrested. At the time, I figured it was natural for her to be curious what was being said about him. But this was more than two years later. It made me realize Hunter's presence tonight had probably made her miss him. As much as he'd lied to me and kept things from me, he'd been a good father to Izzy. He'd never missed a game, and they used to play basketball often together.

I sighed and shut the laptop before flicking off the TV. Why did the men in my life have to be so difficult?

The buzzer rang half an hour early. Considering I was running late and had just gotten out of the shower, I hoped it was my neighbor in 4D who'd forgotten her key again.

"Hello?"

"Morning, sweet pea." His voice was extra gravelly through the intercom. My nipples perked up.

I looked down, and spoke to them. "What am I going to do with you guys? Haven't we talked about this? You get your hopes up too fast, and then you're sorely disappointed." I pressed the intercom. "Fourth floor." I buzzed the front door open.

A few minutes later, Hunter stepped off the elevator and sauntered down the hallway toward me. He had a natural, confident swagger that made even his damn walk sexy—not to mention he had his work boots on again today. Those things *really* did it for me for some odd reason. And since I was standing there doing nothing but holding the door open, I couldn't help admiring the rest of the package. Unfortunately, that didn't help my nipple situation any.

Hunter's eyes dropped and took lingering note before his gaze returned to mine with a triumphant smile. I rolled my eyes and stepped aside for him to come in. Of course, he stopped in the doorway so we were toe to toe. Leaning down, he kissed my cheek and then leaned in—it seemed to be his thing, a few words that made the hair stand up on my neck after a superficially innocent kiss.

Only this time, he didn't say a word. Instead, he took an audible, deep inhale and groaned out the exhale. I felt the rumble from it shoot down to my toes, making some interesting stops on its way.

Seriously? I was a puddle from a fucking sniff. I needed an extra thirty seconds to collect myself after he walked inside.

"You're early."

He held up a bag I hadn't noticed. "I brought breakfast."

I read the logo. "Jamba Juice?"

"Steel-cut oatmeal with bananas, shredded coconut, and brown sugar."

My eyes widened. "That's my favorite breakfast in the world."

"I know. Bella told me."

"You called my mother to ask her what I liked for breakfast?"

"No. She called me last night to invite me for dinner on Sunday, and I mentioned we were going to Izzy's game. She might have suggested I pick up breakfast on my way and told me what you liked."

I spoke under my breath. "Of course she did."

Hunter smiled. "Come on, let's eat before it gets cold."

It would've been stupid to let a perfectly good breakfast go to waste as a form of protest against my mother and Hunter's new-found friendship. So I sat down and dug into the awesomeness.

I hadn't realized I'd been quiet for so long while I shoveled oatmeal into my mouth until I caught Hunter's lip twitching while he watched me.

"What?"

"I take it you really do like this stuff?"

I spoke with a full mouth. "It's better than sex."

"Then you haven't been fucked properly."

Mid-swallow, I choked on the oatmeal, sputtering and gasping.

Hunter dropped his spoon and looked like he was about to dive across the table to deliver the Heimlich.

I put a hand up to stop him and spoke with strain. "I'm fine. Water."

He grabbed a glass and filled it while I worked to catch my breath. My throat burned as I downed the water.

"You sure you're okay?"

I patted my chest as everything finally made its way down the right pipe. "I'm fine."

Hunter sat back down. "You shouldn't try to talk while swallowing."

"*You* shouldn't say inappropriate things."

"You started it. Answering the door with your nipples all perky, smelling so fucking good, talking about sex. I think you're the one who's inappropriate here."

My eyes bulged. "You showed up half an hour early, so I'd just gotten out of the shower, and my nipples were still hard as a result. That smell you like so much? *It's called soap*. And I wasn't talking about sex. I made a statement that was a *metaphor* to describe how much I like the oatmeal."

Hunter scooped a heaping spoonful of oatmeal from his container and spoke before shoveling it into his mouth. "The only thing I heard from that explanation was *nipples* and *sex*."

"How was your date last night?" Hunter side-glanced at me before returning his eyes to the road. We were sitting in traffic on the bridge on our way upstate for the game.

"It was wonderful."

He chuckled.

"What?"

"You're a shit liar."

"What are you talking about? I'm not a liar."

"You pick imaginary lint off of your clothes when you lie. You just did it when you said your date was wonderful."

"You're out of your mind."

He shrugged. "If you say so."

A few minutes of awkward silence passed before he spoke again. "Did you go back to his place?"

"That's really none of your business."

"You wanna know what I think?"

"Not really, no."

"I think you kissed him goodnight but compared it to our kiss and realized as much as you want to want this guy, you don't."

My gaze narrowed. "We had sex, and I didn't think of you once."

"Really?" He glanced over at me.

"Really," I said. I turned my head toward the window to keep my heated face from his view.

Hunter leaned over and breached my personal space while driving. "What's that you're doing with your left hand right now?"

I froze. I was picking imaginary damn lint off of my jeans. Having no response to being caught lying, I simply scowled at him.

He gloated a smile in my direction.

After a few minutes, he sighed. "Let me take you to dinner tonight."

I ignored him. "Did you take the garter I caught from Anna and Derek's wedding? I couldn't find it when I left my hotel room."

"Nope. Didn't see it."

"Damn. I really wanted to keep it."

Hunter changed the subject back. He really had a one-track mind. "So...what do you say? Let me take you to dinner tonight."

"No."

"You'll let the poor bastard you don't even like kissing take you to dinner, but you won't let me take you out?"

I nodded. "That's right."

"I'm attracted to you. You're attracted to me. I don't get it."

I decided to be honest and not filter my response. "When I was twelve years old, I came home from school early. We had a half-day for parent-teacher conferences. My mom kept a calendar on the refrigerator with all our schedules and activities. With four girls, there was scribble on most days. But that particular day, Mom had forgotten to write that we had a shortened day. Both my parents worked, and I was a latch-key kid, so I walked home from school and let myself in. There was noise coming from my mom's room, so I figured she'd left the TV on like she sometimes did. I went to turn it off and walked in on my father having sex with one of my mom's good friends."

"Shit. I'm sorry."

"My father begged me not to tell my mother, swearing it was the one and only time. He said if I told her she'd be heartbroken, and I'd break up the family."

"That's shitty. He should have manned up and told her himself, not put that on you."

"Yeah. I know that now."

"Did you tell her?"

"Not for a few weeks. One night the woman was over, and I saw the way my Dad was looking at her. I couldn't let my mom be humiliated like that. I knew it wasn't a one-time mistake he'd made, even though I was twelve. When I finally told her, he admitted it and said he was in love with her friend. Dad moved out, and Mom went into a state of depression that lasted a really long time."

"Sometimes doing the right thing sucks."

I forced a smile. "Yeah." I stared out the window, watching the trees pass for a while. "My husband didn't cheat on me, but he also didn't tell me the life we were leading was funded by money he'd stolen from unsuspecting clients, or that he'd been running a scam for years. Nor did he mention that the penthouse we lived in was on the verge of foreclosure or that he'd run up a fortune in debt on credit cards under my name. I had to move two weeks after his arrest, my bank account was overdrawn, and my credit was complete crap because he'd been having the credit card bills sent to his office and wasn't paying any of them. Even borrowing money from my mom, I couldn't get an apartment on my own because of my bad credit. Lucky for me, my wonderful husband's best friend was very supportive and was nice enough to help me find a place to live. In exchange for that kindness, he thought I should have sex with him."

"The men in your life have been shit. I get it."

"Yeah." I sighed. "I have definite trust issues. But it's more than that. I didn't go away to college like I would've liked to because I didn't want to leave my mom alone.

She never asked me to do that. In fact, she pushed me as hard as she could to go away. When I married Garrett, he wanted a stay-at-home wife even though I was just getting my therapy career started. So I left my job because of him. I'm just at a point in my life where I need to focus on me. I love my job. Izzy needs my attention. I can't get involved with anyone, even if I'm attracted to him."

Hunter nodded, and I could see from his profile he was disappointed. "There's just one thing I don't understand."

"What's that?"

"Why go out with Marcus then?"

"You won't judge me if I'm honest?"

"Never."

"Because he's a really nice guy, and although I don't want to be attached to anyone, I also don't want to be celibate. I'm not worried about getting lost in him. Does that make sense?"

We arrived at the school for Izzy's game. Hunter put the car in park and turned to face me. "It makes a lot of sense. All of it. Although, I live three-thousand miles away, and I'm definitely not looking for a relationship either. Just like you have your baggage, I have mine. I'm only in town for two months. We could agree to be not-celibate together—just sex and fun, with an expiration date. It would keep you from fucking some guy you're not attracted to, and we could get lost in each other in the bedroom only." He held my gaze. "Think about it. *Sex, not love.*"

Chapter 14

— Hunter —
12 years ago

I had no real interest in the party. Not even in the cute little redhead who used her elbows to squeeze her enormous rack together every time she batted her eyelashes at me while we spoke. But Jayce asked me to stick around, at least until the girl he wanted me to meet showed.

My big brother wasn't a love 'em and leave 'em type of guy. I could count on one hand the number of girlfriends he'd had, even though attracting them was never an issue. Jayce was just the serious type. A lot of that came from the weight he'd carried on his shoulders the last few years before Mom died. He'd refused to live on campus, even though he'd snagged a full ride, including room and board. After she passed, he still wanted to stay home to make sure I had a place to come back to for holiday breaks from school. Our uncle pretty much had to force him to live on campus and try to enjoy himself.

"You want another beer?" Jayce yelled to me from the other side of the kitchen. People were playing beer pong between where the two of us stood.

I shook my can from side to side. Since I'd been nursing it, I still had half left. "I'm good. Thanks."

He grinned. "Lightweight."

Jayce made his way back over and leaned against the kitchen sink next to me. He followed the plastic ball bouncing in front of him as he spoke. "Have you talked to Derek lately?"

"Yeah. He's building a robot or some shit that they do over there in genius land. I'm hoping it's an anatomically correct female robot he can hump because he never seems to do anything other than study."

My brother tilted his beer at me. "It'll all pay off one day. Derek's gonna be loaded, with a hot wife who thinks his geek ass walks on water. You'll see."

I laughed. "We'll see."

"How are your classes going?"

Always the big brother. "Good. You?"

"Easy. Nothing left but electives, so I'm spending most of my time tutoring underclassmen for cash."

Jayce had met the girl he liked through his tutoring job.

"Cash? Are you still charging Pearl, too? You should be taking a different kind of payment by now," I joked and chugged the rest of my beer. "By the way, who named a girl Pearl twenty years ago? Every time you say her name, I picture you dogging some blue-haired old lady like Mrs. Whitton who lived across the street."

My brother shook his head and chuckled. "You're a sick fuck. Mrs. Whitton was eighty-five with a cane. But Pearl is actually her middle name. Probably was her grandmother's or something. It's just what everyone calls her."

One of my brother's roommates yelled from the yard. "Delucia, come out here. We need someone smart to settle something."

Jayce tapped his beer can to mine. "Ain't hard to be the smart one in this crowd. I'll be back."

After beer sloshed on my shoes twice from players bumping into the beer pong table, I decided to get some fresh air. Since the backyard was packed, I went out the front, figuring I'd check my phone to see if Summer had left her party yet. Walking out onto the porch, I stopped digging for my phone when I saw two girls strolling across the lawn.

Summer.

She was walking with another girl, deep in conversation, when she looked up and our gazes caught. Her eyes flared wide before she took off running for the porch. The girl she'd been talking to looked confused as to why she'd been suddenly left hanging mid-chat.

Summer darted up the stairs and jumped into my arms. Thinking back, that might have been the moment I fell in love with her. My heart was so full from her reaction, not to mention my hands were full of a pretty spectacular ass. We hadn't kissed that first day—just sat in the fountain and talked for hours. Then we'd spent the last six weeks getting close on a level I'd never explored with a girl *before* sleeping with her. Hell, who was I kidding? I'd never bothered after sleeping with them either. After a big hug with long legs wrapped around me, I pulled my head back to take a good look at my girl. I wasn't even sure when I'd started to consider her *my girl*, but she was all the same. Plump, smiling lips invited me to taste them. Wrapping both hands around her soft cheeks, I sealed my lips over hers. The party in the background faded as she kissed me back, pushing her full tits up against my chest.

I had no idea how long it lasted, but eventually the sound of someone clearing her throat knocked us back to reality. We smiled like goofballs at each other when the kiss broke. I swiped my thumb over her bottom lip to fix her smeared lip gloss.

"Umm....do you two know each other or is this one of your stupid dares?"

Summer smiled. "Hunter here picked truth the first time I asked him. And actually, he has every time since."

Her friend shook her head. "You and your tests. I'll let you two go back to what you were doing. I'll find us something other than cheap, gross beer to drink."

"Okay. Thanks. We'll meet you inside in a few."

When her friend disappeared, I asked what she'd meant by *you and your tests*.

"When I was in eighth grade, a bunch of boys asked me to play truth or dare. Turned out that was their little trick to get girls to do stuff. Eventually one of us would pick dare because we wanted to sound cool, and then they'd dare us to kiss them. So I started using the game to weed out the boys who were only interested in one thing."

"What do you mean?"

"If I think a guy is cute and has potential, I ask him to pick truth or dare. If he goes immediately for dare, it's because he wants me to reciprocate and pick dare, and then he'll dare me to do something with him or to him— shows he's more interested in fooling around than us getting to know each other."

Her logic was untraditional, but I suppose she sort of had a point. And shit, was I glad I'd picked truth that first day. "Do most guys pick dare?"

"Almost all of them. Well, not Gavin from my art conservation class. He picked truth. But I realized he didn't really count a few days later when I met his boyfriend." She tilted her head and smirked at me. "You're not gay, are you?"

Her ass was still in my hands with her legs wrapped around my waist. I responded by grinding my hips into her so she could feel my erection. "What do you think?"

Summer giggled. The sound was damn awesome.

"What are you doing here anyway?" I asked. "I thought we were meeting up after you went to your party?"

"I was just going to ask you the same thing. Did you already hit your party?"

My brows drew down. I thumbed toward the house. "This is the party I was going to. This is the party you were going to, also?"

She smiled. "Yep. That's so funny. You said you were going to a frat party, and I said I was going to an off-campus party. It didn't dawn on me that we were both talking about an off-campus frat party."

My eyes fell to her lips. "I want to get out of here. Take you...I don't know...anywhere but here. But my brother wants me to meet someone."

"I have to meet someone, too. Maybe we can sneak out right after."

"Definitely."

As much as I hated to, I lowered Summer to the ground. The house was too mobbed with drunk people to maneuver while carrying her. I took her hand. "Come on. Let me introduce you to Jayce. Maybe his girl is here by now."

"That's funny. The guy I'm meeting is named Jayce, too."

Sometimes you just *know*. Like the first time Mom fell down. I helped her up and asked if she was okay. But something inside of me was certain she hadn't just tripped, even though that's what she'd said.

I knew the answer before I asked Summer.

"Any chance your middle name is Pearl?"

She wrinkled her little nose. "How did you know that?"

116

Chapter 15

— Natalia —

I could barely concentrate on the game. *Sex, not love.* Those were the exact same words that Anna had said to me about having a relationship with Hunter. The two of them made it sound so simple. Maybe it was. Maybe I was making it out to be more difficult than it needed to be. After all, it's what I'd have with Marcus if I slept with him. Although, I wasn't quite sure that was the way Marcus would see it. Not that I was so full of myself to think Marcus had fallen in love with me already, but my gut told me he was looking for a relationship. Of course, some men took you out to dinner a few times and pretended that's what they wanted just to get in your pants. I could be wrong, but Marcus's intentions seemed genuine.

The part of me that wanted to sleep with Hunter justified its cause. *Sleeping with Marcus would be wrong—you'd be misleading him.* The *honest* thing to do would be to break things off and have a purely sexual relationship with a man who has the same intentions. Yet the part of me that didn't want to sleep with Hunter—my brain—knew this man could break my heart. I was attracted to him, sure. Who wouldn't be? But it was more than just physical. I actually liked him. He was funny, smart, outdoorsy. Not to mention he'd bonded with Izzy—a guy has to be something special to combat teenage revulsion. Could I go in with my eyes wide open and keep feelings from growing?

"You want something?" I heard Hunter say.

I turned to him with confusion written all over my face. "Hmm?"

"You didn't hear one word I said, did you?"

"I heard you."

"Yeah? What did I ask?"

"You asked if I wanted something."

"Before that."

"*Oh.*"

He smirked and leaned in. "Thinking about what I said earlier in the car, aren't you?"

"I am not."

"Are too."

"Am not."

"Are too."

"How old are you? Because you sound like you're seven."

Hunter stood. "What do you want to eat? Because if you let me decide, I'm buying you a hot dog to watch you eat it."

"I'm not hungry." It wasn't until my eyes followed Hunter down the bleachers that I even noticed the game had stopped. It was half-time, and I'd dazed for most of the first part of the game.

Hunter returned with a brown box holding pretzels and two ridiculously large sodas. He handed one to me. "So, what did you decide?"

"I guess I'm having a pretzel since you bought it for me already."

"I meant regarding my proposal you've been fantasizing about for the last half hour."

"I wasn't..." I thought better of protesting again, which would lead to another round of immature *am not, are toos,* and instead, I came clean. Rolling my eyes, I said, "I've been going over the pros and cons in my head."

He set his pretzel down, dusted off his hands, and turned in his seat to give me his full attention. "Lay 'em on me."

"What? *No.*"

"Why not?"

"Well, for starters, this isn't the appropriate place for it." I looked to my left and right. Although no one seemed to be paying attention, I'd certainly eavesdrop on this conversation if I heard it in the stands.

"Okay. Then where is?"

"Somewhere more private."

"My place after the game today."

"No."

"Why not? Can't trust yourself?"

"Don't be ridiculous. I'll have Izzy, and I told her we would go shopping later this afternoon after the game."

"Tomorrow, then?"

"Date with Marcus."

Hunter made a face.

"When I told you I was going over the pros and cons in my head, I didn't mean I wanted your assistance. I was just being honest."

"Fine. But if you're going to go over the pros and cons without me, I want to plead my case first."

My brows raised. "Plead your case?"

"Yep. You might be missing some critical factors that would sway your decision."

"Oh yeah?" I laughed. "Like what?"

"Well, you should know I'm extremely good at it."

"Every man thinks he's good at it, Hunter."

He ignored me. "And I'm well endowed."

"Show me a man who pleads his case by saying '*I have a tiny penis*'."

"I believe sex without going down on a woman first is bad manners."

I opened my mouth to say something, but nothing came out.

One of the women sitting two rows ahead of us turned and leaned up. "If she says no, I'll give you my number."

My face turned crimson, while Hunter, being Hunter, dazzled her with a smile and wink. "And I haven't even gotten to my best selling points yet."

Luckily, the ref blew the whistle calling the game back to start, and the persistent man sitting next to me redirected his focus. I, on the other hand, stared straight ahead, struggling to follow a bouncing ball. All I could think was *God, I like a man with good manners.*

⸻

"Could we go to the mall tomorrow before going to Sunday night dinner?" Izzy asked from the back of Hunter's rental car. We were almost back to the city after getting stuck in construction traffic.

I turned. "I have plans tomorrow in the afternoon."

"Oh. That's right. The ugly guy."

From the corner of my eye, I caught Hunter smirking.

"Marcus isn't ugly. Besides, I thought you *needed* to go to the mall today for some new practice shorts."

Izzy shrugged. "I can use the ones I have for a while longer."

There was a reason if she was giving up a trip to the mall. "Okay. So if we skip the mall this afternoon, do you want to do something else?"

She looked away. "I kind of want to go to Beacon to watch the boys basketball game."

"The boys basketball game?"

"For technique," she responded, selling it way too hard. "It's good to watch other players for form and technique, right, Hunter?"

Hunter's eyes flashed to me. I squinted back, and somehow we had a two-second wordless conversation. "Watching is always good," he said. "But you might want to watch pro ball so you don't pick up bad habits from high school kids."

I tried not to smirk. Of course I'd let her go to the game instead of shopping with me. She was fifteen and belonged with her friends.

Hunter looked in the rearview mirror at Izzy. "What time is the game?"

"It just started."

"On second thought, watching might be good. You can watch for things they're doing wrong as part of learning."

Izzy pepped up. "That's what I'll do. Could you drop me off, Hunter?"

"Don't you want to go home and change?" I said. "You're in your uniform still."

"It's a basketball game. There are *two teams* in uniforms."

"I don't mind dropping her off," Hunter said. "Besides, it will give us a chance to discuss the business we didn't get to yet."

I furrowed my brow. So Hunter clarified. "Pros and cons."

Hunter waited at the front of the school until Izzy walked inside and then turned to me. "Your place or mine?"

"I'm not having sex with you."

"Do you mean now or ever?"

"You said..." I deepened my voice into a husky impression of him. "...*your place or mine*, and that usually refers to whose house you're going to have sex at."

"So it means it's off the table *now*, but not forever then?"

I laughed. "Why don't we go have some lunch? I owe you at least that for coming to two basketball games and giving up your Saturday morning."

"Alright." He put the car into gear. "I'll take lunch. But know that it didn't feel like I gave up anything this morning, and also...I'm paying."

I'd eaten a pretzel at the game, so I wasn't that hungry. "I'll have a Caesar salad."

The waitress turned to Hunter, who looked at me. "Do you like calamari?"

"Yes."

"We'll take an order of fried calamari."

"Okay." She scribbled it down on her pad.

He looked to me again. "Do you like eggplant?"

"Yes, but I'm not really hungry."

"Me either. Let's share."

"Okay."

"We'll also take an order of eggplant rollatini."

"Umm...can you cancel my Caesar salad then?" I asked the waitress.

After she left our table, I opened my napkin and draped it over my lap, then took a drink of my water. Hunter watched me intently.

"What?"

He shrugged. "Just looking at you."

"Well, don't do that."

"Don't look at you?" He arched a brow. "It's kind of hard to sit across from someone and have a conversation without looking at them."

"I meant don't look at me like *that*."

"Like what?"

"All smoldering and stuff."

"I'm smoldering?"

I exhaled. "Can we just have lunch as friends? No sex talk, no you looking all sexy and staring at me, no pressure."

"I'll try. But the looking all sexy thing just comes naturally."

We laughed, and it seemed to break the tension—until my cell phone rang and I looked at the caller ID. *Super* flashed on the screen.

"I'm sorry. It's my building super. I need to take this."

I answered, assuming it was Jimmy, the regular maintenance guy. "Hello?"

"My favorite tenant, I hear you need my services?" The voice on the other end made my skin crawl. It wasn't the super. It was the creep who owned the building.

"Oh. Hi, Damon. I called the super this morning because of a small issue. But it's not a big deal. I don't think you need to get involved."

"Are you home?"

"No, actually, I'm out."

"What time will you be home? I'll come take a look at that drain for you."

I had no idea what time Izzy would be home, and I tried to avoid being alone with him at all costs. "Umm.... I'm not sure when I'll be back. Probably not for a few hours."

"How about five?"

Ugh. Why couldn't the super just fix it for me like he'd do for every other tenant? "It's really not a big deal, Damon. Jimmy can fix it when he has time. I can use the bathroom sink for now."

"I'll see you at five."

"I might be a little later."

"Call me when you're back at home."

I managed to stifle a groan. "Fine."

After I hung up, I couldn't hide my frustration.

Hunter looked concerned. "What's up? Everything okay?"

"Do you remember when I told you my husband's best friend was nice enough to help me find a place to live? But in exchange for that, he thought I should sleep with him?"

"Yeah."

"Well, that was the asshole on the phone. Damon owns my building. I dread anytime anything goes wrong in my apartment, because instead of the super coming to fix it, Damon insists on showing up. He doesn't go as far as pushing himself on me or anything, but he's tried to kiss me before, and he constantly asks me out, and it just makes me really uncomfortable."

The way Hunter's jaw ticked was endearing. "I'm going home with you later. He can fix the sink while I'm there."

"That's not necessary."

"No, it is. And while I'm at it, I need to apologize for being such a pushy asshole. I didn't see it until you just told me about that guy."

"You aren't an asshole." I smiled. "Pushy, maybe. But it's not the same thing. I've never felt like if I told you no, and sounded like I meant it, you wouldn't back off. Damon, on the other hand, I don't trust. I don't even like to be in the same room as him."

"Yeah, well, I'll back off anyway. You change your mind on wanting to be anything but friends, I'm here. Otherwise, I'll cool it."

As much as I'd said that was what I wanted, and knew it was for the best, it made me sad. I forced a smile. "Okay."

The rest of our lunch was nice, but the mood definitely shifted. There was almost an awkwardness to our conversation. Hunter would relax and start to say something flirty, and then he'd catch himself and dial it back. It was as if he didn't know how to be friends with me. At one particular point, when he was running his finger along the top of his glass and looking exceptionally tongue-tied, I called him on it.

"You have no women friends, do you?"

He looked up from the glass. "Sure I do. I'm friends with lots of women."

"Who?"

"Anna, for one."

"She's not your friend. She's your buddy's wife."

"So it's either one or the other?"

"Do you have any single women you're friends with?"

"Sure. At work."

"Okay. Who?"

"I go to lunch with Renee from the office sometimes. She's a project manager."

"Is she dating anyone?"

"I don't think so."

"How old is she?"

He shrugged. "Mid-sixties, maybe."

I shook my head. "She doesn't count. She's safe. How about any single friends in their twenties or thirties?"

"No. But there's a good reason for that."

"What's the reason?"

"Men and women who are mating age and attracted to each other can't be friends. It's primal."

My eyes widened. "You can't be serious."

Hunter leaned back in his chair. "What would I do with a woman I'm attracted to?"

"What do you mean? What do you and your male friends do?"

"Outdoors stuff. I like to rock climb, scuba dive, play golf."

"So why couldn't you and I do those things together?"

"For starters, when the guys and I play golf and one of us has to take a leak, we walk over to the brush and take a leak. When we rock climb, there's no better way to celebrate getting to the top than peeing off the side of the mountain."

"So men and women can't be friends because of your need to publicly urinate?"

"Last time we were diving, Derek sliced his hand on a coral reef. We tossed him electrical tape to wrap around his hand to keep the cut shut and went back for another dive. He probably needed a stitch or two, but if he'd gone to the hospital, we would've called him a pussy for a month."

"And if I was diving with you, you wouldn't toss me electrical tape?"

"Nope. Would take *you* to the hospital for stitches."

"What if I didn't want to go for stitches?"

"Wouldn't give you a choice. You get hurt, I'm gonna take care of you."

"But you won't take care of your best friend, Derek?"

Hunter smirked. "Nope."

"You're really a chauvinist, you know?"

"Taking care of a woman is being a gentleman."

"Not when you do it because you think your sex is superior and the woman can't take care of herself."

"Didn't say that. You cut your hand, I'm sure you can get yourself to the ER for stitches. But I'd want to take you, nonetheless."

I sipped my drink and smirked. "Chauvinist."

Hunter leaned in. "Bet you can give yourself an orgasm. But I'd rather be the one to take you there with my mouth. Does that make me a chauvinist, too?"

The thought of him going down on me had me squirming in my seat, chauvinist or not. Of course, he couldn't be a *gentleman* and let it go unnoticed. Instead, a dirty smile curled at the corners of his sinful mouth.

I was glad the waitress appeared and interrupted. Despite my protest, Hunter paid the bill and then held out his hand.

"Come on, I'm taking you home and coming in while that asshole Damon fixes your sink."

"You don't have to do that."

"Give me this gentlemanly act since you won't let me have the one I'd really prefer to do for you."

Chapter 16

— Natalia —

Turned out I didn't need to call Damon when I got home. Because the asshole was sitting on my couch when I unlocked the front door.

Startled, I jumped back. Hunter, who was close behind me, caught me and immediately shifted so I was behind him.

Every muscle in his body tensed as he growled, "Who the fuck are you?" Hunter was not a man I'd want to meet in a dark alley.

Damon stood and glared right back. "Damon Valente. Who the fuck are you?"

I squeezed Hunter's shoulder. "It's fine. This is Damon. I just didn't expect him to be in the house."

Hunter responded to me by speaking to Damon. "He shouldn't be. How'd you get in here?"

Damon was such a smug asshole. "I own the building. We have keys to all the apartments. Who is this guy, Nat?"

Feeling the need to diffuse the situation, I stepped back in front of Hunter and tried to play it off. "This is Hunter Delucia."

Damon overtly sized him up. "Yeah? I'm the landlord but also a friend of Nat's husband, Garrett."

I put down my purse and corrected him. "*Ex*-husband."

Hunter closed the door behind him and walked to extend his hand to Damon. I breathed a sigh of relief, thinking Hunter was going to make nice. I should've known he just wanted to get closer to get his point across.

He waited until Damon's hand was in his and looked him straight in the eyes as he spoke. "You shouldn't be in here when Natalia's not home."

"Nat doesn't mind."

"Actually, Damon, I do."

The two men were still hand in hand, but it was more akin to the shake before a prize fight than an introduction. Concerned at the tension in Hunter's face, I diverted attention to the problem at hand. Although something told me Hunter would *not* think the problem at hand was the kitchen sink.

I walked to the kitchen and opened the double cabinet doors beneath the sink, revealing the now-half-full bucket I'd put inside.

"It's filling up even without running the water. It's worse when the water's on. The first time it happened, I didn't realize until my feet were getting soaked. It had filled the cabinet and leaked out in less than a minute. So I'm guessing there's a hole somewhere or something."

I let out an unsteady breath when the two men released their shake and Damon walked to the kitchen. He put his hand on the small of my back, with his fingers splaying down mighty close to my ass, as he stood next to me. I reached around and quietly removed it.

Damon turned on the water and crouched down to watch beneath the sink. "Your seal is leaking. Strainer is old and corroded. It needs a new one and some putty." He stood and twisted the water back off. "I'll pick one up and come back tomorrow morning to install it."

Hunter stood in the doorway, his shoulders occupying almost the entire space. "I'll take care of it."

Damon turned. "It's part of her lease. Landlord takes care of plumbing, electrical, and heat. Plus, I promised my friend I'd take care of his wife while he wasn't around."

Hunter's eyes flicked to me and then to Damon. His jaw was set rigid. "*Ex*-wife. And you can let your friend know, Natalia is being taken care of just fine."

Damon's face heated. But Hunter was younger, bigger, stronger, and his tone left no room for negotiation. Pissed, he turned his attention to me. "Don't waste my time if you're going to have someone do the work yourself."

The door slammed shut a minute later. Hunter ran his fingers through his hair. "Sorry about that."

"Sorry? I seriously doubt that jerk will be sniffing around anymore. I can't thank you enough."

"Guy's a dirtbag."

"He certainly is. I think if I'd met Damon the same day I met Garrett, I might have thought twice about my ex-husband's character before the truth smacked me in the head a few years later. You can tell a lot about a person by meeting their best friend."

Hunter nodded. "I agree." He caught my eyes. "For the record, I think Anna's pretty damn great."

God, this man could melt ice with those eyes. "Derek's pretty awesome, too."

Even though I'd told him I would call a plumber to fix my leaky seal, Hunter insisted it wasn't a big deal and he could fix it easily. So while he ran out to get what he needed, I cleaned everything out from underneath the sink and decided to bake him brownies. They were already out of the oven and halfway cooled by the time he returned—even though the store I'd told him about was only up the block.

He had two bags when he entered. "Smells good in here."

"I made you brownies. You've spent time helping Izzy and bought me dinner on your birthday and lunch today. You're going to repair my sink. Not to mention that you drove me around California and let me stay at your house. It's the least I could do."

"It's not necessary." He reached to the plate, grabbed a brownie, and stuffed it in his mouth. "But if you're in a giving mood, I can think of a few other ways you could repay me."

Before I could respond, he shook his head. "Wow. I really can't seem to stop my mouth, even when I try. I hope you were being honest when you said I'm not like that Damon asshole."

"You're nothing like that dirtbag," I assured him. "I'm glad you're back to your normal, perverted self. That half hour you practiced self control was awful."

Hunter unbuttoned his shirt and winked. "I knew you liked my dirty mouth."

Wearing just a white T-shirt, he got ready for the sink repair. He dumped the contents of one of the bags on the counter and opened a bunch of plumbing parts individually wrapped in plastic bags before setting them on the floor where he'd be working. As soon as he laid down and stuck his head in the cabinet, Izzy's cat appeared from nowhere and ran across the room—jumping on and over Hunter during his random chase of air. The sudden pounce on his abs made Hunter jolt upright, and he whacked his head on the cabinet as he sat up. "What the hell was that?"

I walked over and picked up the crazy feline. "Sorry. Are you okay? That was Izzy's cat. He doesn't come out often. He's shy."

Hunter rubbed his head, then raised his eyes to the cat in my hand. His eyes widened. "Does he...have one eye?"

I petted the top of its head. "Yeah. He was a stray that Izzy used to feed when she lived with her mom. Must've gotten into a fight and lost it at one point. He doesn't have a tail either."

"That's one ugly cat."

"Hey, be nice. Catpernicus has feelings, too."

Hunter arched a brow. "Catpernicus?"

"Izzy's into astronomy. We call him Cat for short. He likes to sleep in the closet. Poor thing digs himself under the discarded teenage clothing heap in her room. I think he probably had it rough on the streets."

I dug my nails into the top of Catpernicus's head, and he pushed up and licked the inside of my wrist while starting to purr.

Hunter grumbled, "Lucky pussy," and went back under the sink.

Fifteen minutes later, my sink was fixed.

"I really can't thank you enough."

"No problem." Hunter washed his hands and grabbed the other bag, which I now noticed was still full.

"Did you buy extra parts in case you needed them?"

"Nope. Got a flat-head screwdriver?"

"Sure." I went to the junk drawer and pulled one out as Hunter emptied the contents of the other bag. Inside was a Baldwin lock and key set.

"Changing the lock on your front door while I'm at it, so that asshole can't help himself inside while you're in the shower one day."

I'd never thought of that. But now that he'd said it, I was glad he was doing it, because I wouldn't sleep tonight with that idea planted in my head.

"Wow. Yeah. Thank you. That's great."

—

"I should get going." Hunter polished off the beer I'd given him after he'd finished fixing my sink and changing my door lock. Since Izzy had texted that she was going over to her friend's after the boys' basketball game, I didn't have anything I needed to do for the rest of the afternoon or evening.

"Do you want to stay and watch a movie or something? I could make you a late dinner since we ate a late lunch?"

Hunter crossed to where I was standing to toss out the beer bottle, then brushed a lock of hair from my face. "I should go."

His hand lingered on my cheek, his thumb stroking my skin as our eyes locked. God, I wanted him so badly I ached. I longed for his other hand to cup my face the way he had during the kisses we'd shared. It was so intimate, so passionate. But as always, fear kept me from telling him that or acting on my feelings.

Hunter read the fear in my eyes and nodded with a sad smile. "I definitely should go."

We walked to the door in silence. When he opened it, a sense of panic washed over me. "You're going to Mom's for dinner tomorrow night, right? She invited you?"

"She did. But I'm going to tell her I can't make it. You should take your date, instead."

My date. I had zero desire to take Marcus to Mom's. In fact, I had zero desire for Marcus. Unlike the man who stood in front of me.

"Will I see you again?"

"I'm here for two months. If you need anything, give me a call. Plus, I'll check in on how Izzy's stats improve." He held out his hand for the first time, instead of kissing me like he'd done every other time we'd said goodbye. "Friends, not fucking?"

It wasn't exactly as enticing as *sex, not love*, but it was what I could handle right now. I put my hand in his. "Friends, not fucking."

Chapter 17

— Natalia —

"You really look incredible. I can't keep my eyes off of you. My buddy is going to be insulted that I'm not looking at his paintings."

I'd gone all out getting ready for my date with Marcus. After a night of feeling melancholy after Hunter left, I decided maybe if I made myself look good, I might feel better about my date. Unfortunately, it wasn't working.

"Thank you." I forced a smile.

Marcus and I moved to the next piece of art, and my first genuine smile of the day appeared. His friend was a talented painter. Most of his pieces were Surrealist, with the focus on one exaggerated object that he'd pulled from a classic movie. The box for the movie that inspired each painting sat on a shelf underneath each work. This particular painting was from the cult horror film *The Birds*. The movie box had a swarm of birds flying around the head of a terrified woman. But the painting showed a swarm of birdhouses that were falling apart with bent nails hanging out all over, and instead of a woman looking terrified, there was a scared man with nail scratches all over his face.

"I have a friend who would get a kick out of this one. Do you think the artist would mind if I snapped a picture?"

"No, not at all. There's a sign near the door that says the artist appreciates sharing, but not reproductions."

I dug my cell from my purse and took a few pictures, intending to send them to Hunter later. I hadn't realized I'd been smiling the entire time until Marcus brought me back to reality.

"Your smile is contagious. What does that one remind you of?"

"My friend H..." I stopped short of saying Hunter's name in the nick of time, remembering that Marcus had pointed out my talking about him the last two times we were together. "...my friend had a bad experience with a birdhouse," I said instead.

After that, my shoulders slumped for the rest of the time we looked at the exhibit. I needed to throw in the towel with Marcus. No amount of forcing it was going to make me attracted to him. A certain someone had ruined that for me. Plus, he was too nice of a guy to disrespect. So I waited until the end of the art show. He'd offered to walk me home, knowing I had plans to go to my weekly dinner at my mom's.

"You're a really nice guy, Marcus," I started.

His smile faded. "Uh-oh. As much as it sounds like a compliment, that's never a good line to hear on a date."

I felt bad, but it was for the best. "I'm sorry. I really am. You're a great guy who deserves a woman who's excited to be with you and wants a relationship."

"And that woman's not you?"

I shook my head. "No. I'm sorry. It's not."

"Is there someone else?"

At least I didn't have to lie about that. Not in the physical sense anyway. "No."

Marcus ran his fingers through his hair. "Okay." He looked down at the ground. "Friends, I guess?"

"I'd like that." We hugged and said goodbye. Since it was a beautiful day, I decided to walk home to clear my head. I hadn't had sex in almost two years and just dumped a willing participant because I knew he was interested in more than just sex. I'd rebuked Hunter, who was also a willing participant, because I was afraid I couldn't keep it to just sex. Basically, I'd just turned down two chances to satisfy my libido because of fear of relationships. At this point, I'd be better off going to a bar, picking up a handsome stranger, and having minimal conversation that could fuck it up before getting to the dirty deed.

My mother was relentless when she was on the trail of a fresh bachelor who could possibly give her more grandchildren. But when Mom and my sisters were all on one side, it was more than I could handle. Slipping out to the yard by myself after Sunday night dinner, I sat on the swing on the back deck. I wasn't surprised when Mom followed me.

"Hey. You don't seem like yourself tonight."

"Well, you guys aren't exactly an easy crowd."

"We only want what's best for you."

I took a deep breath and exhaled. "I know, Mom."

We sat in silence for a few minutes before she spoke again. Her voice was softer than usual when she started. "I regret never getting married again."

That caught me by surprise. "You do?"

Mom nodded.

"So why didn't you?"

"I was afraid to trust anyone. You know the old saying that hindsight is twenty-twenty?"

"Yeah."

"Well, it wasn't for me. For years I looked back at my relationship with your father for signs that I'd missed. But even in hindsight, I couldn't see any. Same goes for my friendship with Margie, too. To this day, I don't know how that woman looked me in the face and never showed any signs that she was sleeping with my husband. I think if I'd been able to see it after the fact, it would've been easier for me to trust again. I could've chalked it up to missing the signs. But without that, I was afraid I'd be blindsided again."

I understood that. I'd looked back for signs that Garrett shouldn't have been trusted a million times—not to mention that I hadn't seen what'd happened between my parents coming either.

"It's hard to move on from a mistake without knowing what your mistake was."

My mother shook her head. "The first step is not thinking it's your mistake, Natalia. It took me years to stop thinking, *if only I'd been thinner, or fixed myself up more before he came home at night, or even been more adventurous in the bedroom, maybe he wouldn't have cheated.* But you know what?"

"What?"

"None of that would have changed anything. Because it was never about me. It was about him—his own inadequacies that made him need to prove something to himself. I was a good wife."

My chest felt like there was a weight sitting on it. "I'm so sorry he did that to you, Mom."

She smiled sadly. "Likewise. I hate what Garrett did to you. But the greatest gift a mother can give is teaching her child. I want you to learn from my mistakes, sweetheart.

Move on. That's why I push you so hard to find someone new. When you spend too much time looking back and trying to figure out what went wrong, you're missing out on moving forward."

"I just need to focus on my career and Izzy right now, Mom."

She smiled. "Okay, sweetheart. Whatever you say. Although those things are doing pretty great, if you ask me."

My sisters blasted through the back door, effectively ending our conversation. But Mom had given me a lot to think about.

She was right that I'd also spent a lot of time focusing on missed signs that my husband wasn't the man I'd thought he was. Maybe it was time to focus on finding peace with who he is and move on.

But it was easier to admit that I kept people at a distance because I was afraid of getting hurt by the same thing, than to admit I was just afraid of getting hurt.

Chapter 18

— Natalia —

Hunter Delucia.

That's what the return address read on the package I'd been staring at since the mailman delivered it. Just seeing his name, looking at the heavy ink of his slashy handwriting, made me happier than I'd been in the last week-and-a-half.

Hunter had kept to his word of not making contact, leaving the ball in my court. And even though I'd thought about him more than a few times each day, I still hadn't taken the initiative to reach out.

I sat at my desk in my home office, typing up notes on Minnie Falk, a patient with a severe compulsive counting disorder. Unlike many patients, she didn't have a specific fear of what might happen to her if she didn't perform her counting rituals. Nonetheless, she suffered a profound sense of incompleteness when she didn't do many of her tasks in sets of four.

I sat back into my chair with the package still in my hands and took a deep breath. My fears of Hunter were really no different than Minnie's fears. I obsessively thought about the man, felt the compulsion to talk to him each day, and had a profound sense of incompleteness when I didn't.

What had my advice for Minnie been this week?

We'd been working on interrupting her pattern. She'd quit smoking a few years back and had recently started again when her sister passed away. Although I would've loved for her to quit altogether, my job was to work with her on her OCD behavior, so I focused on her four-cigarettes-in-a-row habit. Today we'd worked on changing that pattern as the first step in changing her compulsion. While she still smoked her four cigarettes in a row, I had her wait sixty seconds between smokes rather than light one cancer stick off another. And after the third one, I'd had her eat a quick snack—just a piece of cheese—to break the pattern a bit more.

Maybe this contact, a package, would give me some relief from the unsettled feelings I'd had as of late, yet still keep some distance between Hunter and me. Anxious for relief, I ripped into the box like a kid on Christmas morning.

Inside was what looked like a black wrist brace of some sort. *King Wrap Strap*. Below the name was a description of the product. *Comfortably stops wrist and thumb from off-hand shot veer*. Underneath it was a note on a piece of Khaill-Jergin stationery, the firm where Hunter worked. The handwriting fit the man—very dark, as if he was heavy-handed with a pen, and tall, slanted downstrokes, masculine-looking. Was I insane to think his handwriting was sexy? The note itself was short and sweet, but boy did it hit the target.

Now you have a reason to think about me.

I smiled from ear to ear like an idiot. It was so sweet that he'd sent Izzy the shooting strap he'd told her about. In fact, overall, since the day I'd met him, Hunter had been nothing short of sweet. Sure, he was forward and crude, but even that had an odd sweetness to it.

It was nearly impossible to get any work done for the rest of the afternoon. I picked up and put down my phone—deliberating over calling him—ten different times.

I should call him to say thank you.

No, I should have Izzy call.

But it would be rude of me not to call. After all, he sent the package to me.

Although the contents was for Izzy.

I'm going to call.

Picks up phone. Puts it down thirty seconds later.

This is ridiculous. Where are my manners? I have to call.

Eventually, after debating with myself for upwards of a half hour, I settled on a simple text:

Natalia: Just received the package. Izzy is going to be so excited. That was very sweet of you to send. I might even get a smile from a fifteen year old this evening.

The dots started jumping around almost immediately. My heart rode along in anticipation.

Hunter: Excellent. And is her stepmother smiling these days?

I had no idea how to answer that. The truth was, I really missed being around him. As I sat at my desk, contemplating my response and chewing on my bottom lip, another text came in.

Hunter: Stop thinking of how to respond and go with honesty.

Natalia: Busy. I've been busy.

Hunter: That doesn't answer my question, Natalia.

I don't know why I decided to text what came next.

Natalia: I ended things with Marcus.

His response was immediate.

Hunter: Have dinner with me.

Natalia: Just dinner?

Hunter: Well, I'd rather eat you. But if that's not an option, I'll take sharing a meal.

The familiar flutter swarmed in my belly. He was so straightforward and unlike any man I'd ever dated.

Natalia: When?

Hunter: Tomorrow night. I'll pick you up at seven.

Natalia: Okay. But it's not a date, right? We're just two friends having dinner.

Hunter: Put whatever label on it that makes you happy, sweet pea. But wear something sexy.

"You smell so fucking good." I nearly whimpered at the sound of his throaty voice in my ear. True to form, Hunter pulled me against him the minute I opened the front door. Wrapping me in a hug that bordered on crushing me, his hot breath tickled my neck as he spoke.

Jesus Christ. Have the four cigarettes in a row, Minnie, if it gives you this type of relief.

"Thank you," I managed to squeak out and then cleared my throat. "Come in. You're a few minutes early, and Izzy hasn't gotten home yet. I don't like her to come home to an empty house if I can help it. She isn't usually this late. I'm sure she won't be long."

I closed the door behind him and walked to the kitchen, needing a little space. Looking over my shoulder, I turned back to ask if he'd like a glass of wine and found Hunter's eyes glued to my ass.

I raised a brow in question when they eventually rose to mine. Of course, he didn't bother to pretend it hadn't happened. That wasn't his style.

"You have a great ass," he said instead.

"This isn't starting out like two friends having dinner. You've been here thirty seconds, and you've already told me how good I smell while pressing our bodies together and commented on my ass."

"Didn't say this was a dinner as friends." He shrugged. "You did. Besides, you're wearing perfume and a dress that is sexy as hell. You're ready for a date."

I rolled my eyes and continued to put that distance between us. "Would you like a glass of wine or not?"

"Sure."

He followed me into the kitchen. Standing across from the refrigerator, he leaned against the counter in a confident stance.

Lifting his chin toward the sink, he asked, "How's the drain holding up? No leaks?"

I uncorked the wine I'd opened yesterday and poured two glasses. "Nope. All good."

When I handed him a glass, he caught my eye. "Damon come around again?"

"No. I think you scared him away."

"Good."

I sipped my wine. "So where are we going tonight?"

"One if by Land, Two if by Sea."

"On Barrow?"

"That's the one."

"I pass it all the time. I have a client nearby." I squinted. "Looks romantic from the outside."

"Saw it featured in *Architectural Digest* a few years back. Been meaning to go. But haven't had the chance."

"I thought you came to New York all the time."

"I do. Meant there was no one I wanted to take there."

God, he was sweet without even trying.

His words, coupled with that intense stare, made me squirm. I grabbed my phone from the counter. "I wonder where Izzy is. She's not usually this late. What time is our reservation?"

Before Hunter could answer, the front door opened and slammed shut.

"I was beginning to wonde—" Her face halted my sentence. It was red and blotchy, and her eyes were swollen. She'd definitely been crying. I went to her. "What happened? Are you okay?"

"Fine," she snipped.

Hunter and I glanced at each other. His carefree face from a moment ago was gone, replaced by lethal anger.

"Izzy," I said. "You need to give me more than that. Did someone bother you on the way home?"

For the first time, she noticed Hunter was in our apartment. She also caught the look on his face and seemed to realize the man was ready to kill someone if she didn't put his mind at ease.

"Oh. No. Nothing like that."

I blew out a heavy breath. "Then what happened? You're late, and you've clearly been crying."

"I don't want to talk about it."

"Are you sure?"

Izzy slumped into the couch without removing her backpack. "One of the girls on the basketball team was talking about Dad."

I sat down next to her. "Like what?"

"Apparently her dad was an investor of Dad's, and when they sent home the player roster for the team, they listed both you and Dad as my emergency contacts. Her father saw the name, saw me at the game, and since I look just like Dad, he knew. Now everyone knows my father is a criminal." Tears filled her big brown eyes. "And that's not all."

Oh God. More? I wasn't sure my heart could take seeing tears spill over. Izzy was a tough girl. She hadn't cried since her father's sentencing hearing, and even then, she hid them from everyone.

"What else happened, sweetie?"

"Yakshit is going to the dance with Brittany."

"What dance?"

"The Sadie Hawkins dance."

"Isn't that a dance where the girls invite the boys?"

"Yeah."

"I didn't even know you asked Yakshit to go with you."

The tears spilled over. "I didn't."

"Oh, honey." I pulled Izzy into a hug.

She tried her best to hide the sobs. There was no sound, yet her shoulders started to shake. We stayed that way for a solid ten minutes—her sobbing and letting me hold her. I hated the cause and her pain, but I was happy I could give her whatever comfort she would allow.

When she sniffled the end of her tears, I pushed the damp hair from her face. "What can I do to make you feel better?"

"I just want to eat and go to bed."

Hunter had retreated to the kitchen. I assumed to give us some privacy. I looked over at him with an apologetic face just as he looked up from his phone.

"Hi, Hunter." Izzy forced a smile. "I wore my J strap today at practice. Thanks for sending it."

He nodded. "No problem. Hope it helps."

Izzy noticed what I was wearing. "Are you guys going on a date?"

I answered *no* at the exact same moment Hunter answered *yes*. That made her smile.

She got up from the couch, finally removing her backpack before heading to the refrigerator. "What's to eat?"

Hunter answered. "You like Italian food?"

Her spirit chirped up. "Nat made sauce?"

I walked to the kitchen. "No, sorry. I made you a turkey and avocado wrap."

She tried to mask her disappointment. "That's okay."

"Come on. Leave that wrap for lunch tomorrow," Hunter said. "Let's go get some lasagna and meatballs."

"Really?" Izzy's eyes sparked a glimmer of happiness.

He looked at me while answering. "I don't fool around about food."

"Do I need to change?"

"Nope. You'll be the prettiest girl in the room, even after basketball practice."

Lord, I swooned. The only thing sweeter than his compliments to me was him giving one to my Izzy.

"These are as good as Nanna Rossi's." Izzy shoveled another meatball into her mouth and spoke with it full. "Don't tell her I said that."

"I won't. As long as your room is cleaned every Sunday before we go for dinner." Nothing like a little bribery.

"I'll just deny I said it."

I pointed my fork across the table at Hunter. "I have a witness."

Hunter shook his head. "I didn't hear anything. Did you say something, kid?"

Izzy showed off her dimples while shaking her head. "Nope. Didn't say a word."

The two of them had been teaming up against me since we left the apartment. I didn't mind, especially since it seemed to take Izzy's mind off her terrible day.

"Are you Italian, too, Hunter?"

He nodded. "I am."

"Did your mom do a big Sunday night dinner like Nanna Rossi?"

"No, she didn't. My mom was sick a lot when I was growing up."

"Oh. Mine was, too. She had cancer." Izzy had surprised me a lot today with all of her openness. "Did your mom die?"

"Izzy," I tried to gently remind her of her manners. "That's not really dinner conversation."

"It's alright. I don't mind," Hunter said, turning his attention back to Izzy. "She died when I was seventeen."

"Was she sick for a long time? My mom was only sick for, like, a year. She had small cell bronchial carcinoma—they call it oat cell cancer. Barely anyone gets it unless they smoked. My mom never smoked."

Small cell bronchial carcinoma shouldn't roll off a fifteen-year-old's tongue so smoothly.

"My mom was sick for a lot of years. But she didn't go to the doctor. She didn't take care of herself."

Izzy held up her hand to show off her charm bracelet. She wore it every day. "This was my mom's. My dad bought her most of these." She fingered through the collection of dangling charms until she found the pearl-colored ribbon. "Nat bought me this one last year on my mom's birthday.

It's the ribbon that represents lung cancer. Is there a ribbon for what your mom had?"

Hunter looked down at his own wrist. "Not that I know of. But my mom made this bracelet." He wore a beautiful, braided leather band with a thin silver rope entwined through it. I'd noticed it before. "She used to do a lot of craft projects when she couldn't get out of bed."

God, this was the strangest date ever. We were sitting in a fancy, romantic restaurant with a fifteen year old, discussing death. And...it wasn't even supposed to be a date.

Izzy frowned. "Yakshit's mom died early, too. She wouldn't go to doctors either."

Hunter and I exchanged glances. "Sounds like you two are close," he said.

"We were. Until he decided to go to the dance with *Brittany*."

Izzy so rarely allowed me access to her emotions. I jumped on the opportunity to understand what was going on in her teenage head.

"Why didn't you ask Yakshit to the dance if you wanted to go with him?"

She shrugged and pushed pasta around on her plate with the fork. Her voice was a vulnerable tone I so rarely heard. "I was afraid."

"Afraid he would say no?"

She shook her head. "But now he likes Brittany."

"Maybe not. Sometimes people say yes just to go out on a date."

Izzy looked up with a glimmer of hope in her sad eyes. "Like you and Marcus?"

My eyes flashed to the smirk on Hunter's face. I sighed. "Yes. Sort of. He was nice, so I went out with him and gave it a chance." I squeezed Izzy's hand. "You're young. I'm not saying you should go ask out every cute boy at school. But if it was the Sadie Hawkins dance, and you really liked him, you should have asked him. Don't be afraid of getting hurt."

When I looked back up at Hunter, he was staring at me. He spoke to Izzy without breaking our eye contact. "Sounds like good advice, if you ask me."

After dinner, Hunter went back to our apartment with us to make sure we got home safe. Izzy thanked him for dinner and took off to her room the minute we walked in.

I kicked off my heels. "Thank you so much for tonight. I know it wasn't exactly the date you had planned, but I appreciate what you did. You have a sweet side, Mr. Delucia."

He looked over my shoulder and down the hall to Izzy's bedroom. Finding it all clear, he wrapped his hands around my waist and locked them behind my back. "At least you admit now that we were supposed to go out on a date."

I hadn't thought about my words. But the least I could do was be honest. He deserved it. "I wore this dress for you and put on the perfume you told me you liked when we first met."

A slow smile spread across his face. "I know. But it's nice to hear you admit the truth for a change."

"God, you're so arrogant. You couldn't just accept the compliment."

He cupped my face in his hands. "Friday night. Just the two of us."

I nodded. Somewhere between him opening up to Izzy during dinner and the ride home, I'd given in.

Hunter's eyes dropped to my lips. "Now kiss me. I missed this mouth."

For the first time, I didn't think about it. I kissed him—well, at least it started that way. Hunter took it over after about three seconds. It was tamer than the kisses we'd shared before, probably because we were both aware that Izzy was just down the hall and could walk out at any moment. But it was no less passionate. Before it broke, he did that thing that drove me wild—catching my bottom lip between his teeth and tugging. *Lord, the man can kiss.*

"Seven o'clock?" he asked.

I nodded. "It's a date."

He smirked and leaned down for one last peck on my lips. "Yes, it is. It was always a date."

Chapter 19

— Natalia —

I'd never been so nervous for a date in my life. It made no sense. I'd spent time with Hunter, knew he was a decent guy, so why was I unable to sit down and relax? In the last half hour, I'd unloaded the dishwasher, reorganized two kitchen cabinets, and now I was checking the date on each spice in the spice rack. I shouldn't have gotten ready so early. When the buzzer rang, I literally jumped at the sound.

Wine. I need wine.

"Come on up," I feigned calm and casual as I pressed the button to unlock the interior door downstairs. I then proceeded to run to the refrigerator, pour a glass of Shiraz and down it like it was medicine. I made it back to the door just as Hunter stepped off the elevator.

He was dressed more casually than I'd expected—in a pair of jeans and a navy polo. Don't get me wrong, he looked delicious, but when I'd asked him how to dress for where we were going, he'd said a sexy dress and heels. As he strode toward my door, his eyes did a sweep over me, and I felt warmth travel through my body that had nothing to do with the alcohol coursing through my veins.

"I think I overdressed."

Hunter leaned in and covered my lips with his for a quick hello. "Nope. You're dressed just right."

"But you're wearing a polo and jeans. You said a sexy dress, so I thought that meant the dress code was more formal."

"I said sexy because that's what I wanted to see on you. There is no dress code where we're going."

"Where are we going?"

"My place. I'm cooking you dinner."

"I could have worn jeans for that."

He smirked. "Might want to ask where we're going in the future, rather than what you should wear. Because my answer's always going to be sexy dress and heels, even if we're going to McDonald's."

I laughed, stepping aside. "You're impossible. Come in for a minute. I need to tell Izzy I'm leaving."

Inside, Izzy had emerged from her bedroom and was hanging on the refrigerator door. She glanced up. "Hi, Hunter." And went back to staring at the food.

"I made you ravioli."

"I'm on a diet. Do we have anything low carb?"

"What? A diet? Since when? And better yet, why? You're a size two."

"Since this morning."

I walked to the refrigerator, took out the ravioli and sauce and put it on the counter. "Start your diet tomorrow." I kissed her cheek. "Mrs. Whitman knows I'm going out. I won't be home late."

She shrugged. "Whatever."

"No one in the apartment while I'm gone."

Izzy rolled her eyes. "There goes the rager I had planned."

The nerves the wine had calmed were back in full force once I was on the way to Hunter's apartment. I stared out the car window, debating whether I was ready to sleep with him. I'd thought we were going out to eat, and since he knows I have to be home early for Izzy, it wasn't something I'd been worried about. Now dinner was at his house, and I knew all it would take was one kiss and my decision-making skills would be hampered. I needed to make a decision while I was not under the influence of his hard body pressed against mine.

Hunter side-glanced to me and back to the road. "What's going on in that head of yours?"

"Nothing."

We stopped at a light, and Hunter turned to me. He didn't say a word. Instead, his eyes pointed down to where my hands were picking lint off my dress that wasn't there. Then his gaze met mine.

"Shut up," I said.

He chuckled, and the light changed, pulling his attention back to the road. I'd thought I'd been granted a reprieve, but a half a block later, he casually said, "We're not having sex tonight, if that makes you relax a little more."

Did he just say...

"What?"

"Sex. We're not having it."

"Why not?"

"Because tonight I'm making you dinner. We're going to share a good meal and talk about sex. I want to know what you're up for and what you're not. But you have to be home early for Izzy."

"Isn't that a tad presumptuous of you? Assuming you're the one who gets to decide when we have sex. What if I don't plan on *ever* having sex with you?"

"I think your wet panties when we kiss says you do plan on having sex with me."

"My panties are not wet when we kiss." I totally lied.

"Okay. I'll check next time to prove you wrong."

I didn't put it past him to do exactly that. "Let's back this conversation up a little. So you've decided we aren't having sex tonight. What if I told you I *wanted* to have sex? You wouldn't have sex with me?"

He actually considered my question for a minute, which I found rather amusing. "What I meant was, I wasn't going to *try* to have sex with you tonight. But if you try to have it with me, by all means, you'll be getting fucked."

I probably should have been offended for a dozen different reasons, but I wasn't in the slightest. Instead, the ludicrousness of the conversation made me burst out laughing. "You know what?"

"What?"

"I *was* stressing over us potentially having sex tonight. And now I'm not. So as strange as this conversation was, it actually made me feel better."

Hunter smiled as he pulled into an underground parking garage. "Glad to help. And trust me, I haven't even begun to make you feel better yet."

"Wow. This is a sublet?" The apartment Hunter was staying in was really nice. It wasn't huge, but it was modern, with high ceilings and an open floor plan, so it felt bigger than the square footage—though it was the outside space that elevated the place from really nice to damn spectacular. New York and *outside space* weren't normally bedfellows. But this place had a balcony big enough for two lounge chairs, a table that seated six, a barbeque, and a dozen potted plants.

"It's owned by Khaill-Jergin, the builder I work for. They keep this one and a few others as corporate apartments, mostly for when executives from the London office are in town. I lucked out that one was available."

"It's beautiful."

Hunter slid the sliding glass doors open and held his hand out for me to step through first.

"The view is sensational," I said. "Yet it feels serene at the same time."

Hunter smiled. "That was the goal. Each project has an essence statement. This building was *an oasis in the jungle*. It opened five years ago. After I graduated, I did my internship with the architect who designed this building at Khaill. The initial design was done, but the architect winds up doing a lot of revisions while the building is going up. So this was the first project I ever worked on.

"Wow. That's really cool. Honestly, most of the time, I don't even think about the buildings I'm walking past every day. It must be amazing to walk by one and look up, knowing you designed it."

He nodded. I'd become plenty acquainted with conceited Hunter, but I'd never met the humble side of him before. I liked it.

Come to think of it, I liked conceited Hunter, too.

"You warm enough to have a glass of wine out here before dinner?"

"Sure. I'd love that."

Hunter went inside and returned a few minutes later with two glasses of merlot. He came up behind me, handed me my wine, and leaned both wrists on the rail on either side of me, caging me in as we took in the sunset and sipped. The silence was comfortable, although the feel of him so close behind me, and the profound effect it had on my body, was unnerving. After a few minutes and the feel of his warm breath tickling my neck, I felt my breaths coming quicker and deeper.

"Turn around, Natalia."

Hunter's voice was low and *so damn seductive.* I waited for him to step back so I could maneuver around to face him. After a few more heavy breaths, I realized he had no intention of giving me space, so I turned while locked between his arms. Between the close proximity, his light blue eyes, and his intoxicating smell, I needed more wine. Raising my glass to my lips, I proceeded to down the half-full glass.

When I was done, Hunter raised a brow.

I held up the empty glass and shook it back and forth. A snippet of the conversation we'd had in the car replayed in my head. "*I wasn't going to* try *to have sex with you tonight. But if you try to have it with me, by all means, you'll be getting fucked.*"

I bit my lip, and Hunter seemed to read my mind. Taking the empty glass from my hand, he set it down on the floor next to us, along with his own half-full glass. When I unconsciously wet my lips, he muttered a string of curses before planting his mouth over mine.

The taste of wine on his tongue was enough to make me feel like I'd drunk the entire bottle myself. My head was woozy, my body tingled, and I wanted to climb the damn man like a tree. He pressed his body even tighter to mine, and my back arched from the railing toward his as my fingers clenched a fistful of his hair.

He groaned when I yanked. "I can't wait to be inside you. You make me hard as a rock."

With a thrust of his hips, he demonstrated that he wasn't exaggerating. *Oh God.* I was so desperate I could probably come from just dry humping with this man. Resisting taking things further was a challenge I wasn't sure I could endure for too long.

When the kiss broke, Hunter looked just as bamboozled by our chemistry as I was. We stared into each other's eyes for a while.

"You're really good at that," I told him.

His smile was playful as his brows drew down. "What?"

"Kissing."

He leaned in and brushed his lips with mine. "I'm good at kissing other places, too. Just say the word and I'll show you."

I laughed. "Seriously. Why don't you have a girlfriend, Hunter? You're handsome, smart, have a great job, own a beautiful house, you're an amazing kisser, *and* you can fix a sink and build things. You're prime boyfriend material."

His playful look turned serious. He also pulled back a bit, though he didn't release me from the confines of his arms and the balcony rail.

"I don't want that type of relationship." He studied me carefully. "I like you. You're beautiful and smart. We enjoy each other. But I'm not looking for anything serious."

Even though he'd been upfront since we met, and I was not looking for a relationship at all, somehow it stung to hear him say that.

"What does that mean, exactly? That I'll be in your bed one night and someone else the next?"

"Absolutely not. We'd be exclusive. To be clear, that's a two-way street. My expectation, once you're in my bed, is that you won't be fucking anyone else either."

"Okay...and we'd spend time together outside of the bedroom, too?"

"Of course. I'll always make sure you eat before I eat you."

I squirmed a little at the thought. "So the difference between what we'd be doing and a relationship is..."

Our gazes locked. "Expectations."

Since we were laying our cards on the table and having a little heart to heart, I figured I'd push a bit further. "You said you had one serious relationship that lasted years."

Hunter nodded. "That's right."

"I married my only real serious relationship. That disaster is the primary reason I've been avoiding anyone with real relationship potential. I lie to myself and others by saying I don't want a relationship because I need to focus on my work and Izzy. While that's partially true, if I'm being honest, it's also because Garrett burned me pretty bad, and I haven't fully gotten over it yet." I paused for a few seconds. "Does your not wanting a relationship have to do with the one serious one you had?"

He looked away, staring over my shoulder and out into the lit-up city before returning his eyes to mine. "Yes, but not in the way you probably think."

"Did she break your heart?"

"We broke each other's." He cleared his throat and took a step back. "How about we go eat?"

"Okay." I followed Hunter to the kitchen and offered to help. But he'd already done all the prep work for a dinner of chicken and broccoli pesto bowtie pasta. It was put together in a sauté pan, and all he needed to do was warm it up. He turned the gas cooktop on and filled my wine glass again while I sat on a stool at the island, watching him.

"Do you cook often?" I asked his back while sipping my wine and admiring the way his ass filled out his jeans.

He glanced back and caught me checking him out. Flashing a knowing, cocky half-smile he said, "Only when I want to eat."

"You don't order in a lot?"

"I like to try to eat healthy when I'm home. I travel a lot, so I have no choice but to eat out a lot. So when I'm home, I attempt to avoid eating crap. Plus, I like to cook. How about you?"

"I cook most nights to feed Izzy a balanced meal. In the mornings, she grabs a bar and runs out the door at six-thirty before school and doesn't get home from sports until almost seven most nights. Dinner is the only chance I have to make sure she gets decent nourishment. Plus..." I smiled. "I like to cook, too."

"You're really good with her."

I sipped my wine. "Thanks. I'm totally bluffing it. I have no idea how to raise a teenager."

"You'd never know it."

"My mom always said good parenting was spending half the amount of money you think you should and double the amount of free time you have with your kids. Lucky for Izzy, I'm always broke and have no life."

Hunter chuckled and turned his attention back to the stove. He lifted the pan off the flame and flicked his wrist a few times to stir dinner before setting it down again. Then he lowered the heat to a simmer and came to lean across the other side of the island from me with his wine in hand.

"So what are your limits?"

I sipped. "My limits?"

"In bed. What's a no for you?"

I was mid-swallow of my wine, and the casual way he'd asked the question caught me so off guard that I gulped it down the wrong pipe. I sputtered and coughed.

"You okay?"

I nodded and put my hand up while catching my breath. My voice was strained when I could finally speak. "Stop doing that to me. Who talks like that?"

"What?"

"You just asked about my sexual limits so casually, like you were asking if I wanted a glass of water."

"How would you have liked me to ask?"

"I don't know. Maybe less business and more personal, perhaps."

He nodded. "Okay. I can do that." Reaching across the counter, he took my hands into his. "Sweet pea, you have a mighty fine ass. What are your thoughts on my tapping that?"

I felt my face shade pink, and a knowing grin spread across his.

"You're a jerk."

"Pretty sure that's not news to you."

A crackle popped from the pan on the stove, forcing Hunter's attention back to heating dinner. I watched him move around the kitchen with grace as he plated two meals and cut up a loaf of semolina bread. Though there was a dining room table, without discussing it, we ate in the kitchen on the island across from one another. It reminded me of hanging out and enjoying a meal with a friend, rather than forcing the formality of eating in the dining room. I liked that he just went with the flow. Garrett would never have eaten in the kitchen.

"This is really good," I said. "Did you make the cream sauce yourself?"

"I did. Thank you."

Hunter forked pasta and chicken, and I couldn't help watching the way his throat worked to swallow the food.

The masculine bob of his Adam's apple was hypnotic. I couldn't imagine what it would be like to watch him undress if the sight of his neck did this to me.

As we ate, I quietly deliberated saying something. I had no doubt Hunter and I would have great sex, but if I was open with him, the way he was with me, things could only be better. So, deciding to push my embarrassment to the side, I opened up.

"I've never had anal sex."

A slow smile spread across his face. He tore a piece of bread in half and dipped it around in the sauce on his plate. "Opposed to it?"

"I'm not sure *opposed* to it is the right term. *Terrified* might fit better."

He chuckled. "Okay. Good to know. We'll save that for when you learn to trust me in bed. How about oral?"

I couldn't believe I was having this conversation. "Giving or receiving?"

"Both."

"I enjoy both."

His eyes scorched with heat. "Opposed to being tied up?"

God, there was a lot Garrett and I didn't do. "Never tried it. But I'd be open to it."

"*Nice.* Toys?"

My face heated. "I have a vibrator, yes."

"Opposed to using it for me?"

My mouth dropped open. I'd never masturbated with anyone watching. "I'm not sure."

His eyes dropped to my pebbled nipples and rose back to meet mine. "I'll take that as a yes. Any fetishes?"

"Me? No. You?"

"Not really. But would it scare you if I told you I'd love to spank your ass."

I swallowed and whispered, "Oddly, no, not at all."

"After I spank you, I'd take you from behind while you're on all fours. Opposed?"

Jesus Christ. I didn't answer, but that wasn't because I was against it, I just couldn't figure out how to get my mouth to move. Seeming to sense that my silence wasn't a bad thing, his sinful mouth continued on.

"And when I'm done, I want to come all over your ass and back."

"*God*, Hunter."

"When is the next time Izzy is staying at her grandmother's? I want a whole night the first time I'm inside you."

In the moment, I couldn't remember what day it was, much less which weekend my stepdaughter was scheduled to visit her grandmother. I gulped from my wine glass in a very unladylike manner and answered honestly. "Not soon enough."

Somehow we managed to not claw each other's clothes off after that. When we'd finished dinner, we cleaned up together and then sat in the living room talking. There was no lull in our conversation as we covered everything from work to our last vacations and places we'd like to visit. Hunter, it seemed, was an open book to most anything, except for his one serious relationship. And I, of all people, understood wanting to forget past mistakes.

Even though I hated to go, I asked him to drive me home about eleven. He walked me up to my apartment, and we said goodnight at the door with yet another amazing kiss.

"I'll call you." He kissed my forehead. I really loved when he did that for some reason.

"I won't be able to answer most of tomorrow. It's visiting day. I take Izzy to see her dad, and it's a four-hour drive each way, plus the actual time while she visits."

I caught Hunter's jaw clench, but he nodded and said nothing further on the subject. "I have to fly back to California on Tuesday for a few days to work with a client on some last-minute drafting revisions. Look at your schedule and let me know if you're free next weekend."

"Okay."

I checked in on a sleeping Izzy and took a quick shower. I was too awake to go right to sleep, so after, I sat on my bed, booted up my laptop, and opened my calendar in Google. Next weekend was marked off as Izzy's monthly visit with her grandmother. She normally went on Friday, and I picked her up on Sunday, unless she had a game early Saturday morning. Then I dropped her after the game. I clicked to my bookmarked favorite sites and opened the athletics schedule for Beacon. Surprisingly, the only game this week was on Thursday evening. There was no Saturday game.

I reached for my phone and texted Hunter, figuring he would probably be home by now.

Natalia: Izzy's weekend with her grandmother is next weekend.

The dots started to jump around.

Hunter: When do you drop her off?

Natalia: After practice on Friday—usually around seven. Then pick her up on the way to Mom's house for Sunday night dinner.

Hunter: I'll pick you up at eight Friday night. Pack a bag. You're staying the weekend.

My little heart went into a pitter-patter frenzy. Before I could respond, a second text came in.

Hunter: On second thought, bring nothing. You won't be needing any clothes. I'll pick you up a toothbrush.

Natalia: LOL. I'll bring a bag anyway. Just in case there's a fire and I have to run out of the house.

Hunter: Good thinking. Wouldn't want any neighbors to see that ass. Because for what's left of my two-month assignment, it belongs to me.

I smiled like a teenager. I liked the sound of that. A lot. But in the back of my head, a tiny little warning went off.

Just make sure all you give him is your ass, Nat. Not your heart.

Chapter 20

— Hunter —
11 years ago

It never dulled.

Not even after eight months of not seeing her.

I should've forgotten all about Summer by now. There'd been others—maybe too many others in an attempt to forget her—but my attraction was still there the first time we crossed paths again.

It was Jayce's graduation party at our aunt and uncle's house. I was sipping a beer in the living room when she walked in. Our eyes locked, and I swear it felt like my heart started to beat for the first time.

Fuck. She's gorgeous.

I watched as she walked over to Jayce and his girlfriend of two months and gave him a big hug. She said something that made all three of them laugh, and then walked over to the couch and parked herself right next to me. Without turning her head in my direction, she took the beer from my hand and brought it to her lips to drink.

She spoke before drinking. "Truth or dare?"

I smirked. "Truth."

After she took a healthy swallow from my beer, she passed it back. "Did you delete the nearly naked picture of me on your phone that I sent forever ago?"

I turned my head and waited until she finally looked at me to respond. "Nope."

Her eyes sparkled. "How often do you look at it?"

"More truth?"

She nodded.

"Every fucking day."

We passed the beer back and forth again. "Seeing anyone?" she asked.

"I have someone I *see* once in a while."

"Is *see* code for *fuck*?"

The corners of my lip twitched. "I was trying to be a gentleman. How about you? You *seeing* anyone?"

She lobbed my noncommittal answer right back at me. "I have someone I *see* once in a while."

I was screwing someone else, hadn't seen or spoken to Summer in eight months—not since the night at the party when I walked away after realizing she was the girl my brother was nuts about—and yet, I had the urge to rip the head off the nameless, faceless guy she was sleeping with. Yeah, time hadn't dulled shit.

I stood. "Going to grab another beer. You want your own, or are you planning on just taking mine the rest of the night?"

Summer flashed an impish smile. "Planning on taking yours the rest of the night, unless that's a problem."

"No problem here."

I took five minutes to sort out my head before returning to the couch. I glanced over at my brother with his arm around Emily—he looked happy. He'd pined over Summer for six more months after that party. Now that he'd seemed to move on, was the ban lifted? Jayce had no idea anything had ever happened between Summer and me—and truth be told, not much had. But was it ever okay to go for a girl your brother was once crazy about, even though she'd never returned the feelings? I wasn't sure my moral compass always pointed me in the right direction.

Summer hadn't moved from the couch when I returned. I sat, cracked open a new beer and took a sip before passing it to her. "My turn. Truth or dare?"

She took a long chug from the can. "Dare."

The challenge exited my mouth without any real thought. "Text the guy you're *seeing* and tell him you're done with *seeing* him."

Summer looked back and forth between my eyes before digging into her purse and pulling out her cell. She scrolled through her contacts and typed a message. When she finished, she turned the phone toward me so I could read the text she'd typed to a guy named Gavin.

Hey. Sorry to do this via text. But I need to end what we have going on. Have a nice summer break!

After I finished reading, she hit send.

I drank from the beer. "Gavin's day just got shitty."

We smiled at each other as her phone pinged with a response. I loved that she didn't bother to open it and ignored the sound of a dozen new messages over the next half hour we sat together.

When the party was in full swing, Summer and I separated, each spending time talking to our friends and hanging out with Jayce. But there wasn't a second of the day that I didn't know exactly where she was. My eyes were like a magnet to her. And it didn't appear I was the only one. Sometimes our eyes would meet, and we'd smile. Other times, one of us would look at the other, mid-conversation with someone else, and even though our eyes couldn't connect, our hidden smirks said we were on the same page.

At one point I was talking to my brother when I felt her eyes on me. I still hadn't worked out how anything between Summer and me would sit with Jayce, so I decided to feel things out.

"You and Emily look happy."

"She's great." He had a bottle of seltzer water in his hand, and I noticed a shake when he raised it to his mouth, almost a tremor. Considering our mother had had Parkinson's, it was something we both noticed.

"What's going on there?" I lifted my chin toward his hand.

"Just a little too much to drink last night." He tipped his bottle to me. "A little too much graduation celebration. Sticking to seltzer today."

What college guy who lives in a frat house hasn't had those nights? I thought nothing of it, seeing as I'd had shaky morning-afters myself. So, I went back to poking around.

"Emily going to grad school?"

"Not right away. She's taking her nursing boards but wants to work for a while before doing a graduate degree."

"How'd you two meet anyway?"

"Tutoring." He smiled warmly. "She sucks at math."

"Ah. Like Su...Pearl. How's she gonna make it through her last year of college without you around to tutor her?"

Jayce looked over my shoulder. I knew by the look in his eye who he was gazing at. "I'll make the time if she still needs help. I'd never turn down an opportunity to spend time with Pearl."

Shit. "Better not let Emily hear you say that."

He shook his head, still staring at Summer over my shoulder. "Yeah. No shit. No one likes to find out they're second choice."

I drank too much.

The party was winding down, and I wasn't the only one who had overindulged. Jayce, who'd said he wasn't drinking today, had just tripped over his own two feet, and his tipsy girlfriend laughed so hard, she fell down on the floor with him when she tried to help him up.

Needing some fresh air, I sat on the front porch alone, nursing a beer and licking my wounds. I'd done my best to ignore Summer after my earlier conversation with my brother. Then the front door opened, and she sat her fine ass down next to me on the step.

"Here you are. I was beginning to think you were avoiding me."

I was honest to a fault, more so when I drank. "I was."

She bumped her shoulder into mine. "You're not too good at it, seeing as you're sitting on the front porch, and this is the only way out."

I guzzled the last of my beer. "He still has feelings for you."

Summer's face fell. "But he's seeing someone."

"I've been seeing other people. Doesn't keep me from staring at your face every fucking day on my phone."

She tilted her head. "My face? Is that the part you stare at in the photo on your phone?"

My eyes dropped to her cleavage. "There's more than three billion women in the world. Why is it that the only one I really want is the one I can't have?"

Summer stared down at her feet. Eventually she said, "Like I told you eight months ago, I like Jayce. He's a great guy. But whether you and I had met or not, he's just a friend." Her eyes rose to meet mine. "You can't make yourself feel something for someone any more than you can make yourself stop feeling something for someone else."

I knew she was right. We'd had no contact for more than eight months after finding out my brother was crazy about her. We'd both moved on to other people, and she'd never moved Jayce out of the friend zone. It was clear neither one of us had stopped feeling what we'd felt that first day for each other. Heart trumps head, every damn time.

It was me who started the game this time. Summer's hands were splayed flat on the steps on either side of her, next to mine. I lifted my pinky and reached the few inches over to her hand, entwining her little finger with mine.

"Truth or dare," I said.

She lifted those big green eyes to mine, looking up under thick lashes. "Truth."

I arched a brow at her choice. She'd always been a dare girl. After sorting through a million questions in my head, I went with something open-ended. "Tell me a secret no one else knows."

Summer bit her lip and looked shy for the first time since I'd met her. "No one knows I stalked you on Facebook and screenshot a photo someone had tagged you in. You were at the beach and looked really sexy." She paused and lowered her voice. "And no one knows that sometimes I look at it while I masturbate."

Jesus Christ.

I swallowed hard. This girl was trying to kill me.

She looked down at our linked pinkies and squeezed. "Your turn. Truth or dare."

I cleared my throat. Since we were going against the grain, I went with it. "Dare."

A seductive smile spread across her face. "Come home with me."

Chapter 21

— Natalia —

"Are you and Hunter, like, serious?" Izzy asked.

We were about a half hour from the federal prison when she asked the question out of the blue. She'd been her normal, brooding self this morning and had popped her earbuds in before we'd even entered the car, then proceeded to sleep for three hours of the three-and-a-half-hour drive I'd already done.

"No. Not at all." We were the exact opposite of serious. But telling Izzy that Hunter and I had agreed to become fuck buddies wasn't really appropriate.

She shrugged and put her feet up on the dashboard. "I like him."

"He's too old for you," I teased.

"Marcus was a dweeb."

"Marcus was very nice."

Another shrug.

"How about your love life?" I glanced at my stepdaughter. "How are things with Yakshit?"

"Okay, I guess. He asked me if I was going to the dance, and I said no. Then he asked why not. So I said the person I wanted to go with already had a date."

"You did?" I was surprised. Old Izzy would have just given him an attitude and not talked it out. She was really maturing. "What did he say to that?"

"He asked me who I wanted to go with."

My eyes flashed to her. "What did you say?"

Izzy buried her head in her hands. "I blurted out, '*You, you dope. I wanted to go with you.*' We were in Science Research class, and everyone had been talking because the teacher hadn't come in yet. My back was to the door, and I didn't see her come in right before I yelled it. I swear, *the entire* class shut up when I said it. Everyone heard."

"Wow. Oh my. How did that go over?"

"A couple of people snickered. But Yakshit just stared at me. I thought I'd freaked him out. So after class, I bolted and ignored him when he tried to talk to me. I managed to keep away from him all day until after practice. He waited outside the locker room for me to come out."

"Did you two talk?"

"He talked. I was so embarrassed that I didn't say much."

"And..."

"He said he would've rather gone to the dance with me, but he didn't think I liked him. He thought I liked Chad Siegler."

"Who's that?"

"Some boring guy who plays on the basketball team. He's basically Marcus. He's cute, I guess. But boring as shit."

I laughed, even though I probably should've corrected her language. But Izzy and I were talking about boys. Who would've ever thought we'd get here?

"Why did he think you liked Chad?"

"I have no idea."

"Well, is Yakshit still going to the dance with Brittany?"

"He told me he was going to tell her he couldn't go so we could go together. But I told him not to. I said to go with her. The dance is next week, and it's not fair to Brittany if he dumps her to take me. It's my own fault he's going with her because I didn't have the nerve to ask him."

"That's very considerate of you."

She shrugged. "He said he wants to take me to the movies."

"Did you say yes?"

"I told him to have a good time at the dance and ask me after if he still wants to."

"Wow."

She stared out the window in silence for a while before speaking again. "Do I have to tell Dad about him if I go to the movies?"

I knew my ex-husband. He'd be adamant that she couldn't date until she was twenty-one. While I didn't love the idea of her dating, she would be sixteen in two weeks, and it was going to happen whether we allowed it or not. I was basically a single mom and the only mother figure she had—except for her grandmother who treated her like she was still three years old. We were going to have to trust each other.

"That's up to you, Izzy. But he won't hear it from me if you decide to not share it with him. However, you and I need to talk about these things. Okay?"

When I glanced over at her, I saw she was relieved. "Okay."

Our visit with Garrett was typical. He tried to talk to me, and I retreated to a table alone, keeping a watchful eye on the two of them while reading a book. When the visit was almost over, I went over to their table to walk out with Izzy. Neither of them looked happy. But it wasn't the same type of upset that sometimes hits Izzy when it was time to go—that was usually sadness. Instead today, my stepdaughter had her arms crossed and looked *pissed*. And my ex-husband was scowling.

"Why don't you ask her yourself?" She squinted at her father.

Shit. This was about me.

He gave her a stern look and a matching tone. "Give us a few minutes alone, Isabella."

Izzy looked up to her father. I'd never seen her defiant toward him before. "*No*," she spat. "I'm not going to leave you alone so you can give Nat the third degree. It's none of your business what she does or who she spends time with."

My eyes widened.

Garrett spoke between clenched teeth. "Go wait by the door, Isabella."

Izzy stood, and for a second, I thought she was caving. Until she turned to face me. "You ready, Nat?"

I glanced back and forth between my ex-husband and stepdaughter, trying to figure out the right thing to do. I hated for her to leave him angry. If she regretted whatever had been said, she didn't have tomorrow to make it all good again. It would be another month before we were back for our next visit.

Hoping I made the right decision, I looked at Garrett. "Izzy is growing up to be a pretty amazing person. She's really matured and has come into her own lately." My eyes caught with hers. "So while I hate you two fighting, I support her, and if she's ready to leave, we're going to be going now. Goodbye, Garrett. See you next month."

Izzy gave her father one last look. "Bye, Dad." And we walked out together.

I expected her to break down after we made our way out of the prison. But she didn't. Izzy was quiet as we collected our things from the locker and walked to the car.

Once we were inside, I turned to face her before starting the car. "Do you want to talk about it?"

"*He's such a jerk.* I was telling him about how my jump shot has improved, and you know what his response was?"

"What?"

"He asked who the man was that was in our apartment."

Marcus had only been inside our apartment once, and my gut told me this was not about Marcus. "How did he know there was a man in our apartment?"

"Damon told him you were dating a plumber or something."

Ugh. Damon.

"I'm sorry he tried to get you in the middle of things and it ruined your visit."

"*Dad* ruined my visit. He wasn't even listening about my game. Then he got pissed when I told him it was none of his business who was in our house."

Oh shit.

"What did he say to that?"

"He said you were his wife, and it was his business. That I was his eyes and ears while he couldn't be home right now. So I told him you were his *ex*-wife, and it was his own fault he couldn't be home right now. That I wasn't his eyes and ears, I was *his daughter.*"

God, I was so proud of her. But my heart also broke that Garrett was trying to use her during the one shitty hour he got to see her each month.

"You're a hundred percent right, Izzy. But that couldn't have been easy to say."

"It's the truth."

When had she become such a grown up? "Izzy...thank you. Thank you for defending me. But I just want to put it out there—I'll never be upset if you want to tell your father our business. While I don't think *I'm* his business, you are, and I suppose he has every right to know if a man is hanging around while you're home."

She again stared out the window, so I started the car to give her some time. We were going to be physically next to each other for the next few hours, yet I thought she might need some privacy to replay things in her head.

But she didn't put in her earbuds and fall asleep this time. Instead, she looked deep in thought.

After about an hour, I pointed to a bunch of fast food signs on the side of the highway and asked if she wanted to stop and get some lunch. She nodded. Rather than go through the drive-thru as we normally would on the way home, I parked in a spot at Wendy's. If she was ready to talk some more, it would be easier sitting across from each other.

I grabbed my purse from the back and opened my car door to get out. Izzy's voice stopped me.

"Nat?"

I turned back to find that Izzy hadn't made any attempt to get out of the car. She faced forward, but when I looked closely at her, I saw tears welling in her eyes. I pulled my car door shut.

"Talk to me, sweetheart. It's normal that you're upset after what happened today."

A fat tear streaked down her cheek, and her bottom lip quivered. Seeing her pain when she turned to face me choked my throat with my own tears.

"What rights does Dad have?" she croaked with a shaky voice.

At first I didn't understand the question, but then I remembered the last thing I'd said was that he had *every right* to know if a man was hanging around her. I thought that's what she was referring to.

"Well, he's your father, so I guess I feel like he has a right to know you're safe and well protected. No matter what happened between me and him, or what he's done wrong, I would feel wrong letting him worry about your safety."

She shook her head vigorously. "No. What right does he have *to me*?"

"You mean legally?"

She nodded.

We'd never discussed the legal aspect of how things were decided by the court. All she knew was she lived with me and visited her grandmother and father. "Well, right now I have full physical custody of you. So no one else has the right to have you live with them. You go to visit your grandmother once a month because that's what I arranged with her. I think it's important to keep in touch with her, and she loves you very much. She wanted to have physical custody of you, but she's seventy-two, and you'd never lived with her before, so the court agreed that you should live with me."

I waited until she looked up at me and made sure she heard the next part loud and clear. "And I wanted you to live with me because I love you."

She smiled through her tears and nodded, so I continued.

"But there are two types of rights people have over minors—physical custody and legal custody. Your dad and I share legal custody of you."

"What does that mean?"

"It means that your dad and I both get a say in the important decisions about you—like schooling, medical care, and that type of stuff."

"Even though he's in jail?"

"Yes. I didn't try to fight him for full legal custody. He's always made good decisions for your well-being, and he does love you. I didn't want him to feel like I was trying to steal you from him. He made mistakes. *Big ones.* But he's still your father."

I thought I'd done a good job explaining it, but when I finished, she looked even more devastated than when I started. Tears streamed down her face.

"Oh my God, I'm so sorry. I didn't mean to upset you. Was that too much information?" I leaned over and pulled her into my arms. "Come here. Talk to me. What part upset you?"

She sobbed on my shoulder for a few minutes, and I couldn't hold back my own tears. It hurt so damn much to see her in pain. Kids shouldn't have to hurt because of the actions of adults who were supposed to protect them. Yet it happened every day.

I never thought I'd long for angry, pissed-off Izzy to appear. After a while, the sobbing slowed, and she sniffled before lifting her head from my shoulder. Her eyes were puffy and red.

"You're going to send me back to live with him, aren't you?"

The question caught me off guard. It had never occurred to me that Izzy might not want to live with her dad when he got out in a few months. It was only in the last few months that she'd started to open up to me, and I'd started to see that she really didn't hate me—she just hated the circumstances surrounding why she had to live with me, and I was the only person around to blame.

I searched her face. "You don't want to live with your dad?"

She shook her head.

"You're upset with him now. I don't think you're in the right frame of mind to think about things like this."

"He's not a girl. He wouldn't get stuff. Can't I just stay with you and visit him on the weekends or something?"

Jesus, I was not ready to answer that question. Even more so, I wasn't sure I *could* answer that question. Garrett would certainly want custody of his daughter when he got out, wouldn't he?

"Izzy, I...I don't think that decision is up to me, or you, alone."

Her hopeful face fell. "It's up to Dad?"

"I guess if you and I decided it would be in your best interest to stay with me, and your dad disagreed, a judge would have to decide."

She looked down, seeming to think that answer over for a minute. Then she hit me point blank, staring straight into my eyes. "Would you want me to live with you, if that's what I wanted?"

The answer fell from my lips before I could even contemplate it. "Yes."

But I did not have a good feeling that things would go smoothly if it turned out this was what Izzy wanted.

Chapter 22

— Natalia —

I was a jittery, nervous wreck.

Somehow I'd managed to keep busy this week and hadn't wasted much time dwelling on my upcoming date, or rather upcoming *weekend*, with Hunter, until now. It was two in the afternoon on Friday, and I'd already finished all of my appointments and written up all of my case notes. Hoping to relax and unwind, I'd drawn a bath and tossed in a sweet pea bath bomb I'd picked up on the way home yesterday.

Like the rest of my apartment, the bathroom was small, so it steamed up just from filling the tub with hot water. Since Izzy wasn't home, I left the door open to let out some of the steam and shed my clothes before settling into the hot water. Closing my eyes, I took a deep breath and inhaled the amazing scent of my grandmother's garden. Totally what I needed.

My phone buzzed from the sink, interrupting my peace, and my eyes fluttered open. Finding a penetrating eye staring at me from the corner of the tub, I jumped from the water, sloshed half the bath all over the floor, and nearly slipped on the wet tile.

The cat.

The damn cat.

You'd think the presence of only *one eye* would have given me a clue.

Catpernicus had strolled in through the open door and perched himself up on the edge of the tub, nearly scaring the life out of me. With the way he continued to eye me (no pun intended), I grabbed the towel from the rack to cover myself.

Seriously? I was on edge today.

I took a few deep breaths and went to grab my phone, the buzzing of which had been the catalyst to my near disaster, and suddenly realized my cell was no longer on the sink. Dread settled into my stomach, but I looked around everywhere, leaving what I feared most for last.

Not on the floor.

Didn't fall into the sink.

No miraculous leap into the nearby garbage can.

My eyes dropped to the tub.

Shit.

There sat my phone—on the bottom of the half-full bath.

In my frenzied scramble to get out, I'd grabbed the sink and must've knocked it into the water. I scooped it up, but of course, it was too late. The phone was dead, and I couldn't imagine there would be a resurrection.

Though I was aggravated with myself, there was really nothing I could do about it at the moment, so I patted my phone dry and attempted to settle back into the tub. Finding it impossible to relax, I decided to finish my grooming. I shaved every piece of hair from my legs and armpits, and then scrutinized the Brazilian wax job I'd had done yesterday to make sure it looked just right. Catpernicus sat dutifully on the edge of the tub, licking and cleaning his paws. I'd arranged for my neighbor, Mrs.

Whitman, who also had a cat, to take him for the weekend. I wondered if perhaps Catpernicus was getting ready for his own date.

Packing my bag was a challenge of its own. I picked out my laciest lingerie, but wasn't sure what, if anything, I'd be wearing beyond that. Which resulted in overpacking— something to lounge around in, something to go out, jeans and a T-shirt...what if it rained? I imagined the look on Hunter's face if I showed up with rain gear and two suitcases. The poor man would probably have a heart attack, thinking I was moving in.

Butterflies took up residence in my belly for the rest of the afternoon. We'd texted a few times this week and decided that rather than him picking me up, I'd go to his place right after dropping off Izzy. Hunter lived pretty close to Garrett's mother's house. I'd be taking Izzy straight from practice, and I didn't want her to see the suitcase, so I stashed it in the trunk. I needed to be careful with the example I set, especially now that she was almost sixteen and interested in boys. Teenagers listen to your actions, not what you tell them is right or wrong.

On my way to pick up Izzy, I stopped by Verizon and got a new, ridiculously overpriced iPhone. They weren't able to save anything from my old phone, so I had no numbers or contacts, and I'd basically be starting from scratch. I didn't even know the first digit of Hunter's telephone number.

It was probably best that Izzy had transformed back to a disgruntled teenager and was in a mood when I picked her up from practice. My emotions were already all over the place, and I wasn't sure it would be wise to discuss boys or her dad. When we pulled up at her grandmother's house, I double parked.

"Oh, I almost forgot. I dropped my phone in the bathtub. I don't even know your number." I dug my new cell from my jacket pocket. "Can you program it in?"

She took it and typed as she spoke. "When did you take a bath?"

"This afternoon."

"But you showered this morning. You were in there when I woke up."

"Umm...I was stressed so I tried a new bath bomb."

"Everything okay?"

"Yeah." I lied. "Just some work things were bothering me."

I walked Izzy to the door, spoke to her grandmother for a minute, and then forced a hug and a kiss. "I'll call you tomorrow to check in."

"Are you doing anything this weekend?" she asked.

I smiled, happy to not have to lie. "I plan on spending the weekend in bed."

Was it possible to feel your heart bouncing against your ribcage? I wasn't sure, but that's what it felt like was going on. Either that or I had a massive case of indigestion. I parked my car in a garage on the same block as Hunter's place, and everything hit me when I handed the keys to the valet. He asked me what time I would be picking it up.

I swallowed. "Not until Sunday."

I was really doing this.

Butterflies swarmed in my belly, stronger and stronger with each step I took toward Hunter's building. I took a deep breath as the doorman greeted me.

"You must be Ms. Rossi?"

It wasn't the same doorman who had been working the night I'd visited. "Yes. How did you know that?"

He smiled warmly and took off his hat. "Mr. Delucia called earlier and said you would be arriving about now. He was unable to reach you and wanted me to let you know his flight was delayed, and he'll arrive home about nine."

"Oh." Disappointment settled in. I'd taken all afternoon to psych myself up for arrival, and another hour would surely fray the last of my nerves.

The doorman reached into his pocket. "He asked that I get the key from the super so you could let yourself in and wait. Would you like me to take you up?"

"Oh. No. I can do it myself." I took the keys and felt the need to explain myself for some unknown reason. "I dropped my phone in water. That's why he couldn't reach me."

During the elevator ride up, I dug my new phone out of my pocket again. I hadn't checked it since the store activated it, other than to have Izzy enter her number. Sure enough, I had a new message from Hunter that had arrived in the last few minutes.

Hunter: Just landed at JFK. My messages aren't showing as delivered. Hope all is okay.

I saved his number to my contacts and typed back.

Nat: I broke my phone and just picked up a new one an hour ago. Lost all my contacts.

Hunter: Flight was delayed. Going to be about another hour before I get there. Sorry. Benny the doorman should have a key for you to let yourself in.

The elevator dinged and the doors slid open as I typed.

Nat: On the elevator with key in hand as I type this.

Hunter: Nice. I was starting to worry you were blowing me off.

His apartment was a few doors down from the elevator, so I let myself in before responding again.

Nat: I still have an hour to reconsider. Anything can happen...

Hunter: How about you spend that hour getting undressed and thinking about all the things I'm going to do to you when I get home.

Now *that* was tempting. I bit my bottom lip and played with him a little.

Nat: You're not even going to feed me first?

The dots started to jump around, then stopped, then started again.

Hunter: I'd give you the visual of what I just imagined feeding you, but we need to stop texting or I'm not going to be able to walk off this plane in a few minutes without embarrassing myself.

Oh my. He didn't have to describe it, my own image was just as vivid. Another text came in before I could respond.

Hunter: See you soon.

Sigh. I left my suitcase at the front door and walked to the balcony. I pulled the cord to open the privacy blinds that covered the glass doors and appreciated the spectacular view. It was odd to be inside Hunter's apartment by myself. After a bit of city gazing, I decided to look around a little. And by look, I mean *snoop*.

It wasn't his home, so the place was pretty bare of personal belongings. Yet that didn't stop me from checking out his medicine cabinet. An extra box of toothpaste, large bottle of mouthwash, unopened vitamins, two untouched deodorants—pretty much just the basics. Although I suppose if he had medicines, they'd likely have traveled with him, so I wasn't really learning anything. In the bedroom, there was a fair amount of clothes in the closet, and the chest of drawers had the usual assortment of socks and underwear. Looking around the room, there wasn't much else to look at—other than the nightstand.

The one on the far side of the room was empty. I was just about to call my little snooping session a bust when I stopped at the other nightstand. Slipping it open with my pointer finger, I hit pay dirt. Inside was a bag, sitting on top of some papers. I took note of how the bag had been placed inside and then lifted it to check out the contents. Inside was the largest box of condoms I'd ever seen, a bottle of lubricant that could be heated, and...bath bombs. I swooned seeing that Hunter had picked up the same scent as I had soaked with earlier today—sweet pea. It also made me happy that the only condoms in the apartment seemed to be an unopened box that he'd purchased with me in mind.

Before replacing the bag, I fingered through the papers, being careful not to disrupt them too much. Inside was a short-term lease agreement for the company-owned apartment, a rental car agreement, and a piece of mail addressed to Hunter. As I started to place the bag back where I'd taken it from, I happened to notice the postmark on the envelope—which had been mailed almost ten years ago. Scanning the return address, I recognized the name—Jayce Delucia—Hunter's brother. I knew he'd died years ago. My hand rubbed at a spot on my chest, feeling emotional that Hunter carried around an old letter from his dead brother. He wasn't just a handsome guy blessed with natural charm—he was a man of many layers. And unlike most men, the more I looked beneath the surface, the more I liked what I saw.

I was a snooper, but I wasn't a total asshole, so I put the letter from his brother back and arranged the drawer the way it had been before sliding it shut. I had no idea what to do with myself after that. Hunter wouldn't be here for another forty-five minutes, at least, so I decided to call Anna. It would be fun to play guess where I am.

"My nipples are killing me," she said as she answered, rather than hello.

Nothing surprised me with her. "Well, okay then. That's where this conversation is going. I was going to take it in a different direction, but I can work with this. How's your asshole doing?"

She groaned. "Seriously, why can't men be the ones to produce milk? I mean, we do everything. I carried this little pipsqueak for ten months, popped her out of my tiny little vagina, and now my tits are killing me because all she does is suck on them all day." I heard a sweet little yelp in the background when she finished her rant.

"Is that my niece?"

"It is." Her voice softened. "She sucks like a Hoover."

"Aww. I miss you guys. Tell me what she's up to these days. Is she walking? Talking?" I joked.

"Not quite. But she's got pooping and sucking down pretty good."

I laughed and settled into Hunter's couch. It was so good to hear her voice, like wrapping myself in an old blanket from childhood. "How are you feeling?"

"Aside from the cracked nipples, I actually feel really good. I've been walking the baby in the stroller a lot, and with breastfeeding burning up all my calories, my body is starting to shrink toward its normal shape."

"Wow. That's great."

"What's going on with you?"

"Eh." I feigned no big deal. "I'm just sitting at Hunter's place, waiting for him to come home so we can screw like rabbits."

A shriek so loud came through the phone that I had to pull it away from my ear. Needless to say, we did a lot of catching up over the next half hour. Though Anna had been initially leery of me and Hunter getting together, she was genuinely excited. *Maybe too excited.* She had me moving out to the west coast, marrying her husband's best friend so the four of us could be inseparable, and pushing a baby carriage next to her. The reality was, Hunter and I were only going to be fuck buddies.

I attempted to set her expectations straight, although the hope I heard in her voice told me that wasn't going to be an easy task.

"Why don't you meet him at the door naked?" Anna said.

I laughed. "He's been traveling all day. He's probably starving."

"My point exactly." My little niece began to mewl in the background. We'd been talking on the phone for a long time. "Damn. She's wet. I need to change her. Can you call me back in a few minutes?"

"Hunter should be home soon. How about if I call you tomorrow."

"Oh my God. Call me right after it's over."

I chuckled. "Sure. I'll call you while he's taking off the condom."

"Okay!"

I wasn't quite sure if she knew I was joking or not. "I'll call you tomorrow, crazy lady."

After I said goodbye, I went to the bathroom to freshen up. While I was in there, for a half a second I gave serious consideration to what Anna had suggested. I knew without a shadow of a doubt that Hunter would be thrilled if I answered the door buck-ass naked. But I was still on edge and needed the passion to build between us before I could let go that much.

As I was brushing my teeth with my finger, I heard the front door quietly open and close. *Oh my God. He's home.* I was half giddy, fully nervous, and buzzing with a sudden surge of adrenaline. Closing my eyes, I took a few deep breaths and then looked in the mirror before heading out to see the man responsible for my heart hammering a million miles a minute.

Only, when I walked out, it wasn't Hunter standing in the living room. It was a woman. Just as I emerged from the bathroom, she dropped her coat to the floor.

And I froze in place, standing there staring at her beautiful, naked body.

Chapter 23

— Natalia —

"Shit!" The woman mumbled as she bent to pick up the trench coat pooled around her bare feet. "I thought someone else was staying here." She seemed to have a British accent.

I blinked a few times, at first stunned at the turn of events, but then in an attempt to unglue my eyes from the statuesque redhead. She was drop-dead gorgeous. Tall, thin, with creamy porcelain skin, perky boobs, and legs that ran for miles. I didn't tend to be overly self-conscious, but standing in a room with her fixed that real quick.

Before I could form a coherent sentence, the woman spoke again while pulling on her coat. "I'm so sorry. I'm in the flat next door. A guy I work with sometimes stays in this one, and I knew he was in town. When I asked the doorman who was staying in this apartment, he told me it was him."

"How did you get in here?"

She pointed over her shoulder. "The door wasn't locked. I knocked first, but no one answered, so I opened it."

"Who are you?"

"Brooke. Brooke Canter." She cinched her coat at the waist. "I do apologize. I thought you were someone else. I'm mortified."

The dread that settled in my belly knew the answer, but I asked nonetheless. "Who did you think was staying here?"

"Hunter Delucia."

Seeing my face falter, the woman's eyes closed. "Shit. Hunter *is* the sublet here, isn't he?"

I nodded slowly.

"We used to..." She shook her head. "Never mind. I should get going."

Before I could say anything else, the embarrassed woman scurried back out the door. I, on the other hand, seemed to be immobilized.

"Such a goddamn idiot." I jabbed my finger at the elevator panel a second time, grumbling to myself. The damn thing wasn't moving, and all I wanted to do was get the hell out of here before Hunter showed up. I shouldn't be so upset, but I couldn't help it. It was stupid of me to expect that someone who'd proposed we have a short-term affair hadn't had others. It didn't even sound like she'd spoken to Hunter since he'd arrived in town weeks ago, but that didn't make it hurt any less.

The elevator car finally started moving. In my haste to get out of the apartment, I thought I might've forgotten to grab my new cell. As I dug frantically in my purse to check, the elevator doors slid open on the ground floor. Frenzied, I found my phone, grabbed my roller bag, and stepped off, without first looking up. Which was the reason I crashed right into a man.

Of course, that man had to be Hunter.

He grabbed my shoulders and steadied them to keep me from falling over. "Hey...where you running off to?"

He said it playfully and with a smile on his face, but when he got a look at my scowl, his smile wilted fast.

"Move." I demanded.

"Natalia? What happened? What's going on?"

"I'm leaving."

"Why?"

"You don't need me here."

"What are you talking about? Why are you so upset?"

His hands were still on my shoulders. "Let go of me!"

He lifted his hands in surrender. "Okay. But talk to me. What's going on?"

I leveled him with a scathing look. "I met your neighbor."

His brows drew down as if that wasn't enough information. Who knows? Maybe it wasn't. I hadn't gone door to door to see what other women he was fucking on the floor. I rolled my eyes. "Brooke. The redhead."

Hunter's eyes shut.

I waited until they opened again to finish my description. "And she's a natural redhead, in case you'd forgotten. Lucky me, I got to verify that first-hand."

I started to walk around Hunter, but he grabbed my arm. "Natalia."

Stopping, I answered like a sullen child. "What?"

I'd been speaking to his chest, and he kept quiet until I looked up into his eyes. His tone was firm, yet calm. "Let's talk about this. You can decide to go after, or you can stay, but either way, please hear me out."

I was weary, and he read it on my face.

"Please," he pressed.

Our lives were intertwined through mutual friends. It only made sense that things end on a better note than my storming out. I nodded, and the look of relief on his face made me realize he was a lot better at controlling his temper than I was.

Almost as if he was afraid I might change my mind, he pushed the button to call the elevator, slipped the handle of my roller bag from my hand, and put his other hand at the small of my back to usher me inside the car.

You could've heard a pin drop on the ride up. Yet even being pissed off and hurt, I found sharing a small space with Hunter had an insane effect on my body. He was just so *right there.* He filled a room with his intoxicating smell and the way he planted his feet wide in that masculine, alpha-male way.

I was relieved when we arrived at his floor. I needed air that wasn't shared with this man to keep my head on straight. Our silence continued as we walked down the hall. Still feeling off kilter, I didn't even realize we'd passed the door to his apartment until he was knocking on another door.

"Why are you knocking?"

Before he could respond, the stunning redhead swung open the door. Her eyes lit up to find Hunter on the other side, until she caught the look on his face and me standing next to him.

"Brooke." He nodded.

She looked between the two of us. "I'm so sorry. I don't know what I was thinking."

"When was the last time we saw each other?" Hunter asked, again in that calm but firm tone.

"A year ago, maybe?"

"How about the last time we talked?"

She shrugged. "A few emails on the Cooper project, but I don't think we've spoken in a year either."

Hunter nodded. "Thank you. I'm sorry to bother you."

His hand still at my back, he guided me to the next door. His hold only briefly loosened so he could unlock it, and then he was ushering me inside. Setting my luggage down, he turned to face me, brushing the hair from my eyes.

"What happened?"

"I was in the bathroom, and I heard the door open, so I thought it was you. When I came out, she was standing in the living room and had just let her coat drop to the floor. She was completely naked."

He nodded and seemed to contemplate that information for a minute before speaking again. "If I'd been waiting for you and some dude let himself in and I walked out and was greeted by his cock, I'm pretty sure I'd be pissed off. Pretty sure he'd also have gotten a black eye before I stormed the fuck out."

Ten minutes ago, I couldn't have imagined he could say anything to make me feel better. But somehow, him putting himself in my place alleviated a lot of the anger. I was still hurt, but he'd cooled my fire.

"Did she have to have such an amazing body and be such a knockout?"

"She doesn't hold a candle to you. Not by a mile."

Either he had poor vision or was a good liar, because he sounded pretty damn sincere.

Reaching out, he took one of my hands in his. "It was once after a holiday party a long time ago. I didn't even know she was in town and wouldn't have cared if I had."

I nodded.

He pulled me to him, and I didn't fight it when he wrapped his arms around me for a long, tight embrace. Somewhere along the line, I lost the rest of my fight, and I hugged him back.

"Sweet pea," he lowered his head to my neck. "Never knew what it smelled like until I met you, and now I can't stop smelling it everywhere and thinking of you."

Hunter took a shower after the drama had passed. He'd been at a construction site all morning and then traveled all afternoon to get home. The entire week I'd been imagining we'd rip each other's clothes off the minute we were finally alone in his apartment, but the impromptu visit from the neighbor had dampened the expected mood—at least until he emerged from the bathroom wearing nothing but a towel and looking insanely hot.

I've never been a good poker player. I wear my emotions on my face. Hunter caught me visually gulping his body, and perhaps I unknowingly drooled a little as I stared at the carved lines of his chest. *Jesus.* Men didn't look like him in real life. Maybe the men on the advertisement painted outside the gym I belonged to but seldom visited... but not real, live men. His abs were defined and neatly cut into eight peaks and valleys that I wanted to trace with my tongue. If it were possible, his broad shoulders looked even wider without a shirt, and I couldn't even begin to explain what the deep-set V that disappeared into his low-hanging towel did to me.

"Are we good?" Hunter's voice was hoarse. "Because if you keep looking at me that way, I'm going to bend you over that couch you're sitting on and give you the rest of the tour of my body from the inside out. But I'd rather not fuck you the first time when you're pissed off."

My eyes jumped to his, and he smirked. "Don't get me wrong, I'd like to fuck you pissed off. Preferably with both of us pissed off. Just not the first time."

I swallowed. "We're good."

He kept the distance between us, which made me think he needed it to keep his control. "You hungry?"

Taking a lesson from his playbook, I arched a brow in response.

He chuckled. "You're going to be the death of me. I just know it." He scrubbed both hands over his face. "Did you eat dinner yet?"

I actually hadn't, but food wasn't on my priority list at the moment. "I'm not that hungry."

"I'll order us something." While he was talking, my eyes dropped back down to follow the light line of hair that ran from his belly button into his towel. Hunter mumbled as he walked to the bedroom, "You're making it very difficult to do the right thing."

Hunter grabbed two throw pillows from the couch and tossed them on the floor. "Alright if we eat in here?"

"I'd like that."

He put on some background music and grabbed a bottle of wine while I unloaded the takeout Chinese food. I loved that one night he made me dinner and served it on the kitchen island, and the next he handed me chopsticks and a container. There was something so intimate about eating at the coffee table. I'd ordered cashew chicken, and he'd ordered shrimp chow mein. Every once in a while, he'd hold out his container, and we'd swap and exchange smiles.

When I wasn't running away from him literally or figuratively, I really did enjoy his company.

"How was your trip?" I asked.

"Busy. The client changed his mind about forty times before settling on what I'd proposed in the first place."

I flashed a cheeky grin. "Sounds familiar—you must bring that out in people."

He chuckled. "How was your week? Visit with the ex go okay?"

I set the container down. "It never does."

"What happened?"

"I take her to visit her father because I care about her. Garrett uses Izzy as an excuse to talk to me and tries to pump her for information. She's starting to see him for who he is."

"That sucks. Sounds like he doesn't appreciate what he has left."

"Yeah. He really hurt her this time. On the drive home, she pretty much told me she wants to stay with me even after Garrett gets out."

"How do you feel about that?"

"Honestly, I hadn't given it any serious thought until she mentioned it. Until recently, she'd spent much of our time together silently hating me from her bedroom. But when she put it out there, I realized I can't see my life without her in it anymore. And as much as she tries to push me away, she wants a mother figure in her life. Maybe Garrett and I can work it out." I shrugged. "It works for plenty of divorced couples that the mom keeps custody and the kids visit the dad on the weekends. I happen to not share DNA with her, but I don't see her as any different than my own."

Hunter looked at me funny.

"What?" I said.

"You're a great mom."

I felt my heart squeeze. A great *mom*. No one had ever said those words to me. "Thank you. Like I've told you, I don't have a clue what I'm doing, but I try to always put her first."

Hunter set his container down on the table and finished the last of the wine in his glass. "Come here, MILF." He held out a hand to me.

When I placed mine in it, he somehow maneuvered to tug me up and onto his lap so I straddled him.

"Never fucked a hot mom before."

I smiled. "You're so crass."

Hunter locked our fingers together, and his face turned serious when he looked into my eyes. "We okay?"

"Yeah," I sighed.

"Your eyes are saying something different."

"What do you mean?"

"They either tell me you want me or tell me you want to run away from me. There's never an in-between with you. When I was a kid, me, my brother, Derek, and all the neighborhood kids used to play this game called Red Light Green Light 1-2-3 where one person was 'it', and the goal was to get to him while he sang *red light green light 1-2-3*. But at any time, *it* could yell *red light* and turn around. Then everyone had to freeze in place and stop advancing."

My forehead crinkled. "I know the game, but what does it have to do with me?"

"You're *it*. I keep advancing, but I feel like any minute you're going to yell red light again, and I'm going to need to freeze—possibly with a bad case of blue balls."

While his analogy was a little crazy, he wasn't that off base. I'd been sending him hot and cold signals since the first day I met him, looking for any excuse to run the other way. But it all boiled down to one truth.

I looked at our joined hands and raised my eyes to meet his. "You scare the crap out of me, Hunter. But I can't seem to walk away."

He held my gaze. "It's not an adventure without a little fear."

At that moment, I truly decided to take a chance. I'd been burned, but I'd healed. I'd been pushed down, but I'd gotten back up. I wasn't ready to think about the rest of my life anyway, so why not enjoy an adventure? Taking a deep breath, I quietly sang to Hunter, "*Green light, green light, 1-2-3.*"

There was a hesitant look in his eyes, and his forehead crinkled.

"I got rid of the red light. It's all green from here on out."

Hunter cupped the back of my neck and pulled me down to him. Our lips collided in a kiss that began differently than all of our others. Normally we started with pent-up frustrations that took the form of clashing of tongues and teeth. But this time it wasn't building frustration that fueled our passion; it was the release of the frustration that had been holding us back.

Our kiss was slower, deeper, more sensual. The kind of kiss that makes you feel like you've never really been kissed before. I felt his cock swelling between my parted legs and unconsciously began to rub myself up and down on it as our kiss intensified.

Hunter's fingers fisted in my hair, and he groaned. "Slow down, babe."

"I don't want to slow down anymore," I whispered, grinding down harder.

If I'd had my way, we'd have finished what we started right on the living room floor. But apparently Hunter had other ideas. He lifted me from his lap and scooped me up into his arms.

He never took his eyes off of me as he walked us to the bedroom. "I need to be inside you in the worst way, but you riding me on the living room floor—as tempting as that is—will not bode well for a solid first performance. Although you can be damn sure that'll be happening this weekend at some point. Right now, you're going to get my mouth first so I can make sure you're taken care of before I embarrass myself like a teenage boy when I finally get inside you."

Hunter set me down on the bed and started to undress. First came the shirt. He lifted his hands behind his head and tugged, pulling it off in one fluid motion. Sitting on the edge of the mattress, I was eye to eye with his happy trail—and boy, did it make me happy. Next came the pants. My eyes stayed glued to his hands as his fingers worked the button and zipper of his jeans. The sound of every metal tooth separating vibrated in the pit of my belly.

Hooking two thumbs into the sides, he pulled them down his thick thighs and stepped out, kicking them out of the way. When he stood back up, wearing only black boxer briefs, my mouth fell open. Hunter was packin' an enormous bulge, the tip of which was peeking out from the top of his underwear band. Moisture glistening at the top of the crown mesmerized me.

"*Fuck*." Hunter groaned. "You have no idea how bad I want to fist a handful of your hair and fuck that open mouth of yours."

I looked up from under thick lashes. "What's stopping you?"

He bent his head back and mumbled something to God before beginning to undress me. My body tingled from head to toe as he slipped off my sandals one at a time, dropping a kiss on the top of each foot before moving on to my jeans. He slid them down my body and rubbed his fingers appreciatively over the lace of my panties before taking those, too. When he removed my shirt and bra, I was too captivated by the way he was looking at me to even realize the last of my clothing had come off. His eyes darkened and dilated, eclipsing almost all of the baby blue with heated desire.

As he dropped to his knees, his voice was gruff. "Lie back. Spread for me, *Natalia*."

I'd always wondered why he chose to call me Natalia, instead of Nat like everyone else. Yet the way my name rolled from his tongue at that moment made me grateful that he did. Nudging my knees open, he feathered tender kisses up the inside of my thighs. By the time he reached the apex of my center, my legs were shaking. After such a gentle climb up, I'd expected to feel a sweet kiss or the warmth of his tongue between my legs. But there was nothing gentle about the way Hunter dove in.

My back arched off the bed at the unexpected roughness and desperation of his touch. He lapped at my arousal, sucked hard on my clit, and buried his entire face in me. It was like he'd been starving and snapped when he took a taste of his first meal. The build inside of me was as fast and furious as Hunter's appetite.

"*Hunter*." My breath shook.

"Come on my tongue, baby."

Oh God. "Hunter..." I moaned his name.

He responded by slipping two fingers inside while his mouth moved up to focus on my throbbing clit.

He pumped in and out a few times.

"*Oh God.*"

"Your cunt is so tight. I can't wait to have you squeezing my cock."

That was all it took. It didn't matter that I normally hated that word. The desire in his strained voice made it sound sexy as hell, and it threw me over the edge. My orgasm crashed hard, pulling me under with a powerful wave that seemed to go on forever. Hunter's relentless tongue never stopped working and fell into rhythmic unison with his pumping fingers to draw every last contraction from my body.

Even though I'd been lying on my back, exerting no energy, my body had a sheen of sweat, and I could barely breathe when he finally slowed.

"You good?" Hunter kissed the sensitive skin above my pubic bone.

"I'm...I don't know what I am. My brain hasn't started to function yet."

He chuckled and climbed farther up my body, kissing just below my belly button. Then he lifted a knee up on the bed to get leverage and hoisted me from the edge all the way to the top, just missing the headboard. The girly, anti-feminist part of me that I hated to admit existed loved that he could hurl me around like I was a feather.

Hunter climbed over me, hovering above with his weight on his forearms on either side of me. "Will it bother you if I kiss you after that?"

No one had ever asked me that question. But Garrett had always gotten out of bed to brush his teeth afterward, and I'd done the same after oral sex, even though we'd never spoken about it.

"I'm not sure. Are you saying you'd rather not?"

Shifting his weight to one arm, he reached down between my legs and rubbed his fingers against my wetness. Going slow, almost as if he wanted to give me a chance to stop him as his hand neared my face, his fingers traced my lips, coating my mouth with my own juices. His eyes traced his fingers as if he was spellbound.

"Lick your lips," he groaned.

The way he looked at me made me bold. Watching him watch me, I ran my tongue slowly from one end of my top lip to the other before bringing my tongue back into my mouth. I closed my eyes and sucked my own tongue, swallowing before opening again. Then I did the same thing to the bottom.

"That's the sexiest fucking thing I've ever seen in my life." His mouth crashed down on mine.

Any modesty I had about kissing after such an intimate act went out the window, seeing the effect I'd had on Hunter. He kissed me for the longest time, long, lush, passionate strokes of his tongue that had me lost in the moment all over again. He ground his erection against me, and I slipped my hands into his underwear to dig my nails into his ass.

"Need you," he groaned.

He pulled off his underwear and reached to his end table for a condom. Using his teeth to tear the foil, he sheathed himself in one motion and spit the wrapper to the side before returning to settle between my legs. I spread wide, knowing it had been a very long time for me.

My eyes were riveted to the man trying his hardest not to come undone before me. He lined up the wide crown of his cock at my opening and ever so slowly pushed inside. I'd seen the outline of it, saw the tip of it peeking out from his underwear, so I knew he was large. But feeling it stretch me as his hips rocked back and forth, easing inside, had me realizing I'd misjudged his girth.

I licked my lips at the thought of how wide he was.

"Jesus Christ," he breathed. "I'm trying to go slow."

My eyes fluttered closed as he thrust in deeper.

"Look at me, Natalia," Hunter commanded. "Watch what you do to me."

Fighting my natural instinct to hide inside myself, I held his gaze. Hunter moved in and out of me, each thrust going deeper and deeper until he seated himself fully. The way he looked into my eyes made me feel like he could see right into me. It scared me to feel so open, so vulnerable, but at the same time, it was beautiful and made me feel safe. I finally realized why I'd been so terrified. It wasn't because I was afraid to fall for him—it was because I'd already started to. And no matter what we'd agreed upon, we were sharing more than our bodies.

His arms began to shake.

My nails clawed at his back.

His thrusts grew harder and faster.

I watched as his jaw tensed while he barreled closer to his own release. The sight of this man coming apart was nothing short of magnificent. Hedonistic. Mind-blowing decadence.

"*Fuck*," he roared, sinking so damn deep that I gasped.

I clenched around him, another orgasm hitting suddenly, just as Hunter bucked one last time and came inside of me. Even through the condom I could feel the heat of him pouring into me.

We held each other, our gazes never breaking stride, as we caught our breath. When he eventually pulled out, he kissed me softly on the lips and then the forehead before getting up to dispose of the condom and grab a towel to clean me up.

Returning to bed, he lay on his back, pulling me to his chest and wrapping two arms around me to hold on tight. "That was incredible. I'm glad you didn't run away again."

I smiled, though he couldn't see it. "Me too. You wore me down, and now you've worn me out, Mr. Delucia."

"Took a year, sweetheart."

"Yeah. I guess it did. But I'm here now."

He kissed the top of my head and snuggled me closer. "Good. Stay for a while."

Chapter 24

"I love you because you make me laugh and have a big heart." Summer walked to the bed—where I lay still naked with my hands clasped behind my head—and straddled my hips. "But this..." She reached down and cupped my dick. "This big thing is a really nice added bonus."

I gripped the back of her hair and pulled her head down to mine. "Oh yeah? You love me, huh?" We'd been seeing each other for six months, but we'd never exchanged those words before.

She smiled and tilted her head. "I guess I do."

Pulling her closer, I kissed her lips gently. "I guess I love you, too, then."

She leaned back and swatted at my abs. "Hey. That doesn't sound very romantic. *I guess I love you, too, then.*"

"Alright. How about this? Summer Pearl Madden, I love you because you never say no to a dare and you laugh at your own jokes even when they aren't funny." I reached up and groped her breasts. "But this...these big tits are a really nice added bonus."

She laughed. "Are you nervous about today?"

"Nah. He's happy. He'll be happy for us."

Jayce and Emily had gotten engaged last night. It was unexpected, but the two of them seemed to be in their own

208

little world. After six months of hiding my relationship with Summer, I planned to come clean with my brother. Even though we were an eight-hour bus ride apart most days, Summer and I had grown inseparable since the night of my brother's graduation party. We video chatted for hours some days, and one of us was on a bus every other weekend, making the long haul for a visit. The *I love yous* we'd just exchanged cemented in my mind that I was long overdue to come clean.

I reached for my cell on the nightstand and checked the time. "Shit. I gotta run. My uncle asked us to meet him at his office at one, so I told Jayce to meet me at the Starbucks around the corner at twelve so I could tell him." I held Summer by the hips and lifted her off so I could sit up. "What are you going to do today while I'm gone?"

She pouted. "Study for math. If I don't pass this final, I won't graduate."

"I'll help you when I get back."

Summer laid on her belly on the bed and watched me dress. "I love when you tutor me."

I yanked on a pair of jeans. "You like that it's free. I might start charging you."

"I'm good with that. So long as you accept sexual favors as payment."

I sniffed a T-shirt hanging from an open drawer. I wasn't sure if I'd tossed it there while getting undressed or if it was falling out because I'd grabbed something underneath and not bothered to fix the mess it made. Deciding it passed as clean, I tugged it on.

"That's such a guy thing." Summer scrunched up her nose. "Sniffing clothing before putting it on."

I eyed her lacy black thong on the floor next to the bed and scooped it up. Cupping the thin material in two hands,

I brought it to my nose and took a loud, exaggerated whiff of her panties.

She shook her head but smiled. "You're gross."

"Yeah. You think that's gross?" I stuffed her underwear into my jeans pocket. "I'm keeping these until later, and I'm going to snort them like a fucking perv on the long bus ride home as some sort of demented foreplay before I come back and eat you."

Jayce seemed distracted as we waited in line for coffee. "My treat," I said when we got to the register.

"Thanks."

He was quiet even when we sat down. "What's up with you? You look like someone killed your dog."

Jayce forced a smile. "Just tired, I guess."

"New fiancée wearing you out already, old man?"

My brother stared down at his cup. "She's pregnant."

Not exactly the direction I expected this conversation to go. "Wow. Umm...congratulations."

He raked fingers through his hair. "I really like her a lot."

"You don't love her?"

He shook his head. "No. I wish I did."

"Then why did you ask her to get married?"

"It was an accident."

My brows rose. "An accident? How, exactly, do you accidentally propose to someone."

His head dropped into his hands. "I don't know. She told me she was pregnant, and she was upset. Obviously, it wasn't planned. She was crying and said she'd always dreamed of getting married and having kids but not starting a family so young and on her own. I would never abandon her, and I didn't want her to feel like she was doing it on her own."

"So you asked her to marry you?"

Jayce yanked on his hair. "*Fuck!* I hated seeing her bawl, and it's my responsibility, too."

"Maybe she feels the same way? She might be scared and not want to marry you either. What did she say when you asked her?"

He slumped farther into his chair. "Her face lit up, and she jumped into my arms and said she loved me."

Shit. Jayce is a stand-up guy. As much as it seems ludicrous that someone could *accidentally* ask someone to marry him—it made total sense when it came to my brother. In fact, he was such a good guy that I knew the answer to my next question before I even asked. "Did you tell her you loved her back?"

He looked at me. *Of course he did.*

When he picked up his coffee to drink, his hand was shaking so badly that he sloshed it all over the place.

"It's gonna be okay, bro."

"How?"

"You'll talk to her. Tell her you care about her and you plan to support the baby, but you're not ready to get married."

Jayce stayed quiet for a long time. He looked deep in thought. "Why can't I love her?" He mumbled. "She deserves better than a guy who can't give her his heart because someone still has a piece of it."

I closed my eyes.

My fucking heart broke for so many reasons.

Chapter 25

— Natalia —

I woke to an empty bed.

I'd left my phone somewhere in the living room, and there wasn't a bedside alarm clock. The blinds were drawn, but the slats were open, and since no light was coming in, I guessed it wasn't yet morning. But where was Hunter? I waited a few minutes to see if he'd just gotten up to get a drink or use the bathroom, but he didn't come back, and the apartment had no sound of anyone moving around. Unable to fall back asleep, I wrapped a sheet around my naked body and went to look for the man whose arms I'd drifted off in.

All of the lights were off, but the city from beyond the sliding glass doors illuminated the apartment enough for me to see that Hunter wasn't in it. Finding my phone, I checked the time—four-thirty in the morning. We'd only fallen asleep a couple of hours ago. Perhaps Hunter was an early riser gym rat?

This girl wasn't, so I decided to head back to bed and get the answer when I woke back up in a few more hours. I was almost at the door to the bedroom when movement from the balcony caught my attention. Hunter was sitting outside.

I watched him for a few moments as he stared off into space. He looked deep in thought, almost troubled. Eventually I walked to the door and slid it open. He turned at the sound.

"Hey. What are you doing out here?" I asked.

"Just getting some fresh air."

I pulled the sheet tighter around me. "It's freaking cold."

"Didn't even notice."

"You looked lost in thought. Anything you want to talk about?"

Hunter's eyes met mine. He seemed to deliberate for a moment, but then he shook his head and looked away as he spoke.

"No. Just couldn't sleep." He stood. "Come on. Let's get you back to bed."

He was quiet as we walked back to the bedroom and even quieter as we slipped back into bed. Just like last night, he lay on his back and pulled me to him so my head rested on his chest. I listened to his heartbeat for a while, and even though I found it soothing, I still had an unsettled feeling.

Turning over from my side to my belly, I put two hands on Hunter's chest and used them to prop up my head so I could see his face while I spoke.

"Do you have trouble sleeping often?"

"Sometimes."

"Is it trouble falling asleep or staying asleep?"

"Both."

"Is it because you have a lot on your mind?"

"Maybe."

"You know what I heard helps with that?"

"What?"

"Giving more than a one-word answer," I said sarcastically.

Hunter's lip twitched. "You know what I heard helps?"

"What?"

He did some ninja-like move that flipped me onto my back, and suddenly he was hovering over me. "Strenuous physical activity."

"Umm...how often do you wake up? Because if that's the case, I might not be able to walk by Monday."

The cloud that had shadowed his eyes only a few moments earlier seemed to lift. "Would you think I was a total dick if I admitted I'd love for you to burn every time you sit down on Monday?"

"You want me in pain?"

"No, I want you to remember what it felt like for me to be inside you."

I was certain that wouldn't be a problem. I raised my hands over my head and arched my back, hoisting my breasts toward his face. "Do your best, Mr. Delucia."

Hunter had a few hours of work he needed to do, so I went down to the Italian grocery store I'd spotted at the corner to pick up something for lunch. We'd stayed up until after the sun rose and finally fallen back asleep until after ten. I'd woken to Hunter's erection prodding me from behind as we spooned. The man had an insatiable appetite for sex.

I picked out all of my favorite finger foods to snack on for lunch—black olives, stuffed grape leaves, fresh mozzarella and tomatoes with basil, marinated mushrooms—rather than just a boring sandwich or something. By the time I got to the cash register, my handheld basket weighed a ton, and I'd managed to ring up eighty dollars worth of crap.

Hunter had given me a key to get back in, but my hands were too full, so I used my foot to knock. He came to the door with a pencil behind his ear, a pair of low-hanging sweatpants, and no shirt. *Damn.* All these good Italian snacks—and him.

"Sorry. I didn't want to put everything down to use the key because one of the bags is starting to break. I think the olive container spilled because my hand is holding the groceries in."

Hunter grabbed the two bags from my left arm and attempted to take the other.

"No, I got this one. I don't want it to break."

In the kitchen, Hunter peeked into the bags. "What is all this stuff? I thought you were going to the deli to get lunch?"

"This is lunch."

He furrowed his brow and reached into one bag. "Cannolis?"

"It's dairy. One of the four main food groups."

Pulling another item from the bag, he held up a container of rainbow cookies.

I pointed. "That falls into breads and cereals."

He lifted a brow.

"What? It has the same ingredients. Flour, salt, eggs..."

He set it down and pulled out a package of stuffed grape leaves. My mouth watered. "Fruits and vegetables."

He shook his head. "It's the leaf of a fruit. Not quite sure it counts as a fruit or vegetable itself."

I took them from his hand. "Semantics."

Chuckling, he reached in again. This time, he came up with a large jar of Nutella. "This one I know."

"You do?"

He ignored me and opened the jar, peeling back the silver freshness seal before sticking his finger in and scooping out some of the heavenly creamy stuff inside. I knew from the cheeky grin on his face when he looked up that his interest had nothing to do with the deliciousness of the spread. Leaning in, he ran his finger along my exposed collarbone before bending to suck the hazelnut off.

"Body paint. This goes in the bedroom for later."

I laughed because I thought he was kidding, but he disappeared into the bedroom with that jar. My mind started to race with what I'd be painting and sucking later.

When he returned, he squeezed me from behind and kissed the top of my head. "Thank you for going to the store. I'll help you unpack and then finish up. I only need ten more minutes or so."

"Don't be silly. Go do your work. I'll get everything unpacked and put away and make us a nice spread of snacks."

Hunter kissed my forehead. "Thanks." He walked halfway to the dining room table and turned back. "Almost forgot...Derek called while you were out. He's coming to town for business in two weeks. Wants to meet us for drinks."

"Okay. That sounds great. Anna mentioned he had a trip coming up."

I took my time with the groceries and made a sampler platter of all the goodies. Hunter had blueprints spread all over the table, and when I saw him begin to ravel the top one back into a roll, I brought lunch and some plates to the table.

"Looks awesome," he said.

"Did you get done what you needed to do?"

"Yeah. This project's been going on for years. We're the third builder on it. Whenever there's more than one builder, there's a reason." He wrapped a rubber band around the roll he'd been working on and tapped it to the table. "Owner is from Dubai and doesn't realize New York City has a byzantine building code. The building is old and needs structural reinforcements for everything he wants to do. Which is fine, but when you change the weight of what you're building three times during the renovation, and the first builder used beams that barely supported the first set of plans, you're basically starting over. And even though almost all blueprints and plans are done on a computer now, he wants to see every set of changes on an old-school, pencil-and-paper blueprint drawing."

"What does he keep changing that makes it so heavy?"

"The house on top of the building."

I'd thought I'd heard him wrong. "He's housing something on top of the building?"

"Yeah. A house." Hunter chuckled. "He's building a house on top of the roof of an old cast-iron building."

"A whole house?"

"Pretty much."

"Why? Is the building not residential?"

"No, most of it's residential except for the commercial storefronts on the bottom two floors."

"So why not just renovate an apartment instead of building a house on top of the roof. I don't get it."

"Building is a playground for the extraordinarily wealthy in New York. You can't look for logic. The answer is always the same—because they can."

"That's crazy."

"Keeps me employed. This particular building is actually really beautiful. I'll take you to see it one day, if you want. The top floors are closed during renovations, and we're at a standstill until the city approves the recent round of changes."

"I'd like that. Even though I've lived here all my life, I don't really take the time to appreciate the architecture."

"Ever think about living somewhere else?" Hunter asked.

"I used to. I went to college here in the city, and Anna went to school out in California. We'd take turns visiting each other over breaks and had big plans for me to move out to the west coast so we could live next door to each other again. We planned to be pregnant at the same time and for our daughters to be second-generation best friends."

"Could still happen. I'm sure Anna and Derek will have more kids."

A picture of Anna and me sitting in Hunter's yard with babies on our laps, while Derek and Hunter stood nearby at the barbeque making dinner, suddenly flashed before my eyes. The thought warmed me, even though it also scared the crap out of me that my head had gone there. Hunter wasn't in this for the long haul. This was just a fling. Wasn't it?

I smiled hesitantly, afraid to get my hopes up, but deep down knowing they already were. "Maybe. You never know, I guess."

Chapter 26

— Natalia —

Hunter and Derek were already seated at the bar when I walked in. Spotting me, both men stood. As I made my way over, I realized it was the first time Hunter and I had been out in public with a friend. Over the last few weeks, we'd spent as much time as we could together—meeting for breakfast if we couldn't see each other at night, taking a dozen kids out to dinner for Izzy's sixteenth birthday, watching her basketball games, sneaking in a daytime movie between my counseling sessions. We even had lunch on the roof of his jobsite one afternoon, not to mention we'd spent so much time in bed, it was surprising I could walk. Yet we'd been in a private bubble. Unless you counted Izzy, we were always alone.

So as I approached the two men, I wasn't quite sure how to greet Hunter. He settled that internal debate for me the moment I neared. Taking my hand, he pulled me flush against him, gave my hair a little tug, urging my head back, and planted a possessive kiss on my lips.

I smiled, more than satisfied with his greeting, and let out a breathy "hey" before turning my attention to Derek. "How's my sweet little Caroline's baby daddy?"

Derek smiled and bent to kiss my cheek. "I'm good. Will I sound like a total wuss-bag if I say I miss the way she smells?"

My heart let out a beautiful sigh. "Not at all. You sound like the perfect man."

"Hey...what about me?" Hunter chided.

"Awww.... You're slighted because I paid a compliment to another man? That's cute. But my heart just melted a little hearing him say he missed the way she smells. It's the most romantic thing I've ever heard. Not sure you can top that, pretty boy."

Hunter wrapped his arm around my waist and pulled me to him. "I miss the way parts of you smell, too."

I elbowed him. "That's not romantic; that's perverted."

"What's the difference?"

We all laughed, and Hunter pulled a bar stool around so the three of us could sit in a little circle at the bar. We caught up on baby pictures, Anna's newest obsession with everything in the house needing to be organic, and Caroline's most recent checkup.

"I almost forgot—Anna wants me to call while I'm with you guys. She gave me specific instructions to order you both mimosas and call on speakerphone."

Hunter had already ordered a glass of wine for me. I held it up to my lips before sipping. "We can skip the mimosas. I'll tell her you ordered them if she asks."

"Oh no. You have no idea how hormonal my wife is right now. I'm not taking any chances." Derek motioned for the bartender and asked for three mimosas before calling Anna on speakerphone.

"Hey, babe. You're on speakerphone."

"Do they have mimosas?"

"They do. Got myself one, too."

"After we hang up, send me a picture of the two of them with their drinks."

Derek arched an eyebrow at us as if to say *I told you.* "Will do."

"Hi, Nat!" Anna yelled.

"Hi!"

"Hi, Hunter. Are you taking good care of my girl?"

"I'm trying," he said and gave my knee a little squeeze.

"I wish I could be there with you guys right now. But it's too soon to fly with Caroline with all the recycled germs on a plane. So, since Derek had to be in town for business this week anyway, this is as close to the four of us sitting together as I could come up with. Derek, do you have my props ready?"

He shook his head, indicating that he thought his wife was loony, but reached into his pocket, nonetheless. "Got it."

"Okay. Show the first picture."

Derek held up a picture of me and Anna. We were probably only about four or five and were pushing our old baby carriages with our dolls inside.

"Nat, I've known you my whole life," Anna said. "You're the best friend a girl could ever have. When I was putting together what I wanted to say today, I tried to think of an example of when I'd asked you for help and you were there for me. But I couldn't. Because even though I've needed your help often over the last twenty-plus years, I've never had to *ask* for it. You're there giving it before I even have the chance." Anna's voice cracked, and I knew she was tearing up. "You're my person, Nat. And I love you and trust you with my life."

I was feeling all choked up myself. "Love you, too, Anna Bow Banya."

She cleared her throat. "Your turn, Derek. Next prop."

Derek shook his head, but shuffled the pictures so he was now showing an old photo of what I assumed was him and Hunter. "You beat up Frankie Munson when he called me a nerd in sixth grade. In eighth grade, when I was too shy to ask a girl to the dance, you asked the hottest two girls to go to the dance with us. In tenth grade, when you were captain of the football team, and I was captain of the debate team, you didn't give a crap that you hung out with a nerd. You've always had my back, bro."

Anna piped in. "Next picture, honey!"

Derek pulled another pic from the back of the stack he held in his hand. It was a photo of me and Hunter from their wedding that I'd never seen. I remembered the moment, but had been unaware anyone was capturing it. He'd just cut in while I was dancing with Anna's dad, and I was insulting him while smiling as I tried in earnest to pretend the way he held me against his body had no effect on me. It was a great candid shot. My head was tilted up to him with a smirk, and he looked down at me with that sexy half-smile he wore so often. There was no mistaking the spark between us.

Hunter and I glanced at each other as Anna spoke. "So, because you two are our people, and we trust you with our lives, we want you to be our daughter's people if something should happen to us." She paused. "Last picture, honey."

Derek shuffled again, and this time it was a picture of baby Caroline. She was dressed in a onesie with a movie logo on it: *The Godfather*.

"Hunter and Nat, will you be our daughter's godparents?"

My smile was so wide, it was surprising my face didn't crack. I jumped from my bar stool and hugged Derek, grabbing the phone and yelling into it at Anna. "Yes! Yes!"

Hunter took the more subdued approach and shook his friend's hand. "Would be an honor, man."

After Derek hung up, I asked the bartender to take a picture with my phone of the three of us holding up our mimosas. Then I shot it to Anna. She sent me one back, holding my soon-to-be goddaughter in one arm and her own virgin drink in the other.

"We haven't finalized a christening date yet, because what started out as a small family gathering, my bride is attempting to turn into our wedding—part two," Derek joked. "But we were thinking three weeks from Sunday, on the 25th."

I mentally did the math. My visit to Garrett was on the 10th last month, so that would put my visit this month the weekend before the 17th. "That sounds great. Maybe I'll pull Izzy out of school that Friday and fly down on Thursday to make a long weekend out of it." I looked to Hunter. "Do you think you'll be able to take a day off to fly out early?"

Hunter looked down, and then his gaze met mine. There was an apprehension in his eyes. "I'll already be out in California."

"Oh. Okay. I didn't realize you had another trip planned." I tried to shrug it off as no big deal, but my hollow-feeling belly got the message before my brain did. "Maybe we can work it out to fly back together."

Hunter's voice was solemn, and he reached for my hand. "I won't be flying back either. Job here in New York will be wrapped up before the christening. My two-month assignment will be done. I'll be home in California."

Wow. *That hurt*. He wasn't being mean or harsh in any way. In fact, the softness of his tone and the way he'd reached out to touch my hand showed me he knew what the reminder would do to me. But that barely dulled the edginess I felt. I was upset—not necessarily with him. I was upset with myself for letting it bother me so much.

Our relationship had been temporary since the beginning. I'd gone into it with my eyes open. The only problem was, somewhere along the way, I'd also opened up my heart.

Hunter said something and waited for me to respond. I blinked myself back out of my thoughts. "I'm sorry. What did you say?"

"I said, maybe you and Izzy can stay with me for the long weekend?"

"Sure." I forced a smile. "We'll see."

For the next twenty or so minutes, I went through the motions of hanging out with Derek and Hunter. I smiled and laughed, but inside, I was waging the battle of head vs. heart. My head was yelling, *He's leaving—who cares?* And my heart was answering—*You do, dumbass. You do.*

Luckily, we all had plans for the evening, and they didn't entail spending much more time with each other. Hunter and Derek had the Knicks game, and I needed to head to Mom's.

"I have to get to dinner. I'm so glad we got to see each other, Derek." I stood. "Thank you for having me as Caroline's godmother. Please give my best friend a giant hug for me when you get home."

Derek stood and gave me a hug. "I will. And I'll see you next month."

I turned to Hunter, grateful for a public goodbye and quick escape. "Give me a call," I said very noncommittally.

Hunter spoke to Derek. "Give me a few minutes. I'm going to walk Natalia out, and then we'll head to the game."

"Sure thing."

So much for a quick escape. With his hand on my lower back, Hunter guided me out of the bar.

I looked at my feet, not wanting him to see what I was feeling written all over my face.

But he cupped my face and pressed his forehead against mine. "I'm sorry if I upset you."

"You didn't," I said. But not even my own ears believed me.

He waited me out, knowing eventually I'd have to look up. When our eyes finally met, he spoke into mine. "I care about you, Natalia. It's not going to be easy for me to leave either. This last month and a half has been great..." His eyes crinkled at the corners. "Especially the last few weeks since I wore you down."

Maybe hearing that I wasn't alone should've made me feel better. But it was the unsaid that cloaked a feeling of melancholy over me like a suit of armor. It was going to be hard on him to leave...but he wasn't considering staying either. Nor was there any mention of attempting something long distance. This was over when our time was up.

I forced a small smile. "I'll give you a call."

He looked into my eyes, briefly closing his before nodding. "Okay."

His lips covered mine in a gentle kiss before going to my forehead for another. "Be careful on the trains."

"Have fun at the game."

It was difficult to walk away, but I knew I needed to be the one to do it. I felt Hunter's eyes on me the entire walk down the block to the train station, certain he stayed outside the restaurant to watch me. But I didn't turn around to check. That was how it was going to have to be between us—I'd need to walk away since he wasn't going to do anything to stick around in my life.

Chapter 27

— Natalia —

I hadn't seen Hunter in five days.

To most couples, that might be normal. Weekdays are busy. I have a teenager to take care of. Then again, we weren't *really* a couple, were we? Since Hunter and I had gotten together, we'd never been apart this long. We'd grab a bite to eat, catch one of Izzy's games, steal a few hours in his bedroom, or even meet for breakfast. It had never been an effort to find the time. Until now. And it wasn't a lack of effort on his part. I was avoiding him, and he knew it—although he hadn't yet called me out on it.

But I had a feeling that was about to change as I pressed the buzzer to unlock the front door downstairs. After five days of me saying I was busy and delaying answering his texts, he'd showed up unannounced at my apartment this morning. Conveniently, Izzy had just left for school, and he knew I rarely had appointments before ten o'clock.

I unlocked my apartment door and waited. Hunter stepped off the elevator and walked toward me with purpose. It pissed me off that my body reacted to seeing him when I didn't *want* to be excited. And that anger was evident in my snarky tone.

"In the neighborhood and thought you'd drop by to say hello?" I asked. I didn't open the door to invite him in.

Hunter looked me right in the eyes. "Nope. Came to talk to you. Izzy gone?"

Anger was an emotion I could tolerate. I folded my arms across my chest. "Yes. But I have to get ready for work. You should have called first."

He took a step closer, into my personal space, and looked down at me. "Why would I have done that? So you could blow me off again?"

A mini stare-off ensued. I refused to back down, even though being so near him made me want to crumble. Straightening my spine, I said, "It's been fun, Hunter. Let's not end this on a sour note."

His eyes blazed. "Can we go inside and talk?"

"I'm not sure there's anything we need to talk about. It was fun. Now it's over."

Then he did the one thing I knew I couldn't withstand—he reached out and cupped my cheek. Stupid tears threatened at the tenderness of his touch.

His thumb stroked my skin. "I'm sorry, Natalia. I really am."

I swallowed and tasted salt in my throat. "Really? It doesn't seem that way."

Hunter closed his eyes. "Can we go inside and talk? Please?"

I nodded, and he followed me into my apartment.

Not ready for the conversation that was to come, I stalled for time and filled the air with anything but silence. "Do you want some coffee?"

"No thanks."

"I'm going to have some."

He nodded, and I retreated to the kitchen, hoping that the few minutes it took would help me figure out what I wanted to say. My head swam with emotions, and I was afraid I might choke up if I didn't rein myself in.

When I returned to the living room, I found Hunter staring out the window. It reminded me of the morning I'd found him outside on his balcony. He was a million miles away.

Sensing me, he turned. "What time is your first appointment?"

I was honest. "Not for a few hours."

A sad but real smile peeked out from behind the cloud of somber he wore. I was too jittery to have this conversation sitting down, so I didn't bother to invite him to have a seat before I started in.

I sipped my coffee and feigned innocence. "What is it you wanted to talk about?"

Hunter reached forward and pushed a lock of hair behind my ear. "I like you. A lot, Natalia. I enjoy your company. You're beautiful and smart...and a *smart ass*, which oddly, I find ridiculously sexy. And the sex..." He shook his head. "I'd spend every waking moment inside of you, if I could."

As perfect as that all sounded, I knew it was just the warm-up. I caught his gaze and prompted him. "But..."

"This was supposed to be just sex—have fun for a while."

That answer infuriated the shit out of me. It was cowardly. "And I was supposed to be married to an honest man who wasn't a thief. Things don't always go as planned, do they?"

He dropped his head. "I'm sorry, Natalia."

"Why?" I bit. "I want to know why."

He looked up. "Why what?"

"Why you can say all those great things about me—how you like me so much, how good we are together—but then you don't even attempt to continue this. Is it because we live so far apart?"

"You were dead set against a relationship with any man when this started. You intentionally dated people you didn't connect with just to keep things on a purely physical level." He ran a hand through his hair. "That's all we agreed to."

"So what?" I raised my voice. "I didn't agree to be divorced at twenty-eight with a sixteen year old. But here I am. And you know what? I'm happy with what I have, even if it isn't the fairytale life I thought I'd get. Sometimes you're planning on driving straight and life takes a left turn, which turns out to be right."

We stared at each other, and I saw so much in his eyes—sadness, anger, guilt, desire. But most of all, I knew I was looking at a man who had feelings for me. I wasn't alone in this. Yet something kept him from even attempting anything more.

"It's not that simple," he said.

"I didn't say it was. But rather than try to figure things out, you'll just say goodbye in two weeks and not look back."

When he didn't man up and say anything, it further fueled my anger. I set my coffee on the nearby end table, and my hands went to my hips. "Tell me, will you have a replacement for me by the time I fly out for the christening? How does that look to you? Do I extend my hand and she and I can exchange compliments about each other's dresses and talk about your stamina?"

"I wouldn't do that to you...bring another woman to the christening. Christ, I'm not even thinking about another woman, Natalia."

I tapped my pointer finger to my lips. "Hmm...is that supposed to be a mutual thing? Because what if *I* want to bring a date?"

That got his attention. His jaw flexed, and I saw a flicker of fury in his eyes. But I wasn't happy with a flicker; I wanted the full damn flame.

So I pushed. "You asked me if I wanted to stay with you when I come out for the christening. Is my date welcome, too? I mean, would it bother you if we were *loud* in your guest room? I tend to moan a bit when I'm getting fucked hard." I paused. "But I guess you know that already, don't you?"

Hunter's already rigid jaw clenched so tight, I thought he might possibly crack a pearly white. Yet he still didn't blow.

I wanted to know the reason he wouldn't fight for us. I needed to know. Frustrated, I lifted my arms and smacked them down against my sides. "Why did you come here, Hunter?"

"Because I knew you were upset, and you kept blowing me off."

"So? Did this help *you* in any way? Did you need to see first-hand that I'm upset or something? Because it certainly hasn't helped *me* any." I turned to storm away, but he gripped my elbow, stopping me.

"Natalia."

I jerked my arm from his grip and whirled back around so fast, he had to retreat to avoid crashing into me.

"Or did you come for a quick fuck? Is that what you came for?" I started fumbling, undoing the buttons on my shirt. "That's all it was to begin with anyway, right?"

"Stop it."

I didn't. I kept right on going. The third button, then the fourth...

"You deserve more than I can give you."

That wasn't an explanation; it was a cop-out. But he'd finally said something that was right. I did deserve better.

"When my parents were splitting up, my father told my mother he'd always cared about her, but he'd never deeply loved her the way he loved Margie. He basically admitted that he'd settled. And let's not even talk about my choice of Garrett. You're absolutely right. I do deserve more. I deserve someone who wants to be with me the way I want to be with them. And maybe it's my own fault for growing feelings for you when you never promised anything more than a physical relationship. But you know what..." I searched his eyes. "I didn't think I was in this alone. I was foolish enough to think you were right there with me, breaking your dumb rule about keeping things to sex only."

Hunter rubbed the back of his neck, looking down at the floor.

I pulled my unbuttoned shirt closed. "You should go."

"Natalia..."

His calm, level tone made me snap. I was riding an emotional rollercoaster, and he was floating through the lazy river. *Screw this.*

"Get out! Go find your new fuck of the month. Oh, wait. It's fuck of the quarter, isn't it?"

I spun around and marched toward the front door, flinging it open without another word. Hunter stayed put for a few long moments and then came toward the door. Only, he didn't walk through it; he slammed it shut. With him still inside.

"I *am* right there with you. I just..."

"Just what?"

"I can't promise more. But I also can't seem to walk out that fucking door."

I was sad and angry. So, how did I respond?

I kissed him.

Probably not the smartest move I've ever made. Yet I couldn't help myself.

It took about one second for Hunter to stop fighting it. He cupped both hands around my ass and lifted me up against the door. My legs wrapped around his waist, arms around his neck, and all of my angry energy poured into the kiss.

I couldn't get close enough. And this time, I was positive I wasn't the only one. Hunter wound his fingers into my hair, tilted my head to deepen the kiss, and pressed his body into mine as he let out a groan. Our hearts pounded against each other. We began tearing away our clothes without ungluing our mouths. Engrossed in the furies of passion, I hadn't even noticed we were moving until I felt Hunter's foot push open the door to my bedroom.

Ever so gently, he set me down on the bed, our tongues still intertwined. I was lost—*we* were lost—in the moment. It wasn't until our kiss broke, and Hunter stood to remove the rest of his clothes, that either one of us had a chance to sober up from the high of arousal.

Our gazes locked, and he froze, his hand on his zipper. "Do you want me to stop? Tell me now."

Ten minutes ago I'd been kicking him out. Now I wanted him inside of me more than my next breath. Of course, in the moment, I could justify anything. What difference would two more weeks make? I already had feelings for him. It wasn't like depriving myself of sexual gratification was going to change that. My eyes dropped to the thick bulge straining for release from Hunter's pants.

Nope. Two more weeks isn't going to make one lick of a difference.

"No," I whispered. "I don't want you to stop."

Heat pushed the hesitancy out of Hunter's eyes. He pulled a condom from his wallet, tossed the billfold on the floor, and made quick work of shedding the rest of my clothes. Hovering over me, he rubbed his thick erection up and down my center before looking into my eyes one last time for confirmation.

I nodded, but as he dipped his head to take my mouth again, I changed my mind. "Wait."

Hunter froze with our noses a centimeter apart.

If I was going to do this, I wanted to be in control as much as I could. "I want to be on top," I said.

A flash of relief crossed his gorgeous face. In one swift move, he rolled to his back, putting me on top. "Ride me, baby," he said, his voice hoarse. "Ride me hard."

I rose to my knees and took him in my hand. He was so thick, my fingers couldn't wrap around his width. Hunter's hands pressed into my hips, and he lifted me to hover high enough to line up his crown at my entrance. The scent of sex wafted in the air, permeating everything.

I looked down at Hunter. He looked so desperate, yet he'd ceded me the control I needed, even if that control was false.

"Fuck," he groaned as I lowered myself onto him.

His fingers pressed into my hips so hard, I'd probably have bruises tomorrow. I *wanted* bruises tomorrow. And I wanted to see every second of what I could do to this man. Looking into his eyes, I took more of him in. He blew out a heavy rush of air that I sucked in as I glided up and down, allowing him to go even deeper.

Hunter was a big man, and in this position almost painfully so. Yet I relished that pain. Leaning back, with my hands on his thighs behind me, I arched my spine. The position sucked him in until I was fully seated with my ass resting nearly on his balls.

"*Christ*. Slow down, Natalia."

The unspoken threat of what would happen if I didn't spurred me on. I rocked my hips back and forth, round and round. The tension in his face drove me wild, with an insane need to make him lose control. I rode him hard; my full breasts bouncing up and down with each rise and fall. Sweat sheathed my skin, and my thighs shook with anticipation.

Hunter's thumb pressed to my aching clit, and he began to rub circles that made my hips follow in unison. My breathing came in short, staccato bursts, and a moan escaped as my orgasm gripped hold of me.

"*Hunter*," I cried.

He answered by fisting a handful of my hair and pulling my mouth down to meet his. His tongue swooped in for a kiss that swept away whatever reality I had left. I was utterly and completely lost in this man.

It was all too much—his masterful fingers massaging my clit, the constant rubbing of that sensitive spot inside of me, his hand wound so tight in my hair, his demanding mouth. Orgasm shot through me, wave after wave of spasms that took over my body. My moans were swallowed between our joined mouths.

Breathless, I gasped for air, and Hunter loosened his grip on my hair so he could watch the last quakes ripple through me.

"Fucking beautiful. *So fucking beautiful.*"

And then he took back the control I'd thought I'd had. He gripped my hips, lifting me up and down as he thrust up from beneath me. Each time he hammered harder and harder, fucking me from underneath, topping me from the bottom. The sheer determination on his face was the sexiest thing I'd ever seen.

"*Fuck.*" He gritted his teeth. "*I'm gonna come.*"

He bucked one last time and let out a load groan as he planted himself deep inside my body. Watching him release, the tension on his face giving way to pure bliss, was absolutely exhilarating.

Spineless, I collapsed on top of him, unable to hold myself upright. Hunter buried his face in my neck, whispering sweet everythings between kisses over and over. God, this man could be so beautiful.

Sated, I reveled in the tender moment and basked in the afterglow. We were good together. I liked to think it was our chemistry and not his past experience that made our intimate times so amazing. I was far from a virgin, but being with Hunter made me feel like everything leading up to him had merely been practice for the real thing.

It was that thought that scared me out of my lust-induced haze and back to reality. If Hunter was my real thing, why did I have to go back to imposters?

Chapter 28

— Hunter —
10 years ago

Summer wasn't happy with me.

She'd said she understood why I hadn't told Jayce about us. But now two months had gone by, and hiding her—hiding our relationship—during summer break made things a challenge. I couldn't go down to San Diego to visit her too often because I'd snagged an internship at an architectural firm I wanted to work at after graduation. And if she came up north, we didn't exactly have a place to hang out considering I lived with my aunt and uncle, and so did my brother. At least until today.

Jayce was moving out. Amazingly enough, he'd come clean with Emily and admitted he wasn't ready to get married. She had been very understanding. Honestly, forgetting the selfish reasons I had, I really hoped things worked out between the two of them—any woman who could be that understanding while fielding pregnancy hormones was worth working things out with.

"I miss you," Summer whined through the phone.

Summer was not a whiner. I needed to fix the mess I'd gotten myself into and tell the truth once and for all. I loved this girl.

"Yeah, babe. I miss you, too. I'm going to sit down with Jayce today after I help him move. Then I'll talk to my aunt and uncle, and I'm sure they won't mind you coming to stay for a visit here."

"Really?" She perked up.

"They might make you sleep in the guest room."

"I don't even care. I just miss your face."

"I miss the whole package."

Jayce popped his head into my bedroom doorway. "Give me a hand carrying my mattress down the stairs?"

I covered the phone. "Yeah. Give me two minutes."

He nodded and disappeared.

"I'll call you tonight."

"Okay. Good luck today."

"Thanks."

I tossed my phone on the bed and passed Uncle Joe on the stairs. He lifted the small lamp in his hands. "Wouldn't let me help him with the mattress. Little shit thinks I'm too old to carry more than five pounds."

I chuckled. "Don't worry. When I move out, I'll put my feet up on the couch, and you can load the entire truck yourself."

Our cousin Cara's room was the first door at the top of the stairs. She lay on her belly in the center of her bed, kicking her feet in the air while reading a magazine.

"Don't worry, Cara," I called as I passed. "We got it."

I chuckled and kept going to Jayce's room at the end of the hall. His door was open, but he wasn't inside. I looked around the other rooms on the second floor, but he was nowhere to be found. So, I took a seat on his bed and looked at the half-empty room. Even though we were only in the same place for the summers, it would be weird to live here alone. Jayce had been the constant in my life, before and after Mom died.

A noise from within the room surprised me, considering I'd thought I was alone. It sounded like Aunt Elizabeth's dog had gotten a fur ball caught in his throat again. I looked under the bed—no dog. Then got up and looked on the other side of it. I nearly fell over, finding my brother lying on the floor. He was pale as a ghost and foaming at the mouth while his body twitched.

I screamed out the window for my uncle, and opened my brother's mouth to see if he was choking on something. There was nothing visible, and I had no idea what to do, so I lifted him from the floor and started running down the stairs with him shaking in my arms.

Luckily, medical care was only a floor away when you lived with a doctor. Uncle Joe sprang into action and had me set Jayce on the couch so he could examine him while I called 9-1-1. By the time I'd hung up, the twitching had stopped, and the color had started to return in my brother's face.

"What the hell happened?" I asked.

Even Cara had gotten up to check out the commotion.

"He had a seizure." Uncle Joe looked at Jayce. "Just keep still, son. Do you remember if you fell before that happened? Hit your head or anything?"

My brother was disoriented and didn't respond.

"Why did that happen? What's wrong with him?"

"I don't know, but we'll get to the bottom of it."

***

Four days.

Four fucking days.

I was seriously close to losing my patience. What the hell takes so long? Over these four days, they'd wheeled Jayce around for all types of scans, drawn blood, and hooked him up to a bunch of machines. Eight different doctors had asked him the same questions over and over. But no one had said shit.

"Dude. You're going to be the one sitting in this bed with a breakdown if you don't relax soon."

Typical Jayce, more worried about me than himself.

"Plus, you've been wearing those clothes for four days. You're starting to stink up my room."

I dragged a hand through my hair. "Why didn't you tell me about the shit you told the doctors? I had no idea you had any other symptoms going on."

He watched me pace back and forth at the foot of his bed. "This is why. You're gonna wear a path in the floor if you don't sit down and stop worrying."

A few days ago might've been his first seizure, but apparently Jayce had had other shit going on for a while and failed to mention it to anyone. Muscle spasms, tremors, weight loss—I'd noticed two of the three and asked him about them.

"Your fucking hand shaking—the first time I noticed it you told me you were hungover. Had you even been drinking the night before? I should've made you go to the doctor. Why didn't you tell me?"

My brother's face turned serious. "You want the truth? I didn't want to know."

"Great." I shook my head. "Now you're Mom. Ignore medical care and leave everything to chance."

"What difference does it make to know? If I have Parkinson's like Mom, there's no cure for it anyway."

"No. But there's treatment. And then you could know what to look out for."

"The doctor said seizures aren't even a common symptom of Parkinson's. So you're blowing the entire thing out of proportion."

Uncle Joe walked into the room carrying a file. He looked exhausted. He'd been here twenty of twenty-four hours for the last four days. But unlike me, he'd at least showered and run home for a change of clothes. I'd refused, sleeping on the chair in the waiting room when they kicked me out of his room at night.

He looked around. "Where's Emily?"

"I made her go home and get some rest." Jayce lifted his chin toward me. "Like this pain in the ass should."

Uncle Joe looked at me. "I think that's a good idea. Why don't you go home and get some rest. I want to talk to Jayce alone anyway."

"Why?" I eyed the folder. "You have results finally?"

Uncle Joe looked to Jayce. "I know you boys are close. But medical information is private."

Jayce looked between our uncle and me. "It's fine. Hunter can stay."

"You sure?"

"Yeah."

My uncle pulled up a chair alongside Jayce's bed. "Why don't you have a seat, too, Hunter?"

When someone tells you to have a seat, bad news comes next. "I'd rather stand."

He nodded and looked down at the unopened folder on his lap for an excruciatingly long time. Taking off his glasses, he rubbed his tired eyes before starting.

"We all assumed your mother had Parkinson's disease. She had the classic symptoms. And, well, you know she refused to go to a doctor for a workup."

"She didn't have Parkinson's?" I asked.

"Obviously, there's no way to be certain, but I no longer think so."

"Does that mean I don't have Parkinson's?" My brother said.

Uncle Joe shook his head. "No. You don't have Parkinson's, son."

Jayce's head tilted back to the ceiling, and his shoulders slumped with relief. "Thank God."

The excitement I felt was short-lived after I took a look at my uncle's face. He wasn't relieved like we were. I suddenly thought sitting down was a good idea.

"There are some conditions that have very similar symptoms to other conditions. Even yesterday when I learned all about the symptoms you've encountered over the years, it still sounded like Parkinson's. And while seizure isn't a common ailment of those suffering from the disease, there is a known comorbidity between Parkinson's and epilepsy."

"So I have epilepsy?"

"No, you don't have epilepsy either. I'm sorry. I'm confusing things by going into all of this explanation. I just wanted you to understand that sometimes symptoms can present in a manner that leads to a diagnosis, but without proper testing, there's no way to truly confirm what you're dealing with. Your mother is gone almost two years now, and we're still guessing since she refused testing. We'll never be one-hundred-percent certain, but the genetic condition you have now leads us to believe she didn't suffer from Parkinson's either."

"Genetic condition? What's wrong with me?"

My uncle's eyes teared up. "You have a genetic condition known as Huntington's disease, Jayce. Yours is considered juvenile Huntington's disease because of your age when you first started to experience symptoms. It's an inherited defect in a single gene, an autosomal dominant disorder. It causes progressive degeneration of nerve cells in the brain, which impacts a person's ability to move, among other things. That's why you've been tripping and had some hand tremors. At the start, it can mimic things someone might do when they've had too much to drink."

"At the start? What else is it going to do to me?"

"It's difficult to know for sure, especially in cases of juvenile-onset Huntington's, because it's rare. But most people will have impaired movement and cognitive issues."

"Cognitive? It's going to affect the way I think? Like how? Mom always seemed depressed, but we assumed that was because she didn't feel good."

"Most likely that was due to Huntington's. Dr. Kohan is going to come in and talk to you in detail in a little while. He's an expert in the field and will go over everything and answer all of your questions. I know the basics, but since juvenile Huntington's is not common and the symptoms present differently, he's in a better position to explain things to you."

My head spun, and my brother looked shell shocked.

"Is there a cure for Huntington's?" I asked.

The look on my uncle's face answered the question. "Not as of today, no. But science makes new breakthroughs all the time."

"But people live with it, right?"

"There is a shortened life expectancy with the disease."

"Shortened?" My brother finally spoke up. "How much shortened?"

"On average, from the time symptoms appear, people live between ten and thirty years when they are diagnosed as adults. But with early-onset like you've experienced, the lifespan is generally ten years or less. I'm sorry, Jayce. I'm so sorry."

The three of us sat in complete silence for a long time after that. Eventually, Dr. Kohan came in and joined us.

He spent another two hours going over things, although I'm not so sure either Jayce or I absorbed much.

I couldn't get past the life expectancy—ten years was the maximum from the time symptoms first appeared. Jayce had said yesterday that he'd started to notice small issues as far back as five years ago. My brother had just turned twenty-one.

"I'll leave you boys my card." Dr. Kohan took a pen from his lab coat pocket and jotted down something on the back. "If you have any questions, my cell phone number is here. Call me day or night. It's a lot to take in. I know that. You're going to have questions once everything really sinks in. That's what I'm here for."

Dr. Kohan and Uncle Joe spoke for a few minutes, and then Dr. Kohan extended his hand to my brother and me. "I'll have my office manager give you both a call to set up appointments for this week in my office to follow up."

"Both of us?" I shook the doctor's hand.

"Yes. I'd like you to meet with our genetic counselor before you get tested. She works in my office on Thursdays."

"Tested?"

The two doctors looked at each other before my uncle spoke gently.

He placed a hand on my shoulder. "As Dr. Kohan explained, Huntington's is hereditary. Fifty percent of children inherit the gene from a parent."

I'd been so freaked out about my brother, that part of the conversation had slid right by me. I'd heard the fifty-percent statistic, but it didn't register correctly. I guess I assumed if fifty percent got it from a parent, and there were two of us...my brother had been the unlucky one. But the actual words our uncle had said sunk in now. *Fifty percent* of *children*—meaning each child had a fifty-fifty chance.

My brother would be dead within five years, and I had the same odds as a coin flip of having the same disease.

Chapter 24

— Natalia —

The bed was empty.

I must've drifted off in post-coital bliss. Lifting my head, I went to turn around and grab my phone off the nightstand, but I nearly jumped out of my skin when I saw Hunter sitting in the rocking chair across from the bed.

Springing upright, I clutched the sheet to my chest. "Holy shit. I didn't realize you were there."

"Sorry. I didn't mean to scare you."

He'd slipped on jeans and sat with the top button open, sans shirt or shoes.

"What are you doing?"

The corner of his mouth curled. "Watching you sleep."

"That's weird. Was it interesting?"

"Riveting." He stood and crossed to the bed, leaning down to kiss my forehead. "I gotta get going. I have to meet the building department in a little while, and you have an appointment in an hour."

"Oh. Okay."

He searched my face and spoke quietly. "Do you regret it?"

I wasn't sure if he was referring to this morning or our relationship in general. "Us or today?"

"You tell me."

I gave real thought to the question before answering. I might be disappointed, but I couldn't say I regretted my time with Hunter. "No. I don't."

"Dinner this weekend?"

"Sure. That sounds good."

He brushed his lips with mine, and then left.

I should've been paying Minnie this time. At a minimum we should've called it even. We'd finished our session, but I'd stayed to chat while doing a little first aid.

The blisters on her fingers from her incessant checking that the front door was locked and the stove was off had opened, and I was concerned that they might get infected. Snapping on rubber gloves, I cleaned out the raw wounds and wrapped her fingers as we chatted away about my life. I'd told her all about Hunter over the last two months.

"There are only three reasons a man is noncommittal. Either he's a fisherman, a milkman, or a priest."

I glanced up at her. "You're going to have to explain that one."

"A fisherman knows there are plenty of fish in the sea, and he doesn't want to spend his life eating cod when there's tuna and striped bass that he still hasn't tasted yet."

I wasn't sure if Minnie realized her euphemism for a player was rather gross—eating fish. But I got her point.

"I really don't think that's Hunter's issue. Although maybe I just don't want to believe he's like that. My gut says it has nothing to do with needing to move on to the next woman."

"Alright. Then maybe he's a milkman. Good woman at home, and yet keeps going out to make deliveries to unsuspecting housewives."

I laughed. "I don't think that's possible. I've been to his house, and there's no sign of a woman. Plus, Derek and Anna would know if he had a serious relationship."

"Then he's a priest."

I cut the tape on the last finger I'd wrapped, and smoothed it down as gently as possible. "He's definitely not a priest."

"I didn't mean he doesn't like a little no-pants dance. A priest is someone who sacrifices for the benefit of others," Minnie said. "They'll give up their own happiness so the people in their flock don't get hurt."

Hmmm. "But why? What could he possibly be trying to protect me from?"

"He knows your story. Maybe he's afraid to let you down, or that he's not good enough for you."

I scoffed at the last part. "Hunter Delucia has more confidence in his little pinky than I do in my entire body."

"Sometimes confidence is worn like a mask to shield people from seeing insecurities."

"I suppose. I just...that doesn't seem to fit either."

"Maybe the last woman broke his heart. Has he ever had a serious relationship before?"

"Once."

"Did he tell you what happened?"

"No. He actually gave a really vague response, and I have no clue why things ended."

Minnie lifted her newly wrapped fingers and wiggled them around. "Might want to see if you can get more information about that."

After Izzy went to bed, I curled up with a cup of tea and picked up my cell. It was almost eleven in New York, but still only eight in California. I'd thought all afternoon about my conversation with Minnie and decided going straight to the tightlipped source wouldn't be half as productive as calling my best friend.

"Hey," Anna said. "It's the fairy godmother."

I smiled. "You know, when I was little, I always imagined my fairy godmother looked like Stevie Nicks."

"I think Stevie Nicks would be a kick-ass godmother. Maybe I should see if she's available instead. Pretty sure she lives in L.A. Then again, who knows, I might have you here after all. Derek said you and Hunter were all kissy face."

My shoulders slumped. "I wouldn't count on it."

"Oh no. What happened?"

"We had a great two months."

"Okay..."

"And...we had a great two months."

"You don't think a long-distance relationship will work?"

"It's not me. It's Hunter."

"He doesn't think it will work?"

"I have no idea. We basically agreed to be fuck buddies for a few months. Now it's over."

"Do you want more?"

"Yes. No. I don't know."

"You sound sure of yourself."

"I like him, Anna. A lot. Way more than I wanted to."

"Oh, honey. Does he know how you feel?"

"I haven't come right out and told him, although he knows I have feelings for him. But he won't even let himself consider giving things a go."

"Why?"

"And there's the million-dollar question."

Even three thousand miles away, Anna knew I was hurting. Her voice softened. "God, I'm sorry, Nat. I told you when you first met that I knew he dated a lot. But so do a lot of guys. I thought...you know, sometimes it just takes the right woman to come along."

Sometimes the unspoken words are heard the loudest. I wasn't the right woman for Hunter. While that hurt to think of, it also reminded me of the woman I'd been curious about.

"Let me ask you, do you know the details of what happened between Hunter and the woman he dated for a long time?"

"Summer? Not really. I know they met while in college, but they'd broken up before I met Derek. The only thing I really know is she called Derek a bunch of times after Hunter broke it off. She'd have a few drinks and call him, all upset about the break up."

"He broke it off with her?" For some reason, I'd assumed it was the other way around and he was skittish because his heart had been broken. Oh wait, maybe that was me.

"Yeah. He definitely broke it off. Although I don't really know why. Derek never said, and I never had a reason to ask. But let me poke around a bit."

"Alright. Don't make it too obvious."

We stayed on the phone for another half hour, chatting about Caroline, the christening, Izzy, and life in general. It felt really good to talk to her, even if I still had more questions than answers about Hunter when I hung up.

Chapter 30

— Natalia —

Izzy got sick with the flu, and it lingered for more than a week.

So the plans I had with Hunter to enjoy our last week and a half had turned into him coming over and watching TV on my couch while Izzy beckoned me from her room every fifteen minutes.

Tonight was supposed to be our first date night now that Izzy was finally feeling better. She had a sleepover for a friend's birthday, so we would even have the full night to ourselves. Unfortunately, not even that enticing thought could get my ass out of bed to start the day. Every bone in my body ached. I felt so awful that I had to use my cell to call Izzy from my bedroom to make sure she was up for school. The thought of standing and walking from my room to hers made me too exhausted to actually do it.

Still in denial that I'd caught the flu from my stepdaughter, I canceled my morning appointments and went back to sleep for a few hours. My hope plummeted around noon when I woke up and dragged my ass to the bathroom, where I took my temperature. A hundred and two.

I can't be sick.

I have a date tonight, and Hunter is leaving in three days.

A wave of chills seemed to answer that thought—but not the type of chills I normally had when thinking of Hunter Delucia. My brain wanted to be frustrated, but honestly, I didn't have the energy to be upset. It was all I could do to choke down two Tylenol and crawl back under the covers.

I couldn't bring myself to officially cancel my date until Hunter texted later in the afternoon.

Hunter: Wear red tonight.

Disappointment settled in. This was how things were going to end for us. We wouldn't even get to go out with a bang.

It hurt the skin on my fingers to type back, if that was even possible.

Natalia: The only red I'll be wearing tonight is from a fever. Sorry. I think I caught Izzy's flu.

Hunter: Shit. Sorry. You need anything?

Natalia: Got a magic pill to make me better?

Hunter: I'm going to refrain from telling you I have something you can swallow that will make you feel better.

I smiled and shook my head.

Natalia: I'm really glad you refrained...

Hunter went silent after that. On any other day, I probably would've wasted two hours overanalyzing the stream of texts. Lucky for me, today I didn't have the energy. The fever had wiped me out, and I fell back asleep for a few more hours, until the buzzer woke me.

I padded to the door with my blanket wrapped around me.

"Hello?"

"Just me," Hunter's voice said. "Got done early so brought you some chicken soup."

The girly part of me wanted to run to a mirror and wash my face and fix whatever smear of yesterday's makeup was likely still on my face. But the sick part of me told the girly part to shut up and sit down. I pressed the buzzer to unlock the door, then leaned against the wall while I waited for the elevator to arrive.

Even sick as a dog, the sight of Hunter striding to my door woke up my body. He wore jeans and a button up that was rolled at the sleeves. And he had on those work boots I loved. He was also carrying bags in both arms.

"Guess you just came from the job site?" I said eyeing the boots as he walked.

"Nope. Had a client meeting, then a meeting down at the building department. Wore the boots because you like 'em."

"How do you know I like them?"

"I watch you." He kissed my forehead. "It's how I also know you like it when I hold your hands above your head while I'm inside you."

I do like that. God, was I that transparent? "What else do I like?"

Hunter smirked. "You like it when I trace your collarbone with my tongue. And you really like it when I tell you all the things I'm going to do to you, even though you don't want to admit you like it when I say you have a sweet cunt."

My jaw dropped open. He was so damn right. I hated that word, but something about him saying that to me in the throes of passion really turned me on. And of course, just like he said, I didn't want to admit it.

I shook my head. "What are you doing here anyway?"

He held up the bags. "Brought supplies."

"But you'll get sick."

"That's a chance I'm willing to take. Now come on, let's get you off your feet."

Inside, Hunter insisted I sit down while he unpacked the contents of the bags he'd brought. "Chicken soup from that restaurant you liked downtown, where we met for lunch a few weeks ago."

"I'm not really hungry."

"You made Izzy eat when she said the same thing."

I pouted because he was right.

He continued to unpack. "Dayquil for keeping the fever down. I remember you tossing out the box the last time Izzy took it. Ginger ale, because the only time this crap tastes good is when you're sick and drinking it with toast. Speaking of which..." He unpacked a loaf of bread from the first bag and moved on to the second one. Butter, Gatorade, Theraflu, vitamin C, tissues, and four DVD jewel cases. The last thing he unpacked was a box of some sort of jewelry crafting.

He held it up. "In case you get bored."

"What is that?"

He shrugged. "Some craft kit they had at the drug store. Figured in case you need something that can keep you busy without getting up."

God, this man could hurt my heart and heal it at the same time. I remembered he'd said his mother did craft projects when she wasn't feeling well and couldn't get out of bed. He really was a sweet, protective, and thoughtful guy. And therein lay the problem. It would be a hell of a lot easier to say goodbye to someone who ran for the hills when I was sick—someone who only stuck around for the good. But Hunter was just naturally a *for better or for worse* type of man, which made it that much more difficult to see him as sex only.

I offered him a sad smile, hoping he'd chalk it up to my not feeling well. "Thank you for all of this. You didn't have to."

His eyes roamed my face. "You're always taking care of someone else. I'm glad I'm here to take care of you."

The thought was sweet, but all I could think was, *I'm glad I didn't get sick in four days.*

The non-drowsy Dayquil made me sleepy. Or maybe it was the action adventure with Bruce Willis and buildings blowing up that had lulled me to sleep. But because I'd slept on and off all day, I was confused when I woke up on the couch. My feet were still propped up on Hunter's lap like they had been when I dozed off, only he wasn't watching television anymore. My eyes fluttered open to him watching me sleep again.

"What time is it?"

"Must be about ten, I guess. Izzy called to check in. I saw her name pop up on your phone, so I answered it before it woke you. She wanted to come home to take care of you."

"Oh. That's sweet. She's really coming around lately."

Hunter nodded. "Told her I had it covered, but I'd make sure you checked in."

"Okay. Thanks. I'll text her."

He nodded. "You hungry?"

"If I say no are you going to force me to eat something anyway?"

His lip twitched. "Probably."

He reached over and felt my head. "Still cool. But it's been four hours since you took the Dayquil. Want a Nyquil dose this time to keep the fever down and help you sleep?"

"God, all I've done is sleep."

Hunter walked to the kitchen, grabbed some medicine, and poured me a tall glass of ginger ale. I managed to accomplish sitting up while he did that.

He sat down on the edge of the coffee table across from me and made sure I took my pills, then took the glass from my hands to set it down.

"You're pretty good at this nurse stuff, you know."

"I prefer playing doctor to nurse, but I'm flexible."

"At least I'm a better patient than Izzy. I'm not calling your name every five minutes to come get my dirty tissues and tell you something hurts."

"No. I think sleeping through the entire thing seems to be more your style."

"Well, now that I've slept the entire day, I'll probably be up half the night." I nodded to the jewelry craft kit he'd brought. "So expect some crappy bracelets when you wake up. Mine won't be as nice as the one you wear."

He looked down at his wrist. "I was ten or eleven when my mom got sick. She had muscular problems that affected her legs, so she was bedridden a lot. My aunt used to bring those kits over all the time. Kept her busy." He twisted the bracelet on his wrist. "Macramé and leather were her favorites. I used to have a lot of them, but over the years they broke or I lost them. This is the only one I have left. I'll wear your crappy one when this one finally goes."

Wow. It was a losing battle to not fall a little harder every day. "You know, Hunter, underneath the jackass suit you wear, you're a really great guy."

He looked at me a moment before standing. "Come on. Let's get you to bed."

Hunter tucked me under the covers and then undressed and slipped in behind me. Unlike the other nights we'd shared a bed, he left his boxers on. Wrapping his arms around my waist, he pulled me flush against his body. His hold was so tight, it made me feel like he was afraid to let go. Or maybe that's what I wanted to believe.

Tomorrow Izzy would be home, so tonight was likely the last full night we would spend together. It wasn't exactly how I'd seen our final act, but maybe it was easier this way.

About a half hour after we settled into bed, I heard Hunter's breaths change, and his hold on me loosened a bit. I allowed myself to succumb to the medicinal haze that made my eyelids feel too heavy to keep open.

Early the next morning, Hunter stirred, but I didn't open my eyes, assuming he was going to the bathroom or something. After a few minutes of him tiptoeing around the room, I felt his lips touch my forehead, and I realized he must've been sneaking out.

He gently pushed a lock of hair from my face and whispered, "Crazy about you, sweet pea. I'm sorry." Then he was gone.

Chapter 31

— Natalia —

I'd just started to feel better when the dreaded day came. Not great—but good enough to shower and spend time in the upright position. Hunter had come by a few times after our night together—he'd even brought takeout and a horror movie for me and Izzy one evening, knowing how much she loved scary movies.

For the last twenty-four hours, I'd been trying to avoid thinking about saying goodbye, wondering what those words would sound like.

Thanks, it's been fun.

See ya around.

Anytime you're in town, stop in. My door is always open to you. And by door, I mean vagina.

Tips are appreciated!

I bounced from sad to angry and back to sad so often, it was just a matter of timing as to which Nat the poor man would get when he arrived.

Unfortunately for him, he buzzed when I was feeling pissy. I didn't bother to wait at the door as I usually did, to admire his farewell strut down my hall. Instead, I left it cracked open and went back to the book I wasn't really interested in on the couch.

Hunter knocked twice before pushing the door open.

I waved but didn't look up.

Awkwardness settled in before he'd even closed the door behind him—at least for me.

He sat down on the edge of the table and took my legs in his hands. "How's the patient feeling?"

"Better." Acting like an insolent teenager, I still hadn't looked up at him.

He waited me out—saying nothing for a few minutes, until I glanced up to see what he was doing. And then he trapped my gaze.

"There she is."

His smile served only to piss me off further. He looked his usual casual, beautiful self, and I wanted him to look like I felt inside—a mess. I hated that he was so unaffected by our saying goodbye.

"Can we just say goodbye and get this over with?" I bit out with as much snark as I could conjure up.

At least his smile fell. "Natalia..."

"Seriously, we're both adults. It was fun. Now we're done. I'm not up to giving you one last blowjob, if that's what you're hanging around expecting."

Hunter's head dropped, and he stared down at the ground for a minute. When his eyes returned to my frigid ones, I saw pain behind them. "I...I never meant to hurt you, Natalia."

My mouth started going without my brain thinking it through. "Well, you did. You know why? Because this was never just fucking. You can say whatever you want, but you knew it from day one, too. You don't have dinner with a woman's family, help her daughter with her hook shots, and nurse her when she's sick when it's just fucking. And at this point, I find it insulting that you would even pretend that's all we had."

Hunter ran his fingers through his hair and blew out a deep breath. "You're right. We were always more. But that doesn't change that I need things to end."

It felt like someone had sliced right into my heart. I swallowed.

"Maybe not. But you know what it does change?"

"What?"

"You owe me an explanation."

Hunter looked me directly in the eyes. "I'm sorry, Nat. I really am."

I couldn't stop the tears that started to fall. But I also wanted some shred of dignity. "Just go. Please."

I felt him staring at me, but I wouldn't look up. Eventually, he stood. He caressed my hair one more time before he leaned down and kissed my forehead. Then he left without another word.

I cried the most awful cry after the door clicked shut. The funny thing was, with everything I'd gone through with Garrett, I didn't cry once. My marriage had imploded in an instant. After the initial shock of my husband being arrested and finding out he wasn't the man I'd thought he was, I'd moved directly to anger—almost skipping the entire phase of loss where I should've been upset.

Yet even with all of the chaos Garrett had thrown my way, I'd never felt hope was gone. I'd felt disappointed, dejected, foolish, *let down in a million ways*, but I'd never doubted that I deserved something better that was out there just for me.

Today I finally realized why I'd felt that way—because there *was* someone better out there who was exactly right for me. The only problem was, that someone had just walked out my door, taking the last of my hope with him.

Chapter 32

— Natalia —

A week later, my health was back to normal, but my heart hadn't even begun to mend. A part of me regretted how Hunter and I had said goodbye, or rather how I'd said goodbye. I'd acted immaturely, blaming him for something that really wasn't his fault. He'd been up front with me from the start. Yet in the end, it was me who hung on to hope that he'd change his mind. It was foolish.

The thing was, I *knew* Hunter had feelings for me. I just didn't know why he wouldn't do anything about them or try to make us work. And because of that, I didn't get real closure. It was more like I was moving on and leaving something important behind.

Yesterday, one of the dads I often spoke to during Izzy's basketball games had asked me if the guy who'd come to the games recently was my boyfriend. It hurt so much to say no—to admit aloud that Hunter was gone from my life for good—that I hadn't even realized why he'd asked me. When the next question came, asking if I had plans Friday night, I was completely oblivious to the fact that he was asking me out to dinner.

The poor guy had to explain what he'd meant, only to be rejected. But there was no way in hell I felt ready to jump back into the dating world yet.

So here I was, alone on Friday night, eating a pint of Cherry Garcia straight from the container while my sixteen year old got ready to go bowling with a boy. At least one of us had a life.

"Be home by ten," I told her. "And Yakshit walks you up to the apartment door and waits for to you get in, or you'll have two parents in prison when I'm done with him."

"You're not even scary. Now, if Hunter said that, Yak might..." Izzy smirked, "...shit his pants."

I laughed, telling her to watch her language. She hugged me goodbye—something new she'd started doing the last few days. It made me wonder if she felt bad that I'd been dumped. Either way, I'd take whatever I could get from her, however I could get it.

Just as ice-cream-overload nausea began to set in, my cell phone rang. A picture of Anna and me, cheek to cheek on her wedding day, popped up. I set the carton down on the coffee table and propped up my feet.

"Thank God. I was on track to finish off an entire pint of Ben and Jerry's without a distraction."

"Mmm.... Chunky Monkey?"

"Nope." I rubbed my bloated stomach. "Cherry Garcia."

"Well, save some for after we hang up, because you're going to need it."

My heart started to pound in my chest. Anna and I had just talked a few days ago after I made my flight reservations for the christening. She'd mentioned that they hadn't seen Hunter since he'd been back, but that he was coming over for dinner last night. Obviously whatever she was about to tell me was about him.

"What? If he brought a date, I don't think I want to hear about it, Anna."

"He came alone. He didn't bring a date."

I felt infinitesimally better. "Is he bringing one to the christening?"

"No. That's not what this is about."

I started to panic. "What's going on?"

"Hunter got drunk last night. I mean, *really* drunk. And he started talking about his brother's death and got really upset. Did you know his brother committed suicide? I didn't until last night."

Before the gravity of her words could sink in, I heard a wail in the background. "Shoot, Nat. Caroline just woke up. I'm sorry. I thought she'd be down for longer. Let me call you back in two minutes. I'll grab her and settle her so we can talk."

"Oh my God. You can't leave me hanging for long. Hurry."

"I will!"

―――――

I'd swapped my pint of ice cream for a glass of wine, downed the entire thing, and was filling glass two before my cell started to ring. "God, that was ten minutes, not two."

"I'm sorry. She was fussy."

"Can you talk now?"

"Yes. She just latched on, so I'm going to have to talk low while I breastfeed. But it's either that or I call you back when she's done."

"Start talking."

"I don't even know where to start."

"At the beginning. Tell me everything."

"Okay, well...it was a strange evening right from the start. Normally he has a beer or two. But when Derek offered him a Stella, he said he'd rather have a Jack and Coke. To be honest, it looks like he's been hitting the bottle lately. His hair's always a little disheveled—you know, he has that naturally messy but owns it kinda look, but last night he looked like shit. He had dark circles under his eyes, hadn't shaved in a while, and it seemed like he'd slept in his clothes. There was some sort of unspoken communication between Derek and Hunter when he said he needed a drink. Derek nodded as if he understood, as if the two of them had done this dance before."

I'd wanted him to struggle after we parted ways, but hearing it didn't give me the gratification I'd assumed it would. Instead, it felt like I'd been punched in the gut.

"I didn't know his brother committed suicide," I told her. "He said he was sick. But I don't understand what brought it all to the surface now. He died years ago, right? Was it the anniversary of his death or something?"

"None of it makes sense. Let me keep going and maybe you'll understand it better."

"Okay..."

"So he throws back the first drink in, like, three minutes. I watched Derek make it. The thing was basically whiskey in a glass with a splash of Coke. Hunter didn't even wince swallowing it down. After the second one, he grumbled that he'd gotten a promotion at work."

"He grumbled about a promotion?"

"Yep. When I congratulated him and said that was great news, he told me life wasn't about the news—it was about the first person you wanted to tell that news to."

Ironic. Two days ago Izzy had been named game MVP, and my first instinct was to text Hunter to let him know. It was a small thing, and it took all of two seconds to remember I had no reason to text Hunter anymore, but my gut reaction had hit me funny, and the rest of my evening had been tarnished by that moment. I'd felt sad after that, instead of happy. I hadn't allowed myself to analyze why it had affected me so much, but Hunter had nailed it—life is about the person you want to call first to tell good news.

I sighed into my cell. "He was sad he couldn't call his brother?"

"No. He was referring to you, Nat."

"I'm confused. I thought you said he was sad about his brother."

"I did. That's the confusing part. One minute he'd be saying he missed you, and the next he'd be talking about his brother. It was like you two were connected in his mind."

I'd gotten stuck a few words back. "He said he missed me?"

"He said he didn't give a shit about the promotion when he didn't have you to share it with."

My heart thumped against my ribcage. "I don't understand. I *never* understood. If he wants to share things with me, then why say goodbye?"

"I asked him that very question."

"And what did he say?"

"He said it was for your own good."

"What does that mean?"

"I couldn't get him to talk about it more. He just kept refilling his glass and talking about random stuff the rest of the night."

"Like what?"

"So much of it made no sense. For example, he rattled on about wanting to put birdseed in the birdhouses in the yard, and then he started to talk about random memories of his brother. Apparently Jayce's birthday is coming up.

I honestly had no idea he'd committed suicide. I guess I never pushed Derek to talk about it much because he was close with both Hunter and Jayce. I knew Jayce had died young, and when I asked how he died, Derek had said he had a genetic disorder and was sick for a long time. Last night, after Hunter passed out on our couch, I questioned Derek about why he'd lied."

"What did he say?"

"He said he hadn't really lied. That Jayce was sick, and that he chose to remember that as *why* he died, even if it wasn't technically the way his life ended."

Jesus. "So he was sick and took his own life?"

"Yes. And Hunter never fully moved on from it. They were close."

Anna was quiet for a while, both of us taking in the enormity of her words. "He'd hung himself, Nat. In his bathroom."

My chest began to shudder with tears. Losing a loved one to illness was tough enough, but adding the tragedy of suicide...the people left behind often felt so much guilt.

"You okay?" Anna asked. I knew from the shake in her voice that she was crying, too.

"No."

"Yeah, I know. It's awful to think about. I couldn't even be pissed off at Derek for keeping it from me. Because once he told me the truth, I felt sick and wished he hadn't. Now I can't stop imagining it."

Anna and I talked for two more hours after that. I made her tell me every detail she could remember from the entire night—three times. I had a rip-roaring headache by the time we hung up, but the ache in my skull dimmed in comparison to the ache inside my chest.

I wanted to fly out to California and hold Hunter while he grieved for his brother. It didn't even matter that we weren't a *we* anymore—I just wanted to be there for him.

That night I tossed and turned in my bed for hours. My mind raced over so many thoughts. Was Hunter's loss related to why he didn't want to have a relationship with me? Could he have attachment fears after such a trauma? He'd lost his mother *and* his brother at such a young age. Maybe the losses had left traumatic battle scars that made him afraid to go to war for his heart anymore?

Even though Anna had cast a bright light on the psyche of Hunter Delucia, I felt more in the dark about the man than ever. It was almost midnight when I grabbed my cell off the bedside table. My fingers hovered over Hunter's name. *Only nine on the west coast—not too late to call him.* If I did, he'd definitely put two and two together and know that Anna had called to tell me about last night. If I didn't, I'd never be able to sleep.

Deciding to text, rather than call, I figured I'd crack the communication door open and he could either chose to talk to me or shut it in my face once again. After another ten minutes of deliberating the right words to send, I went with simple.

Natalia: Thinking of you. Up to talk?

My pulse raced as I hit send and waited for a response. Immediately the text showed as delivered. After another ten seconds, it changed from delivered to read. I held my breath when the dots started to jump around. Anticipation throbbed in my veins as I waited for a response. After a few seconds, the dots stopped moving, and I let out an audible breath. I stayed frozen, staring at my screen and assuming the dots had stopped moving because he'd finished typing and the words were racing through the air on their way to my phone. I waited for them to arrive.

Five minutes.

Ten minutes.

A half an hour.

An entire hour of waiting.

But the words never came.

It would've been easier to accept that he didn't respond if my text had gone unopened, or if I'd never seen those dots jumping around as he considered writing back. Then I could've always wondered if he'd received my text—clung to a morsel of hope that was the case. But there was no wondering. Hunter had read my text and decided not to bother responding.

Chapter 33

— Hunter —
7 years ago

"Come on, Jayce. Pick up the damn phone." My leg bounced up and down as I counted the rings. After the fourth, it went to voicemail. I disconnected and immediately hit redial.

No answer again.

Something was off. I grabbed my laptop and the files I needed to work on and stopped at my boss's office on the way out.

"I need to do research down at the building department," I lied. "Be back in a few hours."

In my car, I turned on some music in an attempt to relax for the thirty-minute drive to Jayce's. But it did the exact opposite. Every song that came on, every mile I drove toward my brother's house, intensified the shitty feeling I had.

Jayce had been depressed lately. I couldn't blame him. He struggled to do simple things now—speaking and sitting up were hard work. Somehow he managed to get himself into and out of bed each day, and he even walked around some still, but by the end of the day, he was exhausted and dependent on the wheelchair he despised. The involuntary jerking in his arms and shoulders had intensified so much that it woke him up at night, so he rarely slept more than an hour or two straight. Other than doctors' appointments, he hadn't left the house in months. Most of his days consisted of watching TV and waiting for the different visiting nurses to come by so he could shave or move to the yard for some scenery.

We tried to get him to move back in with Uncle Joe and Aunt Elizabeth or come live with me. But he refused, preferring to stay in his depressing rental house by himself, rather than be surrounded by family who wanted to help. I visited him a few nights a week after work, and so did our uncle, but not even that cheered him up anymore. I used to think the worst thing in the world was death. But these days, I'm pretty sure sitting around waiting to die is much worse.

Still twenty minutes out, I hit redial on my cell as I drove. *No fucking answer again.* I'd been in a meeting when he called and left a message this morning, so my ringer was off. A sick feeling twisted in my gut as I hit play to listen to the message he'd left again.

"*Bro* (Quiet for ten seconds)

I was never mad about Summer. (A few deep breaths as he struggled to speak.)

I just wanted to make sure you knew that. (Another long pause)

Love you, man."

Huntington's had affected his mind—the way he thought, the things he thought of. Manic ups and downs had developed in his personality. I'd read enough to know everything he was going through was the norm, but something in his voicemail told me his message was more than just a random thought during a downswing. I hadn't spoken to Summer in years. Even though I'd come clean to Jayce about my relationship with her, I'd ended things not long after he got out of the hospital. Why was he thinking about it now? It felt like he wanted to make sure I didn't carry that weight with me after he was gone. I prayed I was wrong.

Every mile added to my bad feeling, and my foot pressed the pedal a little harder. By the time I hit his exit off the freeway, I realized I was going ninety-five miles an hour. I'd made the half-hour drive to Jayce's in twenty minutes.

My brother didn't answer the front door—not that I gave him much of a chance before I used the key he'd given me last year.

"Jayce!"

No answer.

"Jayce!"

No answer.

I flexed my hands open and shut a few times. *So cold.* My hands were so cold.

Not in the kitchen.

Not in the living room or small dining room.

The bedroom door was wide open.

Nothing.

There weren't many more places to look in the small house.

Not in the yard.

I walked down the hall that led from the back door to the kitchen and found the bathroom door closed. Facing it, the hair on the back of my neck stood up.

Fuck. I'm making myself crazy.

I took a deep breath and knocked. "Jayce. You in there?"

No answer.

I knocked one more time, and the door pushed open as I did.

I froze.

My breathing halted.

The earth shifted, and a fault line ran up my heart.

No.

No.

"Nooooo!" I screamed.

I rushed toward my brother's limp body hanging from a rope tied to the ceiling fixture. He'd removed the light to reach up to the beams in the rafters.

Panicked, I lifted his body to give the rope slack.

His eyes were open and bulged from their sockets.

His lips and face were blue.

Dried blood stained the corners of his mouth.

But I refused to believe it was too late.

"No!"

"No!"

"You can't..."

I held him for the longest time, not wanting the rope to tighten around his neck.

I couldn't let go to get something to cut him down.

I couldn't let go to call someone to help.

I couldn't let go to check if he had a pulse.

I couldn't let go.

I just couldn't let go...

Chapter 34

— Hunter —
Present day - two weeks later

This was a fuck of a lot harder than I'd thought it would be.

Sitting on an Adirondack chair in Derek's yard, I looked over at Natalia talking to a bunch of women and wondered if anyone else saw what I saw. Maybe they were blinded by her beauty—the smile that lit up a room, long legs toned just right so they were muscular, yet still feminine, and a dress that hugged her curves yet covered everything in a way that made it sexier to show less skin. But when she'd said hello earlier today, our eyes met for a brief second, and I saw it before she quickly made her escape. She was hurting beneath all those layers of beauty. And I fucking hated that I'd done that to her.

I sucked back my second seltzer water, wishing it were something else. But after weeks of binge drinking—crap I hadn't pulled since right after Jayce died—Derek had made me promise sobriety for the christening. It was the least I could do.

My buddy sat in the chair next to mine, one arm holding his sleeping beauty in a long white dress that hung two feet longer than she was.

"My wife is going to divorce me when she finds out, you know."

"What are you talking about?"

He shot me a look that said *don't be a dick*. "And she's *gonna* find out. She could've just gone on thinking you were a perpetual douchebag who didn't want to be tied down. But nope. You screwed that up. Ever since your drunken night talking about Jayce, she thinks you're broken. And you know Anna. There's nothing she likes better than a project to heal someone. She's not going to stop digging until she knows every little thing about your life. I'm not offering details, but I also won't lie to her. Eventually she's going to ask me the specifics of the genetic disease he had and put two and two together."

"Don't use bad language in front of my goddaughter, please."

Derek shook his head. He stayed quiet for a moment as we looked over at his wife and her best friend. His voice turned serious when he spoke again. "Nat deserves to know."

"No, what she deserves is a whole lot more than I can give her."

"What about you? Don't you deserve some happiness?"

I sipped my seltzer, wanting a drink to take the edge off in the worst way. "Leave the healing projects to your wife."

We couldn't avoid each other at the church. The godparents sat on the end of the pew next to each other. Natalia had Caroline in her arms. She looked beautiful cradling a baby—a real natural. And it had nothing to do with how gorgeous she was. I tried not to look over at her, fighting the urge to stare, because for a brief second, I'd forget she wasn't mine anymore. Then when I remembered, it hurt to breathe.

One of the blankets on top of Caroline dropped to the floor, so I leaned forward to pick it up, dusting it off even though the marble floor was sparkling clean. The church was warm enough, so I laid it on the pew between us rather than covering the baby again.

I finally found the courage to look up at Natalia, and when our eyes met, she waited for me to say something, do something. When I didn't, she broke the ice.

"The dress is beautiful, isn't it?"

My eyes washed over her. "Yeah. Red's your color. You look gorgeous."

Natalia cracked a small smile. "I meant Caroline's dress."

"Oh. Yeah. Her dress is beautiful, too." *I'm such a jackass.*

It was awkward, which felt like crap since our conversation had always flowed easily, since the first time we met.

So, I attempted to make it better. "How've you been?"

The look on her face told me I'd done the opposite. "Lonely. You?"

I couldn't bullshit her and leave her hanging when she'd been so honest. Forcing a pathetic excuse for a smile, I said, "About the same."

Then, like the asshole I am, my eyes dropped to her full lips. Sitting in a house of worship didn't stop me from thinking about how much I'd love to see them swollen from my teeth. When I looked back up at her eyes, they told me she knew exactly the thought in my mind. Lucky for me, the organ music started, beginning the ceremony, or I might've done something stupid and leaned in the little bit separating us...in a church of all places.

My buddy had won the party planning battle with his wife, so it was a low-key celebration after the christening. Just family and a few friends with some food catered back at Anna and Derek's house—and *Adam*. I suppose Adam would fall into the friend category, since he and Derek worked together and are close enough that he was a groomsman in their wedding. But to me, tonight, Adam was enemy number one. I wondered if the asshole knew how close he'd come to getting to sleep with the beautiful woman he was currently talking to. Worse, I couldn't stop thinking about whether Natalia might be in the same frame of mind tonight. She threw her head back and laughed at something the pencil neck said, and I nearly lost my shit. Since drinking wasn't an option, I decided a time out was in order and took a walk.

I found Izzy out front, bouncing a ball near the neighbor's basketball hoop at the curb. I walked over. "How's your free-throw ratio?"

She bounced twice, then swished one into the net. "Never better."

I took off my jacket and laid it on the grass. "Up for a little one-on-one?"

The wiseass looked from side to side. "Sure. Is there any real competition around to play?"

I reached in and stole the ball mid-bounce, showing her where her competition was. "How you been?"

"Good. I got game MVP a few weeks ago."

"Congratulations. That's great."

She shrugged like it wasn't a big deal and tried to swallow her proud smile. I bounced the ball, faking left, then right, took a few steps and shot from three-point distance.

Swoosh.

"Lucky shot," she said.

"Yeah. Okay. Your turn." She grabbed the ball, and I stood in the way of the net with my hands up. "Get past me, MVP."

I'd like to say I let her blow by me to help her confidence. But I didn't have to *let her* do anything. She didn't break a sweat to pass me. And I found out all too quickly that my three-point shot *was* beginner's luck. We played for a while, the game growing more intense with each basket we made. By the time we were done, my shirt was untucked, sleeves rolled up, and I was sweating like an out-of-shape old man. Izzy was barely winded.

"Need a break?" she asked.

I was bent over with my hands on my knees, trying to catch my breath. "What gave you that idea?"

She laughed, and we sat on the curb to cool off.

"How are things going? Is Yakass being good to you, or do I have to fly out to New York to kick his ass?"

"Yak*shit*, not Yak*ass*. And everything's good, I guess."

"You guess?"

"Let me ask you something? Would you really fly across the country to kick a boy's ass if he was mean to me?"

I'm sure she thought I was kidding, but I wasn't. "Absolutely."

"Then I should return the favor. Oh, wait...I just kicked your ass." She smirked.

I deserved that. Picking a few pieces of grass from the lawn, I asked, "How is she?"

"Not so great..." Izzy turned to look me square in the face, "...thanks to you."

"I'm sorry, Izzy."

"I don't get it. I thought you liked her."

"I did. I do."

"So, what's the problem? Is it because you live out here, and we live in New York?"

"It's complicated."

She shook her head. "It's actually not. Adults just make things more complicated than they need to be. You like her. She likes you. You work it out."

"It's not that simple. There're a lot of other things that factor in as you get older."

"Are you going to jail?"

Sadly, she was asking a serious question. "No, I'm not going to jail."

"Did you cheat on her?"

"I don't think this is an appropriate conversation to be having. But no, I didn't cheat on her."

She ignored my comment. "Do you still think about her?"

I nodded. It was impossible to *not* think about her all day long, even though I'd tried my hardest.

Izzy was quiet for a long time, and I knew she was pondering how to put together the puzzle of our conversation. Although without all the pieces, she'd never be able to see the full picture. At least that's what I thought, until she proved kids could see a lot more than adults thought they could.

"My dad messed up in so many ways. He's not the guy I thought he was. Over the last few years, I've sat around and thought about all of things he said to me. Because I'd never suspected he could be a liar, it made me question if I even knew how to tell the truth from his lies. So I doubted everything—did he love me? Did he want to be with me, be with us, or were we part of the act he put on for people? I didn't realize it until recently, but Nat was feeling the same way. That's why it was hard for her to move on, for both of us to move on. My dad claimed he didn't tell Nat the truth because he didn't want to hurt her. And of course, everyone thinks I'm too young to understand anything." She shrugged. "Maybe I am too young to understand a lot of things. But what I've learned over the last two years is Nat doesn't need protecting. She's the strongest woman I know. So if you want to protect her—really allow her to move on without it dragging out for years like things with my dad did—don't leave her questioning. Because while the truth hurts, it's like a Band-Aid when you rip it off. The pain goes away. It's the lies and questioning that keep you aching for a long time."

My mouth hung open. Not only had I had my ass handed to me in a game of one-on-one, I'd just been schooled on life and love by a sixteen year old.

Chapter 35

— Hunter —
One week later

Holy shit.

I'd always suspected it was her.

I came to visit Jayce a few times a year—but every year on his birthday, his grave always had flowers on it before I arrived. They were such an odd combination—a violet, a lily, a carnation, maybe two roses, and some Hawaiian birds of paradise. It wasn't an arrangement a florist would ever put together. And they weren't wrapped in the traditional way; only a string of jute bound the disorganized bundle together. It made me think someone had walked into a florist and just started picking out flowers they liked— or ones they thought the recipient would like—without regard to matching or making a bouquet of any sort.

Which was why I'd always suspected it was her. It was classic Summer—bold and beautiful, as seen through her eyes.

Her back was to me, but I knew it was her from two rows away. Out of habit, I stopped and watched from a distance. I'd done that for a few months after things ended—not wanting to see her, but not being able to keep the hell away.

She paced back and forth in front of Jayce's headstone, and I thought maybe she was talking to him. That seemed about right. I smiled when I saw her wag her finger at the stone. After watching longer than I should have, I turned to walk away. I'd come back later for my visit. But I'd only made it a half a dozen steps when her familiar voice called to me.

"Hunter?"

I froze. *Shit.*

What the hell did I do now? Keep walking and pretend I didn't hear her? I'd been a dick for long enough. Maybe it was time I manned up. Taking a deep breath, I slowly turned back around.

How long had it been? Jayce had been gone more than seven years now. All that time and she looked exactly the same, yet nothing like she used to. She was still as beautiful as ever, but she looked more mature now—almost tamed.

"Hey," I said. Quite an unimpressive opener after so long.

She smiled and tilted her head. "Were you leaving because you saw me?"

Our eyes locked. "Truth?"

"Always."

I nodded. "Yeah."

"I was just finishing up. I come every year on his birthday to yell at him. Just let me say goodbye, and I'll go." She turned to the headstone for a minute and then back to me. I still hadn't budged from where I stood. "All done. He's all yours to yell at." Summer took a step toward the car parked on the nearby paved lane and looked my way again. "You look good, Hunter. I hope you're happy."

She was almost at the car before I finally grew some balls—although I had no idea what I wanted to say.

"Summer...wait."

I made my way to the end of Jayce's row where she stood, only to stare down at my feet like an awkward schoolboy. "You look good," I said.

"How can you tell when you aren't looking at me?" I heard the humor in her voice. She hadn't changed, even after all these years.

I looked up, and she smiled. It was genuine and real. Summer didn't hold anger or grudges.

"Are you happy?" I asked.

Her hand went to her stomach, and she rubbed a small bump I hadn't noticed. "I am. I'm four months pregnant and have morning sickness all day and night. But I'm happy." She pointed over to the car. "That's my husband, Alan."

Wow. I looked over at the parked car. I hadn't noticed anyone sitting in it. *Really on your game today.* "Congratulations."

Her eyes searched my face. "Give me a minute, okay?"

I nodded, mostly because I had no idea what she was talking about. But she walked over to the car and spoke to her husband behind the wheel. Leaning into the window, she kissed him before he started the engine.

When she returned to where I stood, the car drove away. "Come on. Let's go for a walk. Alan's going to give us a little while to catch up."

I started walking along side of her, unsure where we were going or what she might have to say.

"Are you married?" she asked.

"No."

"Divorced?"

"No."

"Kids?"

"No."

She looked over, studying me. "You still have no idea, do you?"

The question could've referred to a million things, but I knew exactly what she was asking. "No. I told you, I don't want to know."

"So you still don't have any symptoms?"

I shook my head. "Not yet."

We walked in silence until the path came to a fork. We turned right.

"Have you fallen in love since we broke up?"

I didn't have to consider it. "Her name's Natalia."

"How does she feel about your decision to not get tested?"

While I thought about how to answer, Summer came to the correct conclusion.

She nodded. "You dumped me because you didn't want to put me through possibly watching you get sick. I tried for months to get you to change your mind. So I'm guessing your warped brain now thinks it's easier to not even *tell* someone you care about. Just love 'em and leave 'em with no explanation so they hate you. Am I right? She doesn't know you have a fifty-fifty chance of developing Huntington's disease. Or that you're too stubborn to get tested."

"What good would it do? So she can worry about me?"

Summer stopped. "I thought you said you loved her."

"I do."

"Then doesn't she deserve the truth and a chance to make the decision with you?"

"No. Sometimes lies save people a lot of pain. You knew, and it made it harder for you to move on. What if I told her and let her be part of the decision, and she convinced me to get tested. What if it's positive and she won't leave me, and then she has to watch me suffer and die at forty?"

"What if it's negative and you've missed a lifetime with Natalia?"

I blew out a deep breath. "It's too big a chance to take. She's got history. You don't understand. Every man has let her down in her life. I can't do that to her—be another man who disappoints her."

She caught my eyes. "Sounds like you already are, Hunter."

The car was waiting again when we returned to Jayce's grave almost a half hour later. Summer motioned to her husband to let him know everything was okay and held up two fingers.

"I gotta go. We have a doctor's appointment in a little while. But I'm really glad I ran into you." She gave me a hug and took two steps toward her car before turning to walk backwards. "Truth or dare. Come on, one last time."

I shook my head. "I'm not giving your pregnant ass a chance to pick dare."

"Fine," she said. "But only because I'm pregnant. Not because I've lost my balls. I'll pick truth."

I chuckled and thought of a question. "Do you want a boy or a girl? And you can't say you want a healthy baby, because we're playing a serious game here."

Summer rubbed her belly. "If I could pick the sex, I'd pick a girl. But I'll take a healthy baby of any sex."

"That's fair."

"Your turn. Truth or dare?"

"Since you picked truth, you know I have to pick dare."

It dawned on me that this had been her plan all along.

"Go after the woman you love, let her be part of your life, and actually live for a change."

"You look like shit."

"That's a nice way to answer the door." I brushed past Derek and plopped down on his couch. We'd made plans to play racquetball tonight, yet he was still in a suit. "I didn't realize there was a dress code."

"Wasn't talking about your clothes. You look like hell. Have you slept lately?"

I hadn't, because the world was out to get me. In the last few days, I'd met Summer at my brother's grave where I'd gotten a lecture. Then I'd flipped on the news to be slapped in the face by a story about the upcoming early release of Natalia's asshole ex-husband, and finally, this afternoon I went to throw on some jeans that were back from the laundry and found a lacy red G-string of Natalia's in the laundry bag.

I'd forgotten I'd found it under the bed when I double-checked the sublet before I left. I'd stuffed it into my suitcase while I was packing and then scooped the contents of my suitcase into a laundry bag when I returned home. The panty find had brought me a momentary rush of excitement, until I realized I'd washed them and could no longer smell her, no matter how hard I tried.

"Just busy at work," I lied.

Derek shook his head. "So full of shit. Whatever. You can try to fool everyone around you, but you can't fool yourself, jackass. I'm going to get changed."

While he was changing, Anna came in the front door with the baby. She held her finger to her lips, motioning for me to keep quiet as she tiptoed past with the baby sleeping in her arms. She disappeared into Caroline's room and came out with a monitor a minute later.

"Sorry. She was a little fussy, so I took her for a walk and just got her to go down for a nap. I didn't want to wake her."

"How's my little peanut doing?"

Anna's face lit up. "She's pretty awesome, if I say so myself."

She walked to the chair and sat across from me. "You want kids someday, Hunter?"

That was a question I always hated to answer. Wanting kids and being able to have them were two different things. So while the answer was that I'd love to have a little rugrat one day, I answered with the half-truth that had become second nature to me.

"Don't think kids are in my future."

"How come?"

Shit. Though I'd known Anna for years now, she'd always been my friend's girl. A red box on the checkers board, when I was black. I hopped over and around her, but never landed there. We didn't have these types of conversations. Obviously she had a reason to take an interest in me as something besides her husband's buddy now, and that interest unnerved me. I looked over my shoulder, hoping to see Derek coming down the hall to interrupt. No such luck.

"Some people are just meant to be cool uncles, not dads."

Most people took the hint at my vagueness. Not Anna.

She squinted at me. "Are you always this dodgy when asked questions? I don't think I've paid close enough attention before now."

My hand automatically went for my tie to loosen it, only I didn't have one on. Before I could figure out how to respond to her non-question, she fired again. "You were great with Izzy. Maybe you shouldn't sell yourself short."

"Izzy's a great kid."

Anna studied me the way a detective examines a suspect. She was zoned in, ready for any telltale sign my face would give.

"Nat's done an amazing job with her," she said.

I looked away under her scrutiny, but she likely saw me flinch at the mention of Natalia's name. "She has."

Anna waited until I met her eyes. I always used the same damn move on Nat when she tried to avoid me.

"Too bad her father is going to be back in the picture soon. They're releasing him next week—a month early due to overcrowding. I'm sure that will require readjustment for Izzy."

I nodded.

But she didn't stop goading me. "And Nat. I'm sure he'll try to use Izzy to creep back into Nat's life as much as possible."

It was impossible to remain steady after that comment. Even if I'd kept quiet, I knew my face screamed that I wanted to strangle someone.

"Natalia's smarter than that."

Anna went in for the kill. "She is...but she's in a vulnerable place right now."

Luckily, Derek finally finished getting dressed. Anxious to get the hell out of here, I abruptly stood. "About time. We're going to be late. They only had an hour of court time available."

Derek looked at his watch. "We have plenty of time."

Jackass.

Ignoring him, I leaned down to brush my lips on Anna's cheek. "It was nice to see you, Anna."

She made a face that said *bullshit* and stood.

Derek snapped his fingers. "I forgot my racquet. Be right back." My soon-to-be ex-friend disappeared again, leaving Anna and me facing each other. After a silent exchange, she reached out and squeezed my arm.

"She's in love with you," she said softly. "But Garrett is a charmer...."

I closed my eyes.

"You ready?" Derek yelled as he emerged from the hall once again.

"Yeah." I locked eyes with Anna. "Have a good night."

Chapter 36

— Hunter —

I couldn't sleep.

The unsettled and jittery feeling inside my gut wouldn't go away. In the seven years since Jayce had died, I'd never once debated my decision not to get tested. I knew what knowing, what waiting for it to happen, had done to my brother. And in case I'd softened, if I'd forgotten a single moment of the agony he'd suffered, I sat up in bed and opened my nightstand to relive every last painful reminder. Slipping the letter that was always with me from my drawer, I flipped on the bedside lamp. It was long past time for a re-read.

Hunter,

This morning it took me three tries to get cereal to my mouth. My hand shook so bad that each time it reached my lips, there was nothing left on the spoon. But on the third try, I managed to keep a little on—only to nearly choke to death because the muscles in my throat can barely manage to swallow anymore.

I'm sorry. I'm so, so sorry.

I don't have much left other than my dignity. I need to take it with me and not leave it behind with my bed-wetting and need for spoon-feeding like an infant. This will hurt you, but I know you will also understand why I needed to do it.

My last prayer said on this Earth will be that you are spared.

In case you are not, I don't have much advice to give, other than to tell you things I wish I could've changed. I wish Emily would never have known about my diagnosis. I blame myself for her miscarriage because of how upset she was for so long. Then I pushed her away by telling her I hadn't ever really loved her. But I did. I just couldn't put her through the years I was about to face. Sometimes when you love someone, you have to let them go for their own good.

Live life, little bro. Don't spend it dwelling on your diagnosis like I did. Time flies whether you're enjoying life or not. The choice is yours.

Forgive me and move on.

Love, Jayce

I read that damn note a half a dozen times. Normally when I did that, I focused on his pain—I'd needed to justify what my brother had done over and over in my mind to accept it was for the best. But this time, I was stuck reading one passage over and over.

Live life, little bro. Don't spend it dwelling on your diagnosis like I did. Time flies whether you're enjoying life or not. The choice is yours.

I'd always interpreted *don't dwell on your diagnosis like I did* to validate my decision not to get tested. What was the point of knowing, when there would be nothing I could do to prevent the onset of the disease? Why live life waiting for a death sentence to begin, when I could move on instead?

Only...

For the first time in my life, I pondered whether I was even living. Sure, I had relationships—sexual relationships—a job I loved, and a few close friends. That had always been enough. But was I moving on and living my life or was I just existing and waiting for a fucking symptom to occur anyway? I hadn't wanted to know so I could *choose* to live every day like it was my last and not have that life chosen for me. Yet if I could choose how to spend my last day here on Earth, I'd want to be with Natalia. So was I really accomplishing what I'd set out to do?

I reread the end of the letter again.

Live life, little bro. Don't spend it dwelling on your diagnosis like I did. Time flies whether you're enjoying life or not. The choice is yours.

I'd equated not dwelling on my diagnosis with not finding out. I'd thought not knowing had been what kept me from planting roots all these years. But suddenly, I realized roots had already been planted, and a strong vine had grown and wrapped around my heart. It wasn't the uncertainty of my health that had kept me blowing in the wind, it was that I hadn't found the one who made me want to weather a storm, allowing those roots to burrow in deeper.

Natalia was the one. I'd loved Summer. She was my first love. But she hadn't been the one. Maybe we were too young. Maybe I'd always thought of her as my first love because deep down I'd known she wasn't my last.

Natalia—she's my one.

I fell in love long before I was willing to accept what it was.

What would change for me now if I took the test and found out it was positive? Would I go back to mindless fucking between two consenting adults? How is that any different than trying to move on without finding out now?

Don't spend it dwelling on your diagnosis…

She wouldn't even have to know I'd taken the test if it was positive.

But what if I took the test and found out it was negative?

The choice is yours…

Didn't the risk of finding out outweigh the risk of losing her?

It was almost one on the morning, but after I finally grew a pair of balls and answered that question, I needed to talk to someone. Reaching for my cell, I scrolled through my contacts until I found the one I needed and hit send.

He answered on the fourth ring with sleep in his voice. "Hunter? Is everything okay?"

I blew out a deep breath. "Yeah, Uncle Joe. Everything's fine. I'm sorry to call so late. But I need to get blood drawn. Can I come by your office first thing tomorrow?"

"Are you sick?"

"No." I paused. "But I need to know now."

No further explanation was required. Uncle Joe took a moment to process what I'd said. "Give me a few minutes to get dressed. I'll meet you at the office in a half hour."

"It's one in the morning."

"I know. But you didn't make this call lightly. I want to hear what's going on. I'll bring coffee. If you still want to get tested after we hash things out for a while, I know a lab that opens at six. I'll draw the blood, take it over myself, and ask them to put a rush on it."

Chapter 37

— Hunter —

"Turn on your TV—NBC."

No *hello*. No *how you doing, buddy*.

I picked up the remote, flicked the TV on, and turned to the station Derek had said. A commercial for Rogaine played on the screen. I muted it to speak.

"I don't have much going for me these days, but I have my hair."

"Just wait."

"You're not making me watch a two-hour, B-flick horror movie again just so I can see your name at the end as robotics consultant, are you?"

"Shut up and watch."

I'd just gotten in from a morning meeting, so I kicked off my shoes and pulled my dress shirt from my slacks. I'd started to unbutton with my cell tucked between my shoulder and ear when the news started to play.

I grabbed the remote to turn up the volume without noticing that my cell had fallen from my hold and landed somewhere on the couch.

What the fuck?

The screen flashed video of a man walking through a gaggle of reporters toward an apartment building. Beneath it read *Convicted Ponzi scheme organizer*

Garrett Lockwood released early. A bunch of reporters shoved microphones in his face, asking questions about restitution to victims as he attempted to walk.

Garrett held up his hand, clearly no stranger to attention, and said, "Guys, I just want to be home with my family. I'll answer whatever questions you have tomorrow."

But that wasn't what had me squeezing the remote so hard I cracked the battery panel cover. It was the building he was walking *home* to.

Natalia's apartment building.

The segment didn't last more than a minute before the news went on to a story about a string of home invasions. I stood staring at the TV, having forgotten all about Derek until I heard a muted voice calling my name in the distance. It was coming from my phone on the couch.

"*Shit.*" I picked up my cell. "Sorry. I dropped my phone."

"Did you see it?"

"What the hell is she doing letting him stay at her place?"

"I don't know. But I can think of one way to find out."

Derek had been busting my balls to call Natalia since things ended. But since I'd confided in him that I'd gotten tested, he'd been relentless.

"You know the results aren't due in until Friday."

"Yeah, I guess Nat will just share a bed with her ex until then. That is, if you get the results you want. You don't mind sloppy seconds, do you?"

"What the fuck? What do you expect me to do?"

"Get your head out of your ass, for starters." He paused. "It's two o'clock here. If you head to the airport now, you can get to her by, what, midnight?"

My heart started to thunder inside my chest. I couldn't do that.

Could I?

Storm to New York to tell a woman I'd essentially walked away from that she couldn't shack up with her ex-husband?

That would take real balls.

Pacing back and forth, I forgot I was on the phone, even though I had it held to my ear, until Derek spoke again.

"You're gonna regret it, man. There's such a thing as taking too long to make a decision."

I dragged my fingers through my hair. *Fuck. He was right.*

"I gotta go."

"Go get her, man. It's about fucking time."

I'd spent six hours on a plane trying to figure out what I would say when I got here. Yet I still didn't have a goddamn clue. I'd gotten tested. If the results were negative, I'd planned to do everything in my power to win Natalia back. But Garrett's release complicated things. Even without me in the picture, she deserved better than that asshole.

I'd caught the interior door from someone exiting as I walked in, so Natalia wouldn't have any notice I was here until I was standing at her door. Wasn't sure if that was a good thing or bad. I jabbed my finger at the up bottom on the elevator panel for the second time and stared at the slowly descending numbers above the doors while I tapped my foot. Sweat started to bead on my forehead even though the air was chilly today.

What if he answered the door?

Worse, what if I interrupted something going on between them?

My heart began to pound as I imagined the different circumstances that could possibly greet me.

When the elevator finally showed up, it stopped and opened on every floor, even though only the fourth floor button was illuminated. Talk about testing patience.

At her door, I took a minute in an attempt to steady myself. It was eleven o'clock at night, her ex-husband could be inside, and I had no damned idea what I was even going to say. *Great plan.* Two deep breaths did nothing to calm me, and since I thought it was possible I might explode if I didn't get to her, I knocked and waited.

I knew I was taking a chance.

I knew I had no right to be possessive when I was the one who'd walked away.

I knew showing up after three weeks and without calling was a dick move.

But I also knew I loved this woman.

Which was why it felt like my heart ripped out of my chest when the door finally opened. And I was staring at Garrett, who stood inside her apartment wearing nothing but his boxers.

Chapter 38

— Hunter —

"I need to speak to Natalia." My fists balled, but miraculously, I managed to keep them at my sides and not punch the asshole in the face.

Garrett squinted and looked me up and down. He stepped into the doorway and pulled the door closed behind him before folding his arms across his bare chest. "We're a little busy right now." He lifted his chin. "Whatever you were to Nat while I wasn't here, you aren't anymore, buddy."

I had two choices: Push past him—which I knew from a quick glance at his physique wouldn't be an issue—and demand to speak to Natalia, or turn around with my tail between my legs and leave, because there was no way in hell this guy planned to let me in.

I wasn't leaving without seeing Natalia. I didn't want a fight with this guy. Yet I needed to talk to her.

Luckily, Garrett wasn't prepared for how dead set I was to speak to her, so it didn't take much effort to brush past him. I caught him off guard, but his hand was already on my shoulder as I yelled Natalia's name inside the apartment.

"Get out. Whoever you are, *my wife* doesn't want to see you anymore."

I pushed his hand from my shoulder and turned to face him. "*Ex-wife*. And I'd like to hear that from Natalia directly. I don't want a scene. I just want to speak to her."

The sound of a door creaking open from down the hallway interrupted our stare-off, and we both turned in the direction of the noise. I was expecting Natalia, but instead Izzy walked down the hall, pushing a set of Bose headphones from her ears.

She either hadn't heard the confrontation brewing with her father or didn't care. Her face lit up when she saw me. "Hunter! What are you doing here?"

I caught Garrett studying our interaction from my peripheral vision. "I stopped by to talk to Natalia. Sorry if I woke you, honey."

She waved me off. "I wasn't sleeping."

I used the opportunity to push for what I'd come for. "Is Nat sleeping? Would you mind telling her I'm here?"

She furrowed her brows. "Nat's not here. Didn't Dad tell you? She's staying at her mom's this week."

I looked at Garrett as I responded to Izzy. "No, he didn't mention that."

Izzy was a smart kid. She picked up on what was going on. Rolling her eyes, she shook her head at her father before looking to me. "Dad wanted to spend time with me, but Nat didn't want to interrupt my school routine." Her gaze shifted to her father. "My father offered to sleep on the couch. But Nat didn't want him under the same roof as her because he would try to play games."

"*Isabella*," her father warned.

"What?" she said. "It's the truth."

I smiled. *Love this kid.* "Thanks, Izzy. I'll see you soon."

She grinned. "You will?"

I winked. "If I have anything to do with it, I will."

—

I'd been sitting on the stoop since dark.

I'd watched the dark blue night sky give way to yellow and orange as the sun rose. It had been years since I'd taken the time to watch a sunrise or sunset. *This* is living—not fucking my way through California waiting for a twitch in my finger to show up. I'd decided over the last three hours that if I was lucky enough to get to have Natalia in my life, I wanted to get up an hour earlier each day so I had sixty minutes more to spend with her.

At almost eight o'clock, I heard the door unlock behind me. I stood from the second step down where I'd been waiting and turned to find Bella. She took one look at me and glanced back over her shoulder, pulling the door closed behind her.

"My daughter is in pain."

I looked down. "I know. I'm sorry."

"Is there another woman?"

"No, ma'am. There is no other woman."

She pondered that for a moment.

"Do you love my daughter?"

"I do."

"Are you here to make things right with her?"

"It's complicated, Bella. I'm not gonna lie to you. But I hope things will turn out okay."

She stared at me for a moment. "You know how Italian mothers make meatballs from scratch?"

I furrowed my brow. "I think so."

"You take the meat and put it in a metal grinder." She used her hands to demonstrate a crank going around.

"Okay..."

Bella pulled her purse onto her shoulder and straightened her spine. "That's what I'm gonna do to your balls if you hurt my baby again." Then she kissed both of my cheeks and walked down the steps, leaving me standing there on the stoop.

She yelled over her shoulder as she hit the sidewalk. "Door is open. She's in the kitchen. No hanky-panky on my couch. I just got new plastic put on."

I chuckled to myself as I watched her walk off. Then I took a deep breath and let myself into the house.

Natalia yelled from the kitchen. "What did you forget this time?"

She had her back to me as she poured a cup of coffee with one hand and held her phone with the other, reading something.

I waited until she set the pot down so I wouldn't startle her and spoke softly. "Hey."

She jumped and whipped around to face me. Blinking rapidly, as if she thought she might be imagining me standing there, she clutched her cell phone to her chest.

I took one hesitant step closer. "Sorry. I didn't mean to scare you."

"Hunter? What the hell are you doing here?"

"Your mother let me in. I came to talk to you."

The initial excitement in her face disappeared as a mask slid over it. She pulled at the tie of her robe to cinch it tighter.

"That's funny. I contacted you a few weeks ago, and you didn't want to talk then. You couldn't even bother to respond to my text. Didn't have much to say at the christening either."

I shoved my hands into my pockets and looked down at my feet. "I saw your ex on TV going into your building."

I'd been up for twenty-four hours with nothing to do but think about what I was going to say to her, but the look on her face told me that apparently *that* was the wrong thing to open with. She was *pissed*.

Her hands flew to her hips "So you thought my ex was visiting me and what... I was *fucking* him?"

Her tone told me *yes* was not the way to respond to that question, even if it was the accurate answer. "I needed to talk to you."

"About what?"

She was angry.

She was defensive.

She looked ready to slap me across the face.

Yet she'd never been more beautiful to me. *God, I am so in love with her.* That thought made it impossible to hold back the smile that spread across my face. Rightly so, upon seeing it, Natalia looked at me like I'd lost my mind.

"What the hell are you smiling at?"

I took two hesitant steps closer to where she stood. "You're incredibly beautiful."

"You're a jerk." Her words were hard, but her face softened a little.

"I am." My smile grew wider.

"What do you want? I have an appointment to get to."

She still hadn't moved, so when I took another step forward she was trapped with the sink at her back and me in front of her. I took her lack of kicking me in the balls as a positive sign. My heart raced, and it felt like if I didn't touch her, it might explode in my chest.

"I missed you." I took another step and closed the gap between us. She still didn't run, so I kept pushing my luck. Reaching up, I cupped both of her cheeks in my hands. My eyes closed at the incredible feel of her soft skin beneath my fingers. I took a deep breath in, relishing her intoxicating scent. She'd definitely just taken a bath. I smiled, opening my eyes, and slowly leaned forward to brush my lips against hers. "Sweet pea," I mumbled. "Love that smell."

The phone in her hand dropped to the floor, yet she made no attempt to pick it up. I took that as another good sign and went in for more. Planting my mouth over hers, I kissed her again. Only this time it was more than a brush of lips. Leaning her against the sink, I kissed her long and hard. I licked her lips, urging her to open, and she moaned into my mouth when our tongues tangled. My hand at her cheeks snaked around to her neck, and I gently squeezed to tilt her head and deepen the kiss. She moaned again, and the sound shot through me.

God, I missed this.

I missed her.

How could I have thought I was living before?

We kissed for a long time, and when it broke, her slack jaw began to tighten almost immediately.

"I can't do this again, Hunter. You hurt me."

I leaned my forehead to hers. "I know. I'm sorry. I'm so fucking sorry I hurt you. I'm crazy about you. I didn't mean for it to happen. Just the opposite. I wanted to *keep you* from being hurt."

After a minute of shallow breathing, she swallowed. "I don't understand, Hunter. You hurt me because you wanted to keep me from being hurt? That doesn't make any sense. What's going on?"

I looked into her eyes. It was the moment of truth. For the last ten years I'd hidden behind a disease I wasn't even sure I had. I wanted to live, and I wanted to live *for* and *with* this woman.

"We need to sit down and talk."

She nodded. "Let's go in the living room. My mother went to my sister's to babysit. She won't be home for hours. We'll have privacy."

I wasn't sure I was doing the right thing. I wasn't sure this wouldn't end in even more of a colossal disaster than the last time, but I needed to take a leap of faith. Sitting on the couch, I clasped my hands, looked down, and silently said a little prayer. I hadn't done that since my brother's funeral.

Then I started at the beginning...

"When my mother was ten, her mother went in for routine knee surgery and died on the operating table. She had a latent heart condition that caused complications with the anesthesia. Because of that, my mother grew up with an irrational fear of doctors. Then, when my brother and I were little, our father died from head trauma suffered during a car accident. Because he was awake at the scene of the accident and died later in the hospital, my mother blamed the hospital for his death, too. It exacerbated her fear of doctors, and she basically never went to one again.

"When I was nine, we started to see signs of her having Parkinson's disease. I don't know how long before that it had started, but at that point, she couldn't hide it anymore. Her hands would shake, and she had trouble walking. Because she refused to go to doctors, my uncle treated her as best as he could and made a diagnosis from observations. But she would never take any of the medications he prescribed and wouldn't get blood work done. She died at home when I was seventeen."

I paused. "I know you know some of this. But I need to tell everything from the beginning."

She reached over and took my hand. Squeezing, she said, "Take your time."

"My brother started showing symptoms of what seemed like Parkinson's in his late teens. He didn't tell us about it until he couldn't hide it, either."

"Oh God. I'm sorry. I didn't realize Parkinson's struck so young."

"It usually doesn't. But Jayce didn't have Parkinson's disease. Neither did my mother."

"I don't understand."

I took a deep breath and held her gaze as I spoke. "They had Huntington's disease. It's a genetic condition. My brother had early-onset, which causes a rapid deterioration compared to adult-onset. It's basically like having Parkinson's combined with ALS. By the time he was in his early twenties, he struggled to walk or feed himself. He'd started to choke trying to swallow his own saliva. He hung himself to end his life. I found him."

Natalia's hand flew to her mouth, and tears began to stream down her face. "I'm so sorry. Huntington's is a horrible disease."

"Thank you."

I looked away, not wanting her to see the tears forming in my eyes, and worked to swallow them. A salty burn scratched at my throat. When my eyes returned to hers, they were met with heartbreak and compassion. As I worked up the courage to finish the story, to tell her the reason I'd basically run away from her, her sad eyes grew wide as saucers.

She'd put the rest together herself.

"It's a genetic disease?" she said.

I nodded.

"So that means it's hereditary, right?"

I looked in her eyes. "It can be. Huntington's has a fifty-percent chance of passing to the child of a person who carries the genetic mutation." I took a deep breath and conjured up every last bit of courage I had to say the words I'd never said to anyone but Derek out loud. "After my brother died, I chose not to have the test. I didn't want to live my life waiting for symptoms. But after I left you and went back to California, I realized I wasn't living my life at all. So I finally had the test done last week. The results should be in by the end of this week."

Chapter 34

— Natalia —

I threw up.

I'd told Hunter I needed to go to the bathroom because I'd felt the familiar burn in my esophagus that happens right before. My vision was still blurry from tears as my head hung in the toilet, staring down at the water.

The bathroom door clicked open, but I couldn't lift my head. Hunter sat on the floor and wrapped his body around mine. The warmth of his chest enveloped me like a heated blanket. I leaned my head against his shoulder and let it all out.

He held me tight for a long time, rocking us and silently stroking my hair. When our eyes met, he spoke low. "I'm sorry. I didn't want to tell you until I knew my results."

"Were you even planning on telling me if the result was positive?"

He didn't have to speak his answer. His look said it all. I wiped my nose. "Well, then I'm glad Garrett finally had a use. How did you know I was at my mother's anyway? I hadn't even told Anna yet."

"Izzy told me when I went by your place."

I leaned up. "You saw Garrett?"

"Yep."

"How did that go?"

"He tried to make me think you were there with him, together."

I exhaled. "Such an asshole. I hate leaving Izzy there with him, but I knew she wanted to spend time with him, even if she'd never admit it. She loves her father, and they have a lot of work to do to fix their relationship."

Hunter nodded. He went quiet for a while after that.

"What are you thinking about right now?" I asked.

He shook his head. "I don't know if I did the right thing telling you. This was really selfish of me. We can't be together if it's positive."

"What do you mean we can't be together if it's positive?"

"I'm not going to subject you to that so that you can wind up being my nurse. I flew to New York because I'm a jealous asshole. I told you because I owed you the truth. The men in your life have all disrespected you with lies, and I couldn't do that. But I won't put you through watching what I saw happen to my brother."

"That's not for you to decide."

Hunter closed his eyes. When he reopened them, he said, "There's no point arguing over it now. I'll have the results in two days."

"Fine." I needed a few days for it all to sink in and to formulate an answer to every one of the arguments he would make against us being together if, God forbid, the test was positive.

We sat on the bathroom floor for another hour while Hunter answered my questions about the disease. He was clearly well educated on the genetics and statistics, along with having experienced it first-hand with his mother and brother. The one positive thing I learned was that Hunter was past the age that would be considered early-onset, which was when symptoms occurred before the age of twenty. Adult-onset generally hit between the ages of thirty and fifty, but could strike even as late as eighty, and the progression of the disease was much longer—taking from ten to thirty years to cause death.

"Come on." Hunter finally stood and helped me up. "Let's get out of this little bathroom."

"I have appointments today that I need to call and cancel."

"You don't have to do that. I need to find a place to stay and crash for a little bit. I've been up since yesterday morning."

"How long are you staying?"

"Not sure yet. At least the next two or three days."

"Stay here at Mom's with me."

"Does she have one of those metal things you use to grind up meat?"

I scrunched up my nose. "Yeah. Why?"

"No reason. She makes good meatballs. But I'd rather get a hotel, if you don't mind."

"Okay."

Even though I'd already taken a bath, I took a quick shower hoping it would help clear my head while Hunter went on my laptop to find a hotel near Mom's house. When I finished getting ready, I found him sitting up on the couch, but sound asleep. I took a moment to appreciate the man and consider how difficult the decision must have been to tell me. He hadn't told anyone except his lifelong best friend since finding out more than ten years ago. That was a lot for one person to hold in. I decided I wanted to show him how much I appreciated him being honest with me, so I straddled his hips and woke him with my lips pressed to his.

"Mmmm…" he groaned, coming to life.

I might've started the kiss, but he certainly took over fast enough. Hunter wrapped both of his hands in my hair and used it to keep me in place while his talented tongue led mine in a tantalizing dance. When I attempted to break the kiss, he caught my bottom lip between his teeth and tugged.

"Where you trying to go? I could get used to being woken up like this."

I rubbed my nose with his. "When I was a little girl, whenever my sisters and I wouldn't confess to doing something wrong, my mom would promise no punishment for telling the truth and say, *'Honesty is always rewarded.'* Then when we came clean for whatever we were hiding, she'd give us a lollipop or something as a reward."

"Oh yeah? You saying you're going to give me a lollipop for dumping my depressing truth on you?"

I pulled back enough so he could see my sinister smile. "Close. I was thinking you'd *be* the lollipop. I'll go to my appointments; you go to your hotel, take a hot shower, and climb into bed naked. I'll wake you with your honesty reward."

Minnie was my last appointment for the day. It wasn't professional to have favorite patients, but I'd come to visit her even if I didn't get paid.

She stared at the elevator panel with stress lines etched all over her face as she waited for the car to arrive. She'd only checked the door lock three times before I urged her to walk to the elevator. Not checking the fourth time was killing her. Obsessive-compulsive behavior isn't about not being able to resist the compulsion. It's about the inability to stop thinking about the compulsion when you do resist it. She hadn't needed to check that the door was locked a fourth time, but she was unable to stop thinking about checking it now. I attempted to distract her while we waited for her slow-as-shit elevator.

"So...Hunter is back."

That did the trick. At least temporarily.

"Oh? I knew he'd come to his senses."

I smiled. "That makes one of us."

The elevator doors opened, and I had to put my hand on her shoulder to guide her to step inside. It wasn't easy for her to leave the floor. But today we were going to go down to the lobby, step off the elevator, and wait for a new one before coming back up to check that the door was locked again. Breaking the pattern a little each week was working, albeit slowly.

"You were right, by the way. He had a secret he was trying to protect me from. He's got a health condition. Well, it's complicated, but he was afraid to get involved with me and drag me into what could amount to some rough years, medically."

Minnie was quiet as we stepped off the elevator and waited for the next one to arrive. I knew from prior experience that focusing was difficult for her until she was on the upswing, heading back toward the relief of her stress. Today it was stepping into the elevator that alleviated some of her anxiety, knowing she'd soon be able to touch that door handle again.

Once the elevator doors closed, she let out an audible exhale and spoke. "Thirty years ago, when I was dealing with my condition alone, I pushed people away because I didn't want them to try to make me stop what I was doing. I knew people would try to help me, but that would mean having to stop checking things, and, of course, that thought alone caused me stress. So I pushed people away rather than face my fears."

I nodded. "I guess that's what Hunter had been doing all these years. He didn't get tested for a long time because he didn't want to have to deal with the results. It was easier to push people away than be pressured to get the tests done when he wasn't ready."

The elevator doors opened on Minnie's floor. She booked out and down the hall, which made me smile. *Baby steps.* I watched from the elevator bank as she checked the handle one more time and then walked back toward me. Her face showed marked relief.

I pressed the down button. "You good?"

She nodded. "Next stop Puff and Stuff." Today we were running errands. While that sounded easy, it entailed working on a number of compulsions. In the cab, she would need to check the door lock four times, at the store there would be four segments of counting her change. I had a small plan for a break in each one. But for now, she was focused. We stepped onto the elevator together and resumed chatting as if an obsessive compulsion hadn't just interrupted us.

"The only people I've kept in my life for the last thirty years are people who would accept me the way I am and not try to change how I wanted to live. I think you know how many people that amounts to."

Minnie had one remaining sister and her mother. No friends or coworkers. She'd alienated the entire world so she wouldn't be bugged to stop her obsessions. But since her mother was getting up in age and her sister had married and moved down to Georgia, she'd realized she was alone most days. That's what drove her to finally seek therapy. She wanted to be able to have people in her life and choose them over her disease.

"Let me ask you something. Would you have pushed away people who never mentioned your checking and let you live the way you wanted to?"

She shrugged. "Probably not. But people can't help themselves. They always want to fix me."

It was like a light bulb went off in my head. I turned to her in the elevator and pulled her into a giant hug. "Minnie, your session is on me today. It's the least I can do when you just solved my love-life problem."

Chapter 40

— Hunter —

I thought it was a dream.

One of the porno variety. But to my surprise, the hand stroking me wasn't my vivid imagination. I'd drawn the blinds to fall asleep during the day, so my hotel room was dark. Just like Natalia had suggested, I'd checked in, taken a hot shower, and then hit the sack naked. I wasn't sure she would follow through with her promise after working all day, but I was prepared if she was.

I could clearly see Natalia's silhouette. She was naked on all fours, with her head looming over my cock. It swelled as her hand pumped a few times, and my skin tingled as her head lowered in slow motion. Right before her tongue peeked out, she looked up at me with her big eyes and held my gaze as she licked me from crown to base.

I groaned.

Fuck. Me.

How could I have ever thought keeping away from her was a good idea?

She swirled her tongue across my crown, wetting it as she got ready to suck me down. I had the strongest urge to wrap my hands through her hair and feed her my cock, thrusting hard, deep into her throat. But I somehow controlled myself. This might have been her reward to me, but it was her game, and I needed to allow her to play it out as she saw fit.

Although, if I couldn't show her what she did to me, it was impossible not to at least express it verbally.

"Fuck. That feels so good. You have no idea how hard it is not to flip you on your back and fuck that beautiful face."

A glimpse of a mischievous smile shone in the dark, right before Natalia's jaw opened wide and she sucked me fully into her sexy mouth.

Jesus Christ.

This.

This was living.

The woman I love coming home from work and waking me up with her mouth. Nothing in the world was better. I was an idiot for not realizing it sooner.

She sucked hard, opening her throat, taking me deep. As she began to bob her head, rubbing my full length along the inside of her mouth and throat, I started to worry I was about to embarrass myself and come within thirty seconds.

"*Fuck.* Natalia, slow down."

If it were possible, saying that made her go even deeper. The head of my cock hit against the back of her throat, and I'm pretty sure my breathing stopped. My balls tightened, and I knew I wasn't going to last long. I was a goner in so many ways for this woman. But I wasn't ready for it to be over. I needed to be inside of her. I wanted to fill every fucking orifice of her body. I wanted to fuck her hard and hear her moan my name in that sexy way.

Using every ounce of my willpower, I sat up as much as I could, lifted her off of my cock, and dragged her up my body until she was fully on top of me. Then I flipped us so she was underneath me.

"You don't want my mouth on you?"

"Oh baby, I want your mouth on me. I want to fuck that mouth as well as your sexy ass and your big, beautiful tits. I have plans to put my cock anywhere and everywhere you'll let me." I rubbed her lips with my thumb. "But I won't last with this beautiful mouth on me, and I need to be inside of you first."

I was positioned on top of her, my cock hard as a rock and practically dripping from her mouth, so when she spread her legs wide beneath me, it was easy to slip inside. I closed my eyes and relished the feeling of connecting with her again. Nothing had ever felt so good in all of my life. Her wet heat and tight pussy sucked me in and made me lose my mind.

And it wasn't just the physical connection that felt so good. Natalia opened her eyes, and even in the darkness, our gazes connected. I'd fucked plenty in my life, but I could honestly say this was my first time making love.

I began to move in and out slowly, as I watched her face. She was so beautiful, so open, so raw and real for me. Emotion overcame me, and I opened my mouth to seal the deal. Wiping a strand of hair from her face, I brushed my lips to hers. "Natalia, I lo..."

Shit!

Fuck.

Fuck.

Fuuuckkk.

I quickly pulled out and jumped from the bed.

Natalia was rightly confused. "What? What's the matter?"

I paced back and forth, ripping out the hair on my head. "I didn't have a condom on."

"So? I'm on the pill. I trust you."

"That doesn't matter," I snapped. "It was totally irresponsible. What if...*fuck*. I can't believe I did that."

"Hunter, it's okay."

"No, it's not. It's not okay. It shouldn't have happened."

I went to the bathroom to privately berate myself. How could I have been so irresponsible? What if I'd gotten Natalia pregnant? What if she'd had my kid, and we were both positive, and I left her to raise it with the disease on her own, and she had to bury two people she loved?"

Stupid.

So fucking careless.

I took a shower to try to relax, but it didn't help. I needed to apologize to Natalia for the way I'd acted and make sure she knew it could never happen again. But when I came out from the bathroom, she was gone.

I hit redial for the tenth time, but she didn't answer.

Such an asshole.

I'm such an asshole.

I finally get my girl back, and what do I do? Fuck it up while inside of her. Who the hell does that? I overreacted. There was no two ways about it. And I was rude and barked at her when I should've been apologizing.

My elbows were on my knees, hands holding my head as I sat on the edge of the bed. She'd been gone more than an hour when the lock clicked open.

I stood immediately, blew out a relieved breath, and headed toward her. "I'm sorry, babe."

Natalia put her hand up, stopping me. "No. Sit. We need to talk."

I did what she asked and waited. Minutes of awkward silence followed as Nat fiddled with the ring she always wore on her pointer finger.

When I couldn't take it anymore, I tried again. "Nat, I'm sorry. I shouldn't have—"

"I don't want to know."

"I was only going to apologize and tell you again why I did it."

"No, I didn't mean it like that. I know you're sorry, and I understand why you got upset."

"Okay..."

"What I meant was...I don't want to know if you're positive for Huntington's disease." She sat down next to me.

I was stunned. "Natalia...I..."

"Let me explain."

Since I honestly had no goddamned clue how to respond—nor was I sure how I'd feel about not knowing after making the monumental decision to find out—I was glad she wanted to be the one to talk first.

"I thought about it a lot today. For the last ten years, you chose to not get tested. You only made this decision because of me. And you plan to walk away if you find out because you think that will spare me. Well...I'm not willing to risk that. I'd planned on telling you that tonight. But then when you got freaked out because you forgot to put a condom on, it made me realize that if we never found out, we'd never be able to have kids." She paused. "Now...I realize I'm jumping the gun here. Who knows, our relationship might not work out for a million normal reasons, so it could all be a moot point. But I needed to give some thought to how I would feel about not having kids because your genetic status would be unknown. And

I decided I don't care about giving birth. I have Izzy, and she's no less of a daughter to me than if I'd delivered her myself—and we've only known each other for five years. If we decided we wanted a child of our own someday—a long time down the road—I'd be fine with adopting."

Hearing her say how much she'd be willing to sacrifice for me made my heart ache and swell at the same time. "Natalia, I don't know what to say. The fact that you would be willing to offer such a huge thing, sacrifice something so important is..." I shook my head. "It means the world to me."

She looked me straight in the eyes. "I want *you*, Hunter. The rest we can figure out. I don't ever want you to be inside of me and feel like it's wrong again. If things between us go the way it feels like they will...one of us can get fixed so we don't have to ever worry about condoms or getting pregnant."

She'd just given me the biggest gift anyone could ever receive. She offered so much and wanted nothing in return except me. I wasn't sure if I deserved it or not, but I was selfish enough to take it.

I'd known how I felt about her for a while now; I just didn't have the balls to put it out there. But it was time. It was long past due.

I walked to her and dropped to my knees at her feet where she sat on the edge of the bed. "I love you, Natalia. I'm so fucking in love with you that my chest feels like it could explode with everything in my heart."

"I love you, too, Hunter."

I kissed her lips softly.

"So we're good?" she said. "You agree we shouldn't find out?"

"Give me some time to think about it. Okay?"

"Of course. It's a big decision, and we have a few days, right?"

I nodded. "The test results probably won't be back until Friday morning."

"Okay. So we'll sleep on it and talk about it again tomorrow with a fresh outlook."

That sounded like a great plan. Then again, you know what they say about the best-laid plans...

Chapter 47

— Natalia —

I was confused when I woke up to the sound of a phone ringing. The blinds were drawn, and I wasn't sure what time it was or where I was at first. But the hard chest acting as my pillow reminded me. Hunter was out cold—he didn't even flinch at the sound of the phone, so I reached over to the nightstand and grabbed his cell. The phone stopped ringing just as I picked it up, but the missed call read *Uncle Joe*. I checked the time before setting it back down. 9 a.m. Damn, we'd both slept late.

I gently nudged my sleeping giant. "Hunter."

"Mmm?" His eyes pinched shut tighter.

"Your phone rang. And it's late. Almost nine."

He opened one eye. "Sit on my face."

I laughed and smacked at his shoulder. "That's your response when I wake you up and tell you that you missed a phone call?"

"What? I like to eat right away when I wake up."

"It was your uncle."

Both his eyes opened, and his face turned serious. "What?"

He leaned up on his elbows. "It's only six in the morning in California. If he's calling me this early, there's a reason."

"I didn't think of that. Well, hurry, call him back."

Hunter swung his legs and sat up on the edge of the bed. But he didn't immediately reach for his phone. At first I thought he was taking a minute to wake up, but then I caught sight of his face. "What's the matter?"

"Uncle Joe ran the test. He said he'd call as soon as the results were in."

"But it's only Thursday. You said results weren't due until Friday."

"He said *probably* Friday. I don't know. He could be calling about something else. But..."

His cell phone started to ring again. We looked at each other for a few rings before he answered. "Hey, Uncle Joe. Give me one minute, okay?"

He covered the phone. "You sure this is what you want? You don't want to know. It's a big decision, Natalia."

I wasn't *sure* of much, but I was certain of one thing. "You'll leave me if it's positive. Your life won't be the same. I'll leave it up to you. But I don't want to take those risks. I don't need or want to know."

He stared into my eyes for a long time before nodding. Then he lifted the phone back to his ear. "Hey, Uncle Joe. Before you say anything, I want to let you know that I've decided to not find out the results. So if that's the reason you're calling, I don't want to know."

I heard a man's voice through the cell, but couldn't make out the words he was saying. Hunter stared off, listening intently.

"Uh-huh. Right."

Hunter's eyes raised to mine and held. "Natalia and I decided we don't want to know."

He looked away again while he went back to listening. I couldn't sit still. I wrapped the sheet around me and stood to pace the floor.

Hunter kept nodding and said yes a few times. At one point, he rubbed his temples with his free hand. It made me nervous that maybe his uncle had called about something else, that something bad had happened.

After a few minutes that felt more like hours, Hunter cleared his throat. "Okay. Thanks, Uncle Joe. I'll give you a call tomorrow." He pressed end call and shut his eyes, looking down.

"What happened? Is your aunt okay?"

My heart jumped into my throat when he looked up. Tears streamed down his face.

"Hunter, what happened?"

Without warning, I was suddenly lifted into the air and tossed on the bed. "My test came back negative."

I shook my head, afraid to believe what I'd just heard. "What test?"

"My DNA analysis came back negative. There's a zero-percent chance that I have Huntington's disease."

Tears streamed down my face to match his. "Oh my God. Are you serious? But you told him you didn't want to know."

Hunter smiled. "He told me tough shit, he wasn't sitting on a negative result until I finally pulled my head out of my ass."

"You really don't have it? You're not just saying that to make me feel better because of our fight yesterday?"

"No, I'm not just trying to make you feel better, babe." He pressed his lips to mine. "But I'm about to make you feel better."

I felt wired with energy. "We should go out and celebrate! I can't believe it!"

"I'm going to do my celebrating inside. Inside of you."

Hunter unraveled the sheet I had wrapped around my body and kissed my neck. "I've never had sex without a condom—except for that minute last night."

I smiled. "So it'll sort of be like your first time then?"

"It's always felt like my first time with you. But this time, I want to come inside of you. I want to bury myself so deep and come so fucking hard that you're legs will shake and the people in the room next door will know my name. I want my cum inside of you, just like you're inside of me— so far that it's lost and never coming out again. I want to mark you as mine."

"*God*, Hunter."

He lifted my hands over my head and clasped them together using one hand while the other reached down between my legs. "Spread for me, beautiful."

I did, and Hunter's head dipped down to suck one nipple into his mouth while his fingers worked my clit. I moaned while he rubbed circles with his thumb. He slipped two fingers inside of me to make sure I was ready and then shifted back to align himself with my opening.

He never took his eyes from mine as he entered me. I was so wet, so incredibly ready for him. I wrapped my legs around his waist as he pushed in deep. Hunter's arms began to shake. "Fuck. You feel...so, so good..."

He started slow, moving in and out and studying the reaction on my face to each thrust. Closing his eyes, he looked like he wanted to savor every minute of the first time inside me bare, but when I moaned and said *come inside of me*, his willpower snapped.

What started out as making love elevated to fucking. *Pure, primal fucking*. Hunter pounded into me hard, his face desperate with need. Our bodies soaked with sweat as we moved in unison, me meeting each of his strong thrusts. The sound of wet, slapping bodies echoed through the room and was the most erotic thing I'd ever heard.

"Hunter…"

"Fuck. Come, baby. Come with me. I'm gonna come inside your sweet pussy."

We both exploded at the same time. I yelled his name and moaned, the heat of him emptying inside of me fueling the most intense orgasm of my life. It was the single most incredible feeling I'd ever experienced.

As we slowed, Hunter brushed the hair from my face and continued to glide in and out while we both caught our breath. "I love you, sweet pea."

"I love you, too. I think you stole a piece of my heart the first night we met."

"I'm charming and hard to resist."

"Umm…I think I did a pretty good job of resisting. You had to chase me for almost a year and come three-thousand miles to wear me down."

"I got news for you, babe. A year was nothing. And I would have chased you across the globe. I thought I couldn't get you out of my mind, but it was my heart that wouldn't let go."

Epilogue

— Natalia —
Two-and-a-half years later

I snuck out while Hunter was still sleeping and ran over to Anna's house to pick up the gift I'd bought him.

He was awake and in the kitchen when I attempted to sneak back into the house. Since the music was on, he didn't hear me come inside, which gave me an opportunity to ogle him from behind. The four years since we'd first met at our friends' wedding had done nothing to dull the desire I felt for this man. Little butterflies fluttered in the pit of my belly as I watched him shirtless, swaying to the music while he fixed his coffee.

Sex, not love. That's how it all started. I smiled, thinking of how grumpy my man had been the last month when I'd declared *Love, not sex* for the thirty days leading up to our wedding.

Hunter yelled without turning around, causing me to jump since I didn't think he'd known I was watching him. But he always knew, didn't he? It was like he had a sixth sense. He walked to me with two mugs in his hands and passed me one as he planted a firm kiss on my lips.

"Where'd you take off to so early?"

I flashed a sneaky smile. "I had to pick something up."

He wrapped an arm around my waist and pulled me tight. "Lingerie for later? Hope it wasn't too expensive because I plan to rip it off of you the minute the minister says you officially belong to me."

I wrapped my arms around his neck. "First of all, it's not lingerie. I'll be commando under my pretty white dress this afternoon. You're not the only one who doesn't want to waste time removing another layer of clothing. Secondly, we have to get through the dinner with our friends and family before you rip anything off. And lastly..." I brushed my lips to his. "I've belonged to you since the day you showed up at my mother's house and won over all of the women in my family."

Hunter's face softened. "I just can't wait until it's official, Natalia Delucia."

"Me too. But let me go get your gift. Izzy's going to be here in about an hour, and then the hair-and-makeup guy and Anna will be here a little while after that."

I'd left his present in the truck, so I extricated myself from my soon-to-be husband's arms and headed back outside. I stopped with my hand on the front door knob and turned back. "Oh, and Izzy is bringing a friend. So, *be nice.*"

"A friend? Her name better be Mary, Martha, or Sally."

I shook my head. "His name is Gaige. And she really seems to like him. So try not to scare him away like you did the last one." We couldn't even talk about what he'd said to the guy he'd caught making out with Izzy on Parents' Day at UCLA without getting into a fight all over again. Turns out Hunter was even more protective than Izzy's father. Thankfully, Garrett and I had struck an agreement on shared custody of Izzy while she finished her last two years of high school back in New York. Once she'd graduated and decided to go to UCLA, the timing was finally right to make my move out to California. I had everything I could ever dream of here—my best friend, my daughter, a beautiful home, a great new job, and the man of my dreams.

Hunter mumbled, "I'll *gauge* how hard I'm going to kick this one's ass."

I ignored him and headed to the car for his gift. I'd thrown a blanket over the cage to keep him warm, but it also served as a wrapping of sorts. Inside, Hunter's face was definitely confused as he watched me drag in a two-foot-by-three-foot rectangular box covered with a blanket.

"Happy wedding day!" I smiled and sat the covered cage down.

"You got me a dollhouse?"

I laughed because that was a pretty damn good guess. It did look like a dollhouse. But the noise that squalled from inside the cage confirmed it was anything but.

"*Fottiti!*"

Hunter jumped back. "What the?"

I cracked up at the big man's reaction. Lifting the blanket off, I revealed his wedding day gift—a giant Scarlet Macaw. It was the most vibrantly colored bird I'd ever seen, with bright blue, yellow, and red feathers.

"This is Arnold."

"You bought me a bird?" Hunter's face lit up like a ten-year-old boy.

I nodded. "Figured it was about time you put all those bird houses to use. You said you always wanted one growing up, but your mom wouldn't let you have one."

"They can live, like, fifty years. She knew she didn't have that long."

I opened the cage and put my hand in for Arnold to perch on. He jumped on right away. "Well, *you do* have another fifty years, Mr. Delucia. *We* have another fifty years to take care of Arnold."

Hunter gazed at me. "We really could have that long together, couldn't we?"

"I hope so."

Hunter leaned in to kiss me, and just before our lips touched, Arnold squawked again.

"*Fottiti.*"

"What is he saying? For titty? I think this bird was meant to be mine."

I laughed. "Oh, no. He's saying *fottiti.* There're two things that made me buy Arnold. *Fottiti* is one of them. When I started looking at birds, I visited a bunch of shops. Last week I was in Tropical Paradise checking out the cages when I ran across Arnold. He kept yelling that word, but I had no idea what it meant...until my mother happened to call and hear it in the background. Apparently, *fottiti* is Italian for *go fuck yourself.* My mother was horrified, but I thought it was hysterical. Turns out Arnold here is eight years old. His previous owners—Guiseppe and Gianna Moretti—sold him back to the pet store because they were getting divorced. I thought poor Arnold here could use a happy home, and we could teach him some nice words to go with his singular vocabulary."

"It's fitting that we have a bird that curses in Italian."

"Isn't it?"

"What was the other thing?"

"Huh?"

"You said there were two things that made you buy him."

"Oh!" I reached into my back pocket. "This is the freakiest thing. It sealed the deal that Arnold was meant to be our bird."

I handed Hunter the paperwork the store had given me. The top page was the bill of sale. It listed all the relevant information, including the bird's name, sex, breed, his sire and dam, and...the bird's date of birth.

I waited for the reaction as Hunter's eyes perused the document. When his eyes went wide, I knew he'd read the date of birth.

"You've got to be kidding me."

"Nope." Our new boy had been born the same day as Hunter's brother.

"You know that's Jayce's birthday."

"Yep. I'd say this foul-mouthed bird was meant to be with us, wouldn't you?"

After Hunter thanked me for his gift—and tried to feel me up in the process—he told me to wait in the living room because he had a little something for me, too.

He handed me a black box with a silver bow. Arnold was perched on his shoulder. I got the feeling he would be spending a lot of time there.

"It's not nearly as awesome as Arnold, but this is for you."

I slipped off the bow and opened the box. My eyes flared. "Is this?"

Hunter flashed an impish grin. "It is."

I lifted the blue familiar garter out of the box. It was the one he'd caught at Anna and Derek's wedding and put on my leg after I'd caught the bouquet. "I asked twice if you knew what happened to this, and you said no."

"I know. I lied. Something just told me I needed to keep it. I think deep down I knew I'd be taking it off your leg someday when I made you my wife. And even though I thought forever was impossible at the time, I held onto that thing like hope I refused to give up."

"That's the most romantic thing anyone has ever said." I reached out and linked my fingers with his.

Of course, he used the connection to yank me against him. "Oh yeah? Does that buy me admission to your pants now?"

I married Hunter Delucia at dusk in a small ceremony in our backyard with our families and friends watching. I'd put tea light candles in all of the birdhouses that hung in the tree we stood beneath. It made it feel like his mother and brother were watching over us from above.

We'd found true love and health and were happy beyond what either of us could have ever imagined. When the minister said he could kiss the bride, my teary-eyed husband cupped my cheeks.

"I love you, Natalia Delucia. You've showed me what living means, and my heart will always be yours."

His lips came down on mine before I could reciprocate the sentiment. But he knew. *He knew.*

I used to think Hunter Delucia had stolen a piece of my heart. But I was wrong. Because eventually, even the heart stops beating. This man stole a piece of my soul—because the soul lives forever, and so will my love for this beautiful man.

The End

Acknowledgements

I owe everything to my amazing readers. Thank you for giving me your time and allowing my stories to become your stories. You've made dreams beyond my wildest imagination come true, and I'm truly humbled that many of you have been with me for so many years. I hope we have many more together.

To Penelope – It always takes me the longest to figure out what I want to say to you in my acknowledgements. Mostly it's because if I listed all the reasons I'm thankful for you, it would be longer than this book. So I'll summarize – it would suck if you weren't by my side each day. Thank you for...everything.

To Julie – Thank you for your friendship and inspiration. Your stories are as one of a kind as you are.

To Luna – Welcome home! Thank you for all that you've helped me with for this book! But mostly, thank you for your friendship and constant support.

To Sommer – I never think you'll be able to top the last beautiful cover you create, yet somehow you do. This one is simply stunning. Thank you! Thank you!

To my agent and friend, Kimberly Brower – I'm proud to have a front row seat as you keep growing and changing the book world. When I look back, I'm in awe at what you've done for me, but when I look forward, I realize it was only the beginning! I can't wait for all the new and exciting things we get to announce this year!

To Elaine and Jessica – Thank you for your hard work and pushing me to keep making each story better!

To Dani at Inkslinger – Thank you for keeping me organized!

To all of the incredible book bloggers – Thank you your constant support. I recognize how lucky I am to have such an amazing group of partners to help share my books. I see you posting tirelessly, day in, day out, and I want you to know I appreciate all that you do. Your passion for books is contagious and your reviews, videos, and teasers set my books on fire! Thank you for taking your time to read my work.

Much love
Vi

Other Books by Vi Keeland

Standalone novels
Beautiful Mistake
EgoManiac
Bossman
The Baller
Dear Bridget, I Want You (Co-written with Penelope Ward)
Mister Moneybags (Co-written with Penelope Ward)
Playboy Pilot (Co-written with Penelope Ward)
Stuck-Up Suit (Co-written with Penelope Ward)
Cocky Bastard (Co-written with Penelope Ward)
Left Behind (A Young Adult Novel)
First Thing I See

Life on Stage series (2 standalone books)
Beat
Throb

MMA Fighter series (3 standalone books)
Worth the Fight
Worth the Chance
Worth Forgiving

The Cole Series (2 book serial)
Belong to You
Made for You

YA/NA Novel
Left Behind